Advance Praise for *If Wishes Were Retail*

"Irresistibly fun and funny, with a ton of heart and depth! This is the kind of book that sneaks up on you and sticks with you!"
—Sarah Beth Durst, *New York Times* bestselling author of *The Spellshop*

"Delightfully charming!"
—Phil Foglio, cocreator of *Girl Genius*

"Habershaw (*The Iron Ring*) offers plenty of laughs in this diverting urban fantasy. After Alexandria Delmore, 17, loses her job at a bagel shop, she sees an ad to be a cashier for a genie who calls himself Mr. Jinn and intends to sell wishes at the Wellspring Mall and applies. Mr. Jinn proves a mercurial boss who's out of date with modern mores and often impulsively abuses his powers, but Alex hopes to get him in line. At first, people are wary of Jinn, but when a video of one of his clients' more malicious wishes coming true goes viral, customers begin trickling in. Jinn's miracles range from the mundane—changing hair colors, healing sunburns, and fixing someone's limp—to grand, including setting up a client with actor Chris Hemsworth, achieving world peace, and curing cancer, but his methods are often unconventional. When the mall gets in trouble for the duo's business of "warping reality," Alex's chances at economic stability and a better future are jeopardized. Even when the consequences of Jinn's actions become dire, Habershaw keeps up the lighthearted, humorous tone. It's a cozy, comical confection."
—*Publishers Weekly*

"My three wishes? Three more books as good as this one from Auston Habershaw."
—Tom Holt, author of *The Eight Reindeer of the Apocalypse*

"*If Wishes Were Retail* taps into a long-storied tradition of smart comedic fantasy in the vein of Terry Pratchett. Habershaw's efficient and accessible prose allows his deeper themes of anti-exploitation, community, and the cost of human greed to take center stage, presented through laugh-out-loud absurdist moments that keep building and building in a page-turner of a novel. *If Wishes Were Retail* is a ten out of ten gnomes—if you can see them, that is."
—Mia Tsai, author of *Bitter Medicine*

"I wish I'd thought of this."
—Daniel Pinkwater, author of *Jules, Penny & the Rooster*

"A love letter to wounded people and community spaces, this suburban fantasy is both delightfully absurd and firmly grounded."
—Dave Klecha, coauthor of *The Runes of Engagement*

Also by the author

The Saga of the Redeemed

The Iron Ring (2015)
Iron and Blood (2015)
The Oldest Trick (2015)
No Good Deed (2016)
Dead But Once (2018)
The Far Far Better Thing (2019)

IF WISHES WERE RETAIL

TACHYON - SAN FRANCISCO

AUSTON HABERSHAW

Interior design and cover illustration by Elizabeth Story
Author photo by Deirdre Habershaw & Jacob Baugher

Tachyon Publications LLC
1459 18th Street #139
San Francisco, CA 94107
415.285.5615
www.tachyonpublications.com
tachyon@tachyonpublications.com

Series editor: Jacob Weisman
Editor: Jaymee Goh

Print ISBN: 978-1-61696-434-4
Digital ISBN: 978-1-61696-435-1

Printed in the United States by Versa Press, Inc.

First Edition: 2025
9 8 7 6 5 4 3 2 1

This book is dedicated to every kid out there sweating a minimum wage job while still in school,

To every gig-worker who gets a three-star review from somebody who thinks that's good enough,

To every person in food service who's been yelled at over a tip,

And to everybody, everywhere, who is working their ass off for some reason they can't remember anymore.

A job is just a job.
A boss is just a boss.
And all of us (every one of us) deserve better.

CHAPTER 1:
INTERVIEW

THE GENIE WAS SHIRTLESS, his skin a kind of burning red-orange color that reminded Alex of hot coals. He had these absurd muscles—huge, rippling piles of them, like a comic book character—and a wispy beard and moustache made of smoke. Alex tried very hard not to stare.

The genie had no trouble starting at Alex, though. "What is a Bagel Hut?"

"Ummm . . ." Alex found herself at a loss. "It's . . . it's a Bagel Hut. You know, where you get bagels?"

The genie squinted at the resume pinched between his long fingernails. His eyes were blazing yellow, like the bulbs of two flashlights. "What is a bagel?"

Alex had envisioned many bizarre ways this interview might have gone, but this one she hadn't anticipated. "It's . . . a . . . I dunno. You don't know what a bagel is?"

"Why would I ask you what a bagel is if I had the answer already? Do you think me a fool? A charlatan?"

Alex had an immediate answer for this particular question, but she held her tongue—an interview skill her mother had told her she needed to work on.

"According to this piece of paper, your only work experience is one summer working in a place called a Bagel Hut, and you cannot explain to me what a bagel is?"

"It's like a donut, but, like, not as sweet."

The genie looked confused. "What is a donut?"

"Jesus Christ, dude—google it, okay? You want me to explain what a shirt is next?"

"What secrets are you keeping from me about the Bagel Hut?" The genie shouted and fire leapt from the corners of his eyes.

"What?" Was she being pranked or something?

"If I were to call upon the master of the Bagel Hut and ask him . . ."

"Her."

The genie's mouth clapped shut. "What?"

"Her. My boss there was a woman. Ms. Partagas."

The genie took a long, slow breath, his absurd chest rising and falling in a way that made Alex think of glaciers and mountains and the movement of tectonic plates. "Do you commonly interrupt your master?"

"*Master*?!"

"Are you reliable?"

Alex knew at this point she ought to have said a variety of things—things her mother had coached her on, like "Ms. Partagas at the Bagel Hut trusted me to do inventory with her on Fridays" or "I'm my class treasurer at school!" But she didn't really feel like putting on a nicety-nice show for this guy, so she only offered the slightest of nods, trying to look away from the genie's blazing eyes, his pointy ears, the gold earrings in his pointy ears . . .

The genie threw the resume over his shoulder without looking. It flipped through the air and landed perfectly at the center of the bare desk that stood in the middle of the bare office, its edges aligned orthogonally with those of the desk itself. "Heed me, Alexandria Delmore: this duty which you intend to undertake is a heavy burden. Wishes are weighty things, and I have need of a mortal of unsurpassed constancy, lest this realm be laid to ruin at the feet of your own ineptitude. Is this understood?"

Alex frowned. "I'm going to be working in the *mall*, right?"

The genie gave her a grim nod. "Just so."

"And you want me to sell wishes?"

"Did not my advertisement in the Between Realm say as much?"

"Do you mean the *Internet?* Uhhh . . . yeah, I guess."

"And did I not swear to you that your toils shall be rewarded handsomely?"

"Also true . . . uhhh . . . genie? Gene? What do I call you?"

"You are not to call me genie—I will be known as 'Mr. Jinn'; is this clear?"

"You got it, Mr. Jinn, sir."

The genie rose from his aluminum folding chair. "I have a question, then, to test your worth. A hypothetical situation, if you will."

"O-okay."

"You are at your post in this Bagel Hut, whereupon you are called by your mistress. 'Lo,' she says, 'thy brother, who labors also for my pleasure, hath displeased me for he has gazed upon my daughter as she walked to the bazaar, and this cannot be. Come and take my sword and dispatch him even now and deliver unto me his traitorous head.' And so you are given the sword and charged with a mighty task. Do you obey the Mistress of the Bagel Hut, Alexandria Delmore?" The genie leaned over her, his eyes burning bright, his sharp teeth clenched in a frightening grin.

"You . . . you want me to *kill* someone?"

"Not I—your liege, Mistress of the Bagel Hut, demands it. Do you obey?"

Alex had no idea what the genie wanted to hear. Did this job involve *killing* people? What the hell? "What *exactly* does this have to do with . . ."

"Answer my question, Alexandria Delmore!" the genie roared loud enough to shake the windowpanes.

"Okay, okay—God! No! No, I wouldn't kill anyone in the Bagel Hut! I mean, obviously, right?"

The genie glowered at her for a long moment. If she didn't get this job, probably the only thing left was working for her dad, mowing lawns and trimming hedges in the summer heat while listening to Lynyrd Skynyrd on loop. Great.

The genie at last nodded. "This is an acceptable answer, Alexandria Delmore."

Alex blinked. "It is? Really?"

"I spent thirty-five centuries trapped in a ring, enslaved to the wishes of my masters. Think you now that I wish for slaves of my own? No indeed! I am most pleased you are not so servile as that. Most pleased!" Fire leapt from the genie's eyes.

Alex flinched from the genie's apparent . . . something. Joy? Enthusiasm? She had a hard time associating the demonic visage of the genie—all fire and smoke and sharp fangs— with positive emotions. "Does this mean I got the job?"

"No."

"*No!*"

"I have scarcely begun my interrogation!" the genie said. "Think you I am to entrust my business to the first child who toddles in off the street? Nay! This must be a thorough examination!"

Alex clenched her teeth and swallowed her rage for a second. "Since we're being so, like, *direct* and everything, can you maybe put on a shirt?"

The genie looked down at his absurd hubcap-sized pectorals. "Are you not impressed with this display of my physical prowess?"

"It's sales, man, not bodybuilding."

The genie nodded slowly, as though turning something over in his head. "The dummy spoke true, then," he muttered.

Alex might have asked—she sort of wanted to ask—but she didn't get the chance. The genie conjured a book from a popular self-help series, this one titled *The Dummy's Guide: 101 Interview Tips for Success*. He glared at it as he flipped through the pages. Silence dragged out.

Alex counted to thirty in her head, then said, "Okay, sooo . . ."

The genie snapped his fingers and suddenly he was wearing a polo shirt with a bank logo on it. It looked like the kind of thing you got in a swag-bag when you attended a business conference or something. It scarcely fit over the genie's bulging physique—if he tried to touch his elbows together, Alex imagined the whole thing would tear to shreds. In fact, it seemed as though the genie was intentionally keeping his elbows far apart. "Is this suitable?"

"Yeah, I guess," Alex said.

The genie nodded at her over the edge of the book and flipped a page. "Where do you see yourself in five years, Alexandria Delmore?"

Alex blinked. Her plans did not go that far. "I don't know. You don't think I'm still gonna be working at the mall, do you?"

The genie frowned. "I will not answer the question for you! I demand you tell *me* your future as you imagine it!"

"Jeez, okay—college, I hope? Getting out of this stupid town? Dude, you are aware I can't *see* the future, right?"

"True." The genie considered this and referred to the book. "The book does not seem to take this into account."

"Is this how this job is going to be *all* the time?"

The genie went back to his interview book. "What is the greatest of your many weaknesses?"

"That question is *such* bullshit, man."

"Answer the question!"

"No—it's a bullshit question! How do you even answer that honestly? Like, say I tell the truth and badmouth myself, then you think I lack confidence or whatever and I don't get the job. Say I lie, then—I say some bullshit like 'I'm just soooo punctual and it's soo annoying!'—and then *you* know I'm lying and *I* know you know I'm lying and we're just sitting here blowing smoke up each other's asses and I ask you, Mr. Jinn, what does that do for either of us?"

"So your greatest mortal frailty is insolence," the genie said. He conjured a pen in his hand and made a little note on a pad of paper that had appeared on his otherwise empty desk.

"What? I didn't say that!"

"Yes, you did."

Alex folded her arms and stewed on that for a second. "Okay, time for my questions: How much does this job pay, anyway?"

"I have told you that your labors shall be handsomely

rewarded!" the genie said in a voice that was louder than necessary.

This time Alex met the genie's gaze, fiery eyes and all. "Yeah, but that's really vague. How much is 'handsomely rewarded,' exactly?"

"Do you accuse me of perfidy?"

Alex rolled her eyes. "Just use normal words, for Christ's sake."

The genie glowered for a moment. Smoke curled out of his nostrils. "You are a vexatious woman."

Alex smiled at him. "Thank you!"

The genie said nothing. He looked around the bare office, as though seeking inspiration. Alex didn't think he'd find much—other than the desk, a bookshelf with only one book (*Your Own Master: The Secrets to Small Business Ownership*) and a cell phone on the floor plugged into an outlet, there was nothing there.

"I will pay you a commission," the genie said.

"How much of a commission?"

"Five percent."

"How much will wishes go for?"

"It varies, but no less than five pieces of silver."

"How much is that in dollars?"

"What are dollars?"

"You are not giving me a lot of confidence in this job, man."

The genie reached up to stroke his smoky beard. This caused the sleeve of his polo shirt to rupture. The genie looked at it; Alex looked at it. It was funny, but she didn't want to laugh because the genie had this look on his face— like he was tired. Like he was tired and trying so hard and still not getting it. She tried to imagine what it would be like, being some all-powerful genie reduced to working in a mall. She suddenly felt bad for him.

"Sorry," she said.

"Why?"

"Why am I sorry, or . . ."

"Why are you sorry, Alexandria Delmore?" He was gazing at her intently.

Alex looked away. "I dunno. I'm sorry your shirt ripped or whatever. That must suck. You specifically wished it up for yourself, so I guess you like it and stuff, so . . . sorry that happened, you know?"

The genie carefully placed his hands upon his knees. He looked up and past Alex, as though gazing at something far away. "I once met a man in Damascus who called upon my master, complaining of his uncle and his greed. This man— a skilled artisan—had made many wonderful things for his uncle and his uncle had refused to pay. He was destitute, and called upon my master in ragged clothing, unwashed and wretched. 'Please, Great Master of the Diwan al-Kharaj' he begged, crawling on the floor like a dog, 'I seek justice! I seek fair repayment!'"

Alex was not sure what she should do. The story had stopped, apparently in the middle. After a few seconds of silence, she asked. "So, what did your master do?"

"He laughed," the genie said. "He ordered the man beaten and cast out of his house as a beggar, for that is what he now was in the eyes of the well-fed and clothed. 'Am I to beggar *myself* to save them from their foolishness?' he asked of me."

"That's bullshit." Alex said, belatedly aware that she probably shouldn't have said "bullshit" twice during a job interview, but that ship had definitely sailed by now. "He had a genie.

Couldn't he just have wished for all the beggars to have money or whatever?"

"Yes," the genie said, eyes wide. "He could have."

Another long pause. "So," Alex said, "was there a point to that or . . ."

The genie suddenly had a scroll in his hand. He unfurled it, revealing a document scribbled in a cramped hand and a foreign alphabet. "You must sign this in your blood."

She got the job. *She got the job!*

Still, brass tacks and all, "For a five percent commission?" Alex recoiled from the little knife the genie presented her with. "No way!"

"Seven percent," the genie said.

"Twenty!"

"Ten!"

Alex stood up. She was tall and wearing boots that added three inches to her height, but even still she barely came up to the genie's shoulders. "Ten and Mondays off!"

The genie grinned, showing a mouth full of razor-sharp teeth. "It is done, Alexandria Delmore."

"Look, call me Alex, okay? Alexandria is my grandmother." She took the knife from him and looked at the bottom of the contract. "What's all this say, anyway?"

"Ah. You will desire it to be translated." The genie snapped his fingers and the words rearranged themselves into legible English script.

It read:

I, Alexandria Delmore, daughter of Charles and Ro-salind Delmore, hereby swear my service to the Jinn formerly of the Ring of Khorad, to assist him in the

*administration and sale of mortal desires in exchange
for currency or property. My duties, hereby agreed to,
are as follows:*

- *To work tirelessly from the opening of the Wellspring
  Mall until sundown each day, excluding Mondays.*
- *To treat with mortal supplicants without complaint.*
- *To obey the Jinn in any reasonable request.*
- *To not divulge the secrets of the Jinn to his enemies,
  should any arise.*
- *To inform the Jinn in case of mortal frailty or illness.*
- *To assist the Jinn with understanding the mortal
  world.*

*In exchange, the Jinn formerly of the Ring of Khorad
will surrender 10 percent of all payment to myself,
Alexandria Delmore, provided I can demonstrate
myself to be a native of this nation and place and
neither a criminal nor a vagabond.*

*This arrangement may be dissolved at will by either
myself or the Jinn, in keeping with their nature
as free beings.*

*I hereby seal this pact with my blood, and may no
man nor spirit question my resolve.*

Alex read it twice. It was sort of . . . disappointing. She was
hoping for something a little more magical somehow. "Do I
have to write my whole name in blood, or . . ."

"Just a drop," the genie said. "A drop will do."

CHAPTER 2:
WHAT THE BAGEL HUT HATH WROUGHT

A FEW SECONDS after her interview, Alex was back in the parking lot of the nondescript office building, her heart racing. She did it. She got a job. What's more, she got *this* job. She took a deep, cleansing breath, and hopped on her rusty, school bus-yellow moped to bike home. It took her three times pumping the kick-starter before the little engine coughed to life and propelled her into the deeper reaches of American suburbia at a modest 20 mph.

Alex's brief stint at the Bagel Hut—her only "real" job—had ended when it was discovered that her father had been "seeing" Ms. Partagas, the manager. What exactly "seeing" entailed was initially unclear—Alex couldn't quite imagine her father, bow-legged and perpetually sunburned, seducing a younger woman. The truth of it had proven to be no less embarrassing. Her father had been taken in by a pyramid scheme selling "natural testosterone powder," having purchased eight cases from Ms. Partagas to the tune of many thousands of dollars. Not only had the powder not worked, it had barely existed— the "cases" contained elaborate packaging for what turned out to be a couple handfuls of rabbit-pellet green pills that absolutely did *not* dissolve in a cup of coffee as advertised.

Her father had then been arrested in the Bagel Hut after screaming a variety of offensive remarks at Ms. Partagas across the counter during business hours. Alex's mother had bailed him out—this process of arrest and bailing out was a seasonal tradition in the Delmore household, indicating the coming of summer in a manner similar to groundhogs and shadows. However, the conversation that ensued following the release of her father was anything *but* traditional and involved a lot of hysterical screaming by both Alex's parents regarding the huge financial burden his attempt to bring "manliness back to the community" had caused. Alex's mother, as it turned out, was completely unaware that her father had sunk so much money into his "little pills," and was shrieking mad about it, especially given that her father's landscaping business was losing customers at a precipitous rate and money was very tight. The argument ended with her father and mother "separating," which meant her father moved into the garage and slept on an air mattress amid at least seven partly disassembled lawnmower engines.

Anyway, all of *this* meant that continued employment at the Bagel Hut proved . . . awkward. Alex liked (had liked?) Ms. Partagas, but Alex didn't think she could have actually looked the woman in the eye knowing that she had suckered her father into near financial destruction, or that her father— the sucker—had called the woman a "foxy, big-bosomed Jezebel" in front of at least three kids she knew from school before getting tasered against the salad bar.

Alex didn't want to hear her boss apologize or explain or justify or anything. Alex just wanted to pretend it *hadn't* happened. Therefore, she hadn't so much quit as just stopped going. Ms. Partagas seemed to have been on the same page, since she mailed Alex's last check home. Alex had opened the envelope worried that it might contain some kind of note. But it didn't—just the check.

All this happened at the tail end of April, about six weeks ago, just before Alex's seventeenth birthday. The birthday party had been a recreation of Cold War Berlin, with each of her parents throwing competing birthday celebrations at opposite ends of the yard. Her mother's side featured pink streamers and unicorn cupcakes while her father's involved the Sex Pistols blaring on a prehistoric boombox and the gift of a six-pack of beer because "you're most of the way there, right?"

There had been no one else at the party besides a couple uncles and a couple cousins. No friends. Nobody her age. Alex's high school experience had been a lonely one, caused largely by the pandemic and compounded by her sharp tongue and generally abrasive attitude—over two years of isolation, her meager circle of friends withered. Some had moved away, some had moved on, some off to college in faraway places. There was nobody left who wanted to deal with all the nonsense that was constantly going down in the Delmore family. *"There's always drama with you, Alex,"* her ostensible "friend" Marissa had texted her. *"Ima pass."*

With friends like those, right?

During the birthday "event," Alex had sat alone in the exact middle of the yard at the old wooden picnic table, not exactly sure who she needed to be pissed at about all of this, but very certain that anger was the appropriate emotion for the situation.

She hadn't even been allowed to drink that beer.

No matter how angry she was, it was made clear to her by both the garage-dwelling and non-garage-dwelling portions of her family that she couldn't remain idle and unemployed, not while her father's landscaping business was on rocky footing, her mother's job at the supermarket was cutting back on overtime, and they were still a few thousand dollars in the hole due to her father's testosterone pill adventures. So, back to the job search it was.

Alex spent the tail end of the school year bouncing from interview to interview. She was surprised how competitive it was; she was even turned down for a job at ValuDay, though they probably employed a million people in those stupid green polo shirts, saying "hi" in a cheery falsetto to every moron who wandered through the doors, and were supposedly "always hiring." Well, not her. Alex, with her surplus army jacket and pierced eyebrow, "wasn't a good fit."

In point of fact, despite all the old people she knew claiming "no one wanted to work," she had not been a good fit anywhere. McDonald's wouldn't hire her because she wouldn't say why she stopped working at Bagel Hut ("my dad threatened to assault my manager with a weed whacker"). Same for the fried chicken place off the highway. She couldn't wait tables because she had no experience. She didn't know much of anything about computers, so Data Dave had told her to take a hike. She hadn't been able to get a steady babysitting gig since she got her piercings in ninth grade. It was all so, so humiliating. A bunch of awkward conversations with people in golf visors and threadbare khaki pants, being told that no, she wasn't good enough to dress up like an idiot and hand out milkshakes to her classmates who were out on dates.

If she had her way, she would have just given up—who cared anyway? Like her miserable minimum wage crap job—even assuming she *could* get one—was going to make such a huge difference. Why be ritually humiliated just so her parents would lose the house *slower*? Their lives were a full-on reality TV disaster now—rip off the bandage quick, Alex figured. Get it over with.

Her mother wasn't having it. At dinner one night—reheated macaroni and cheese in cheap plastic bowls—she raked Alex over the coals. "This isn't about you, you know. I wouldn't be asking you to do this if I didn't *have* to, Lexie." Her mom was still wearing her supermarket uniform—her name on her nametag ("Rosalind") was surrounded by assiduously focus-grouped illustrations of smiling faces full of delighted, meaningless laughter. Alex couldn't stand looking at it.

"I know, Mom," she said.

"You need to broaden your search, that's all."

"But I've already applied to *everywhere* I can bike to! You didn't even want me to interview at that fried chicken place!"

"Lexie, you are *not allowed* to ride that horrible motor scooter on the shoulder of the interstate!"

Alex stabbed her macaroni, the imperfectly heated cheese sauce rendering it spongy more than soft. "Well then *what*? You say you need me to get a job, and then you make it *impossible* for me to get a job!"

"Ask your father for a ride," her mother said, shoveling leftovers into a resealable plastic container stained orange from some distant encounter with marinara sauce. "Bring this to him."

Alex frowned at the food. "Why are you still feeding him if you're so pissed?"

"We can't afford for him to eat out and I won't have him in my kitchen."

Alex took the mac and cheese out to the garage, where she found her older brother Mark and her father already eating a pizza they'd had delivered. "Mom says we can't afford to eat out."

Mark rolled his eyes. "You gonna tattle or something?"

Alex chucked the container of mac and cheese at his head. Her father stood up from a box of "Muscle-T" he was using as a chair and pulled up his belt to better hug his beer gut. This meant he was about to dispense fatherly advice; Alex braced herself. "You got a job yet?" he asked.

"No."

"You wanna mow lawns for the rest of your life?" He gestured to the garage full of lawn-care paraphernalia with one grass-stained hand.

"I don't even want to mow lawns *now*."

"Then let that motivate you, Lexie. You need to broaden your search, that's all."

So, Alex *had* broadened her search. She started looking for jobs that *not everyone* would look at seriously. Gig economy shit—delivering groceries to lazy people who couldn't be bothered to get to the store, walking people's dogs, stuff like that. All of it stunk. It seemed even worse than all the dumbass retail jobs. At least there, you could commiserate with comrades in arms against the menace of the customer. As a gig worker, the customer and the boss seemed like the same exact thing, and you were all alone.

Alex didn't apply. She justified it by telling herself that her parents would freak if she took a job like that—riding around on her dilapidated moped was something her mother actively discouraged, and her father had a dim view of the gig economy simply because of the number of "amateurs" who were going around doing shitty gardening for cheaper than he offered.

That was when she stumbled across the genie. On page ten of a Google search, where only the desperate found themselves. It was a website of a sort—a single, blank, white web page with the words "THIS SPACE BELONGS TO THE JINN, FORMERLY OF THE RING OF KHORAD" and an e-mail address and a brief job description for a cashier. Alex had e-mailed and received an instant reply—*You will attend me on June the 21st, when the bell strikes one hour past midday, whereupon you shall be tested for worthiness.*

An address was provided—one of those places that rented out temporary office space. Initially, she wasn't sure if she should go. The whole thing was weird. Some kind of prank, she figured. But, then again, she didn't have a lot of options. She brought along one of her dad's pocketknives in case she had to stab some creeper, told her mom exactly where she was going, and figured the odds of being raped and murdered in an office park in the middle of the damned day seemed . . . slight. Okay, so maybe *more* likely than genies being real, but the payoff if the job was legit was worth the gamble.

So she'd gone. The genie had been *real*, and it had actually *worked*—she had a job! A job that paid in a commission on wishes that, if anything, sounded like something above minimum wage. A huge win.

She couldn't tell her parents about it, of course—no way. They wouldn't believe her anyway and, if they did, they'd freak out. Alex texted her mom before getting back on her moped: *I got the job! Working at the mall. Sales.*

She hoped that would satisfy her curiosity. God knows her mom was busy enough with her own problems. Alex sort of hoped that, just this once, her parents and their bullshit "separation" would work in her favor.

Home was a fifteen-minute ride away. The sun was out, but it wasn't that hot. It was a glorious day for it, but Alex was too lost in thought to really savor anything. She just kept thinking of some plausible cover story to keep her new job secret and, barring that, some excuse for why she took it. The money, she supposed she'd say.

What the genie was paying wasn't what she was really after, though. It was working for a being who could *grant wishes* and might be able to fix her life. All she needed to do was make friends with a genie. Making friends was not Alex's strong suit, but if it meant not having to deal with her parents anymore, she was willing to *Princess Diaries* herself into the perfect life she always dreamed of.

Alex was daydreaming about this when she pulled into her driveway and saw her father's pickup truck pulled up with the engine running and her brother leaning against it, sucking on his vape pen. The front door stood open. Her father had come home in the middle of the day, left his territory, and invaded her mom's. He was probably hoping her mom was still at work, but Alex knew perfectly well that this was her day off.

Her daydream of hanging out with her new boss vanished in a very genie-like puff of mental vapor.

Shit.

The walls of the house barely muffled the yelling. Alex stood on the front steps, debating whether or not she wanted to go inside.

"I wouldn't," Mark said, blowing a column of sickly sweet blue smoke into the sky. Mark was tanned brown as toast from weeks of working outside and wore a shirt with the sleeves ripped out—a walking, talking cliché, her brother.

Alex considered getting back on her bike and riding around the block a few times, just until her dad was gone back to work.

But then her father rushed out clutching a bunch of papers to his chest, his eyes wild, bald head shining with sweat—like he'd just robbed the place. Alex could hear her mom clearly now. "Are you fucking kidding me, Charlie? Get the fuck out! Go back to your whore! *Go back to your bagel whore!*"

She slammed the door behind him so hard the Easter wreath fell off.

Alex was left, nose-to-nose, with her father.

Her father forced a smile. "Oh, hey, Lexie. Listen, let's go get lunch, huh? You, Mark, and me."

Alex did not want any part of this. "No thanks, Dad."

Her father had his hand on Alex's shoulder, spinning her around, piloting her toward the truck. "C'mon, c'mon—we'll get that pizza your mom hates. With the pineapple."

So it was that Alex found herself sitting between her brother and her father in the front seat of the pickup truck. The interior smelled of engine oil, cut grass, and old coffee. On the dashboard, a bloody Jesus dragged the cross amid a forest of other ornaments—a few cartoon characters, a bobblehead of Donald Trump, and a little placard stating that the only good garden gnome was a dead garden gnome. She remembered liking riding in her father's truck when she was little—a sense of importance and power from the roar of the engine and being higher than everyone else on the road—but both she and the truck had come a long way since then.

"Your mom tells me you have a job now?"

Alex tried to imagine how her mother had delivered this information. *"Lexie had to get another job, you deadbeat sonofabitch!"*

"Yeah." Alex said.

"Whatcha doing?"

"Sales."

"On commission?"

"I guess. Yeah."

"How do you like it?"

"It's okay," Alex said, not bothering to explain that she hadn't started yet.

"What are you selling?" Mark asked. "Like, cell phones or some shit?"

"Language!" her father barked.

"Yeah," Alex said. "Cell phones. Exactly."

Her father mulled this over for a moment. "I suppose that's honest work."

Alex had never quite figured out what constituted "honest work" in her father's eyes. It was all tied in with his abstract sense of "decency," which he frequently extolled, usually when disparaging Alex's chosen mode of dress. In point of fact, Alex could think of few less honest professions at the mall than selling cell phones, but she didn't have very high standards for her father's judgment, especially given he'd been mixing glorified oregano in with his coffee for weeks and hoping he'd grow more hair.

"You know, I got my start in sales, too," her father said. "Sold knives door-to-door. Those kinda knives that never go dull—you know those?"

"Yeah." Alex looked out the window at the gas stations and fast-food joints and convenience stores that cruised by, her mind racing for some way to change the subject. "What do you want all that paperwork for?"

Her father's whole body language changed in a way that told Alex he was lying—he licked his lips and hunched his shoulders and gestured too much when he talked. "Uhhh . . . nothing. Legal stuff, you know? For the business."

"Yeah, what do you care, anyway?" Mark asked. Such a kiss-ass, that Mark.

"You gonna see if you can sue clients for dropping you like a hot rock?" Alex asked.

"Sarcasm isn't pretty, Lexie," her father said.

"Maybe I should take up restaurant management, then."

"What the . . ." Her dad looked away and swallowed some nasty words, but only barely. "What did your mother tell you? Look, you can't believe everything she says, okay? She's up-set—which, you know, is totally fair, but you really can't listen to everything a woman in that state says."

A woman in that state.

Alex wanted to ask him exactly what "state" her mother was in and how, in his opinion, she had come to *be* in that state. But that would be another fight, and Alex didn't *want* to fight with her father. She let her mother do that for her. Every "you son of a bitch" and every "screw you, Charlie" was silently cosigned by Alex, but in light of her dimwitted brother's whole-hearted endorsement of . . . of *whatever* was going on here, her public role had to be that of mediator. So, Alex let the subject drop.

They pulled into the parking lot of the local pizza chain, they went in, they had a Hawaiian pizza to split between the three of them. Her father paid the bill with change from a mason jar. He and Mark went on and on about how the landscaping business was in a death spiral. "I couldn't figure it out," her dad said. "Loyal clients for years—*years*—and then they just up and cancel! I thought it was some kind of gig thing, but it's not."

"Yeah, it's not that." Mark added, waggling his eyebrows.

Her father had that wild-eyed look he got when talking about government conspiracies. Alex braced herself. He leaned across the table toward her and stage-whispered one word: "Gnomes."

Alex blinked. "I'm sorry, *what?*"

"Or fairies. Or leprechauns—I don't know the terminology, okay—but it's *gnomes*, Lexie. My business is being stolen *by little people.*"

"I've seen them!" Mark added. "They're really quick, but I saw one—look!" He slid his cell phone across the table with a photograph of a beautifully manicured lawn with a blurry reddish streak across it.

Alex frowned at it. "Gonna take pictures of bigfoot next?"

Her dad snorted. "You don't wanna believe me, fine. But I'm gonna prove it. I'm gonna expose those little freaks. Hell, I'm gonna *sue* them! Constraint of trade! Labor laws! Uhhh . . . zoning law and stuff!"

Light dawned. *That* was what the paperwork was for . . . somehow. As her father geared up into full rant mode, the plan made progressively less and less sense. Even assuming there *were* gnomes (and, if there were genies, why couldn't there be gnomes?), Alex rather doubted there was any lawyer on Earth willing to take on the case.

That didn't stop him from raving for the next thirty minutes. Right there in the restaurant. People around them moved tables to get away from him.

Alex said as little as possible. She had to fight the urge to scream, to hit him and cry and throw a complete, all-out, Real Housewives hissy fit over how stupid and insane he was and how angry she was with Mark for just going along with it. But she didn't. She played the part of the good daughter, dutifully listening to her father's colossal delusions of how the thing between him and financial success was a couple gnomes doing topiary and not, you know, the fact that he was a short-tempered, sullen asshole in a rusty truck with the business sense of a drunken troll and tried to tell herself that all she needed to do—*all* that had to happen for all this bullshit to stop—was for her to make it into a college somewhere and just fucking *vanish* from this miserable town forever, like everyone else she had ever liked.

Of course, it would take a miracle for that amount of money to become available to her even *if* her father's business wasn't failing. Unless she got a scholarship or something. Unless she was crazy lucky.

Unless she, for instance, got to make a wish.

CHAPTER 3:
THE WELLSPRING MALL

BECAUSE HER MOM was being totally unreasonable about her riding her moped to the mall ("it will get stolen! You'll get hit by a car!"), Alex got dropped off for her first day of work by her dad and brother in the truck. Today, she opted to ride in the back, rattling around with the mowers and rakes and leaf-blowers, rather than have to listen to conservative talk radio and her father's unhinged and quasi-legal schemes for fighting gnomes ("you think rat poison would work?"). They stopped by the curb long enough to let her climb out and leap to the sidewalk. Mark leaned out the passenger's side window. "Good luck earning yourself a full ride to Lesbian College!" he said.

"Screw you, Mark." She straightened her jacket and looked around to see if anyone had heard. There was no one. Mall wasn't even open yet.

She heard a murmur from inside the cab of the pickup. Mark relayed the message. "Dad wants to know when your shift gets out."

"Sunset, I think."

Mark relayed the message again. "He says if it's after six, you gotta call mom."

"Why, he gotta date?"

Mark shrugged, stuck out his tongue, and the truck pulled away from the curb with him still hanging out the window. He threw devil horns with one hand and screamed like a banshee as they sped off.

"Assholes." Alex dug in her coat and pulled out her phone to check the time. She was late. "Shit."

The last time Alex had been inside the Wellspring Mall, she had been maybe nine years old, going to visit Santa for what turned out to be the last time. She hadn't believed in Santa then, but her father was still invested in the whole thing, so he wanted to prove to her that Santa was real. At that time, her father had been dabbling in "sovereign citizenship," which mostly seemed to entail her father bringing a gun everywhere. Like, for instance, in the line to visit Santa, full of mothers and other kids, all of whom Alex had taken it upon herself to inform about the lie that was Kris Kringle. Alex wasn't sure what had happened next, but one of the mothers in line saw that her dad had a pistol stuffed into the waistband of his jeans (probably when he was crouching down to try and shut Alex up), and the next thing that happened was basically a mass panic event as children were scooped up by their mothers and ran for the hills shouting "gun gun gun!"

Her father, assuming they were talking about somebody *else* with a gun, *drew* his gun to blow away the imaginary gunman and, well, things unfolded from there. In retrospect, Alex was amazed her father hadn't been shot by the SWAT team that showed up.

Anyway, the point was that Alex had remembered the mall

as being a lot louder, a lot brighter, and a lot . . . well . . . more exciting. Most of the stores now looked like sterile terrariums of weird lifestyles Alex didn't think anyone actually lived: there were young people in cargo shorts on boats, bony European girls having trouble controlling their hair on the beach, men in suits wearing expensive watches. The brands and the storefronts seemed to glide across her notice, barely registering as shops. Some other stores looked like bad ideas launched by reality show contestants—essential oil emporiums and custom aerial photography of anonymous, tree-laden swathes of suburbia (*we'll even put it on T-shirts!*). A full third of the storefronts were obscured behind big blocks of smooth plywood, all painted gray, with signs that said, *"Coming Soon to Wellspring!"* But nothing was coming soon, Alex was betting. She was walking down the broad, empty corridors of an empire in decline.

The genie had not given Alex any specific indication *where* his shop was in the mall. She didn't even exactly know what it was called. So, she walked around for a while, scanning storefronts for something that looked likely. It turned out the genie's shop—kiosk, really—wasn't called anything at all. It was a drab gray cylinder, barely wide enough to fit three people abreast. At one side was mounted an ostentatious throne of what looked like obsidian or some similarly dark rock.

The perimeter of the cylinder was a glass display case that was filled with testimonials of satisfied customers. These testimonials were all ancient—scraps of parchment and papyrus, illuminated manuscripts, a clay tablet inscribed with cuneiform. They had beside them little notecards that translated what was written—an Egyptian pharaoh credited the genie with the construction of his pyramid, a sixth century Frankish king explained how the genie had crushed some army, an Abbasid Caliph described a golden fountain that would never run dry. The notecards were small and written in an old-fashioned calligraphy that Alex had trouble reading.

"Well," she muttered to herself, "I guess I'm actually doing this."

On top of the counter was a cash register and a fat scroll—two cylinders the diameter of Alex's legs mounted on wooden dowels. She was examining this last bit when the genie appeared in a puff of blue smoke. Alex jumped back against the counter. "What the . . . don't DO that!"

The genie was wearing a leisure suit from the 1970s—white, all rhinestones. The kind of thing Elvis would wear. He looked very serious. "You misunderstand our arrangement, Alexandria Delmore. You do not give me commands. I command *you!*"

Alex looked him up and down and decided she just couldn't keep it to herself. "What are you wearing?"

The genie smoothed the collar of his rhinestone leisure suit. "The attire of your kings. So that my relationship to your people will be clear."

"The attire of our . . ." Alex stopped herself. For the sake of this job, she'd told herself she'd shut up about stuff like that. Well, she'd try, anyway. "What do you want me to do?"

The genie gestured to the throne. "I will sit there, as befits my station. You will greet supplicants as they approach and hear their entreaties."

"Their wishes, you mean."

"Just so."

Okay, so she'd be getting their wishes and then collecting the money—clear enough. "How much for a wish?"

The genie pointed at the scroll. "I have compiled a list of all the wishes I have ever granted and assigned to them a price in order to ensure a fair exchange."

Alex looked at the huge, antique scroll. "I don't suppose you arranged them alphabetically?"

"I have not."

Alex sighed. Of course not. Still—positive vibes! "I'm assuming a limit of three per customer?" She grinned at her boss.

The genie stared at her. "Why would you assume that?"

Alex was suddenly at a loss for words. "Uhhh . . . like . . . because you're a *genie* and . . . like . . . so three wishes? Isn't that how it works?"

"No, that is not how it works."

The genie walked through the counter (*through*, like smoke) and ascended the throne and sat down. "You may begin your duties."

Alex jerked her thumb in the direction of the food court. "I was just going to get a coffee, if that's okay."

"It is not okay. I am not paying you to drink coffee in a café."

"Dude, I'll bring it *back*. Do you want anything?"

The genie seemed perplexed by this. He looked at her, head cocked to one side. "You are offering to purchase coffee for me?"

"I mean, I'm sort of assuming you'll pay me back, right? I'm not working at the mall because I'm independently wealthy." Alex stopped. "Wait—can't you just, like, *wish* us up some coffees?"

"Yes." The genie nodded.

Alex waited a few seconds. "Um . . . *will* you?"

The genie gripped the armrests of his chair. "No." He sounded very firm, almost angry about it.

"Okay, well . . ." Alex backed away from the counter. "I'll be back in five, okay?"

It was a short walk to the food court. Four of the five storefronts in the little, semi-circular alcove were closed, but the fifth—SpeedJava—was open and had a line of mall employees waiting for their morning jolt. Alex was the only one not wearing some kind of uniform. When she got there, a bunch of people in polo shirts turned and stared at her in her ripped jeans, combat boots, and army jacket. The girl at the back— blonde with artificially tanned skin and wearing short-shorts and a crop-top—recoiled from her like she was covered in slime. "Oh my God—where do *you* work?"

Alex smiled sweetly. "Your nightmares, Bunny."

The girl rolled her eyes. "My name *isn't* Bunny."

Alex turned her thoughts to her new boss. If you were a genie, and you wanted a coffee, why *wouldn't* you just wish yourself up a coffee? And what was with the Elvis suit? She knew this was going to be weird, but maybe she was underestimating how weird it could get.

She thought of her idiot family—of her father's absurd paranoia, her mother's rages and terrors, of her brother Mark lighting his tank top on fire with a roman candle and then trying to put it out with a bottle of whiskey.

She thought of that stack of college applications in her room, all filled out and ready to go.

She thought of becoming the valued employee of an all-powerful genie.

It would all be worth it. She could handle it.

But . . . *could* she?

By the time she got to the front of the line, she felt a little tickle in her stomach that she began to identify as unease—

maybe even fear. She was working with a being beyond all mortal control. What if somebody wished for something crazy? Her mind started to list off all the terrible things that could be wished for:

I wish my ex-girlfriend would just die already.

I wish gay people would disappear.

I wish the Earth really was flat.

She thought about her dad—what her crazy, irresponsible, conspiracy-theorist dad would wish for. It made her shudder. *It'll be okay . . . it'll be okay . . .*

Genies have rules. They have standards. They . . . have something.

She hurried back to the kiosk with her coffee, planning to take a good hard look at that pricing guide.

When she got there, she climbed over the counter and went straight to the fat scroll. The genie seemed not to notice she had returned.

The first thing on the list was *Goats—5 pieces of silver per herd*. The second thing was *A Soaking Rain Over One's Fields—50 pieces of silver.* She skimmed the list, scrolling down: Bountiful Harvest, Protection from Smallpox, a Dog of Pure Gold, Hemorrhoids to One's Enemies, Fair Winds for Sailing, a Flock of a Thousand Songbirds . . .

"What the . . ." Alex said. "Who would want *fifty* swift horses?"

"The Emperor of China," the genie said from his throne above her. "He was most pleased. I think that shall be a wish frequently in demand."

"That's . . . a lot of horses."

"Indeed."

The genie supplied no further instructions regarding her

duties. Ironically, Alex was now the Christmas elf to the genie's Santa—collect the money, relay the wish, and then it would be granted. Alex wondered if there was going to be any sitting on laps involved. She hoped not.

It was hard to tell when or if people started showing up to the mall, since they were so far from the main entrances. The closest department store had once been a JC Penny and was now closed, meaning nobody was coming in their side. Gradually, senior citizens and women with strollers trickled by in singles or pairs. Most of them gave the kiosk scarcely a glance. Those who did look caught sight of the genie, his massive arms folded and his eyes smoldering, and hurried away.

Across from them, the woman in the Better Body Outlet arranged a scenic display of pastel-colored bath salts in a rack by the entrance to her store. She kept giving the genie dirty looks and then began stringing dream catchers all around the doorway.

An hour passed.

Alex kept scrolling through the massive pricing guide. Some of the entries were legitimately hilarious ("a rooster that curses like a sailor") and others were . . . well, problematic (transport a "marriage bed" into your home, complete with bride).

When she got to "Fifty Slaves" she had to say something. "You know some of these wishes are illegal, right? Like, if anybody wishes for this, they should legit go to prison."

The genie looked down at her. "What do you mean?"

"I mean that it's *illegal* to *own slaves!*" She pointed at the entry.

The genie stroked his smoky beard. "Of this I was not aware. Truly, one man may not own the freedom of another?"

"Of course not!"

"Not even if they sell their freedom?"

"Why would anyone do that?" Alex asked.

"In exchange for their miserable lives, for instance," the genie said. He sounded as though he were explaining something simple that she should have learned already.

"Yeah, no—illegal."

"What if they are captured in battle?"

"No."

"What if they worship unclean gods? Or perhaps are fornicators with goats?"

"Are you kidding me right now?" Alex didn't know if that was racist or something, but it sounded suspiciously like something her father would say, so she wasn't a fan.

"Are you to tell me there is no means by which a person can be compelled to obey another against their will?"

"Other than prison? No!"

"So be it!" the genie boomed. He pointed at the scroll. "You will cross out 'fifty slaves' and replace it with 'imprison fifty men.' Satisfied, you miserable shrew of a girl?"

Alex clenched her teeth. *Remember the money. Remember the money.* She started hunting around for a permanent marker in the kiosk. There were none, because of course there weren't. At a loss for what to do, and not wanting to talk to her boss again, she slipped a dark lipstick out of her jacket pocket and crossed out "slaves." Then she shuffled the scroll so that somebody wasn't likely to come across that particular wish.

"Your attention, please!"

Alex looked up to see a big, fleshy white guy in a mall security uniform and a stupid looking moustache standing across the counter. He was talking to both of them, sort of, but mostly Alex, since she was closest.

Alex looked at the genie, who wasn't paying attention, then back to the mall cop. "Hi!"

He was standing on a sun-faded and brittle-looking Segway scooter and peering down at a clipboard. "Yeah . . . did you guys sign a lease?"

Alex called over her shoulder. "Oh *boss*—you want to handle this?"

The genie looked down at them. "Does this wretch seek to make a wish?"

The mall cop produced a pained smile. "Ah, no—see, you're not on the list, buddy. You can't be here."

The genie looked nonplussed. "What is your name?"

"Uhhhh . . . Frank?" Frank pointed at his name tag, which read "Officer Coop."

"And who are you, Officer Coop Frank, to deny me space in this marketplace?"

It started to dawn on Frank who—or *what*—he was talking with. Alex watched it happen, almost in slow motion. One second, this fat dude was all bored and calm, and the next second he was wide-eyed and alert. Alex guessed at this point the guy would either back off or double-down.

Frank chose double-down. "You need to *pay* to sell here, Aladdin!"

"Bold choice, dude." Alex muttered.

"Why must I pay?" asked the genie.

"Because . . . because that's how it's *done*, you stupid . . ." Frank sputtered. He tapped a fat finger on the clipboard. "You aren't *on the list*!"

The genie snapped his fingers. "Review your list again, Officer Coop Frank."

"I just . . ." Frank started to snarl and then looked at his clipboard. "What the . . . hey—you can't do that!"

"You are insolent," the genie said. "Begone."

Alex elected to move out from between the genie and the man on the scooter. "Hey, let's all calm down, okay? Maybe if you just, like, give us a rental application or something and we can get this all sorted out . . ."

"You're a tough guy, huh?" Frank said. "Maybe you won't be so tough if I call the cops on you, will ya? Huh?" He plucked a cheap walkie-talkie off his belt.

"Dude," Alex said. "Just chill, okay? He's a genie—he doesn't know how it all works."

Frank pointed a finger in her face. "You shut up!"

The genie rose from his throne. "Enough!"

And then Frank was gone. In his place was a beautiful song-bird, all blue and yellow plumage, perched on the handlebars of the Segway. Frank's clipboard and walkie-talkie clattered to the floor.

Alex gasped. "Holy shit, you didn't!"

"Am I to endure such abuse?" The genie pointed to where Frank had been. The bird was twittering and screeching. It took a little hop and landed on the floor. "If I am to be irritated by such a fool," the genie added, "it may as well be done with a more pleasing sound."

Alex climbed over the counter. The bird squeaked and hopped away from her, its whole little body trembling. "Change him back! Change him back, oh my God!"

The genie folded his arms and sat down. "No."

Alex took off her jacket. This was a crime, right? Turning somebody into a bird had to be a crime. Holy shit, holy shit! She tried to keep her voice calm. "Hey, Frank! It's okay, buddy.

I got you, okay? It's . . . it'll be all right!" She threw the coat over the bird's head. The bird—Frank—held perfectly still. Alex knelt and gently scooped him up.

She brought the bundle back to the counter. "Are you out of your *goddamned* mind?"

The genie raised one smoky eyebrow at her.

"You *can't* turn random people into animals! You're going to get in trouble!"

The genie shrugged. The leisure suit tore at the shoulder as a result of the gesture. "There is nothing they can do to me. No mortal army can oppose me. No human champion is my equal. If they come for me, I shall slay them with as little trouble as I transformed that insolent, torpid wretch into a beautiful songbird."

Alex looked around the mall. The lady in the Better Body Outlet squeaked and ducked behind her cash register.

If Alex didn't fix this, it was going to be the shortest job she'd ever had. "Look, do you actually *want* to run a business here in the mall?"

The genie frowned. "This is obvious. Of course."

"Okay, then you need to play by the mall's rules, right? If you turn the whole place into a battlefield, then *nobody* is going to visit your business. If you want to do this, then you need to turn this guy *back* into a guy and apologize and then you need to get a rental application or whatever from mall management."

The genie looked at her with those light-bulb eyes for a long moment. "You are very knowledgeable in these things, Alexandria Delmore. Very well—I shall do as you suggest."

Suddenly Frank was sitting on the counter of the kiosk, Alex's army jacket over his head. He yanked it off and rolled backward, landing on the mall floor with a hard thump. "Ah-hhh! AHHHHHHH!"

The genie extended a magnanimous hand. "I render my apologies unto you, Officer Coop Frank. I have handled you roughly and not in keeping with your customs."

Frank rose unsteadily to his feet, staring at his hands. "AH-HHHHHHH!"

"In order to make restitution for my insult, I offer you one coupon for a wish at half price." The genie reached solemnly over to a roll of paper coupons that had not been there before, detached one carefully along the perforations, and held it out to Frank.

Frank just ran away screaming. "I'm a man! I'm a MAN! AHHHH!"

Alex felt her pulse rate slow, but not by much. "You really are a people person, aren't you?"

"Transformation into a beast can be a taxing experience," the genie said. "He will recover apace."

Alex remained on edge for the next hour or so, waiting for the other shoe to drop. Frank did come back a few times, but never close—he peered at them from around large potted plants or strolled casually by, about twenty yards away, his face pressed to a walkie-talkie. No manager appeared. No customers dared to approach. If anyone had called the cops, none ever showed up, which was a good sign because Alex didn't know how the genie would react to guys with actual guns.

Eventually, Alex calmed down enough to realize that the genie was going to suffer no immediate consequences from what he had done, but the fact remained that she was working for a guy who was squatting on a spot in the mall. The genie sat on his throne in his stupid Elvis costume and did . . . nothing.

If she was going to keep working here all summer and get the genie on her good side—which was the plan—*she* was going to have to do something about it. The genie refused to let her leave her post, so she spent the rest of the morning using her lipstick to cross out wishes that were flagrantly illegal: *Lay a Plague Upon the House of Thy Foes, Consume an Enemy Host in Colorless Fire,* and even *Strike Dead a Herd of Elephants.* When it was time for her lunch break, Alex argued her way out of the kiosk and went back to the food court. She bought a yogurt and a croissant at the knock-off French café and sat in a hard metal chair bolted to the ground beneath a smoky gray skylight.

The plan was simple: after she ate her food, she was going to track down the manager's office, get a rental application, and fill it out. It seemed a stupid kind of plan, but she didn't have a better one.

"Hey—Alex, right?"

A tanned blond dude in a white polo shirt with the Velocity Burger logo emblazoned on it was standing over her. She recognized him from school—Fontana Russo. He had been a senior when she was a freshman. He also was a grade-A douche-canoe. This was the guy who had tried to talk Miranda Lahey into making out with him after a student council meeting and when she shut his ass down, he went around school telling people how big a slut she was.

Fontana kept smiling at her, like that was supposed to do something. "Did you hear me? I said 'hey.'"

"I'm not deaf, asshole."

"I hear you're working for that genie, right?" Fontana sat on the edge of the table. "You know, I'd watch out, if I were you."

"What do you care?"

"Come on—a thing like that, working here?" Fontana sighed as though he pained for humanity or something. "Can't end well."

"Okay."

"See, I got a job assistant managing at Velocity. I can get you on, if you want to bail."

What was this guy's angle? Alex looked over at Velocity—there was a line six people deep. The people behind the counter were running back and forth, sweating through their shirts, their glassy eyes fixed on some distant, unknowable point in time and space: they were slaves building the pyramids, chain-gang workers digging ditches. "No thanks."

"We pay dental."

Alex pointed at her mouth. "You see something wrong with my teeth?"

Fontana leaned closer. "I dunno, why don't you smile for me?" He winked.

"Jesus." Alex got up and walked away.

"Offer still stands," Fontana called as she left. "Won't last forever, though! You don't take me up on it, *you'll be sorry!*"

The phrase "you'll be sorry" had a certain curl to it—a certain poison behind the words. It sent a shiver up Alex's spine. She doused her hands in hand sanitizer from a little bottle in her jacket pocket. She did it twice.

Then it was a matter of finding the mall manager's office.

The back spaces of the Wellspring Mall—those areas never seen by customers or patrons—were harder to find than Alex thought. They were deliberately designed to fail to catch the eye—beige corridors with no ornamentation, their floors lacking the buff and polish of the grand mezzanines. Doors with no door handles, unmarked and apparently unused, confronted Alex at every juncture. There were almost no signs beyond EMPLOYEES ONLY.

After walking aimlessly for a few minutes, she decided to talk to somebody who worked maintaining the facility itself. She spotted a cleaning cart outside the men's bathroom—perfect. She poked her head inside. "Hello?"

There was no one there.

But somebody clearly *had* been there—the scent of pine mixed with bleach was still wafting through the air. The urinals *gleamed*. Maybe they were hiding in a stall? "Excuse me? Can I ask you a question?"

No answer.

Alex edged her toe over the threshold of the bathroom. Maybe they had headphones on?

She found herself pushed back—not forcefully, but insistently—by a pair of tiny little hands on her hip. "What the ..."

She looked down to see a little bearded man with a long red nose and an athletic sock for a hat. He looked pissed. Faster than she could follow with her eye, he produced a tiny little scrub-brush and quickly buffed the spot where her foot had stepped, his arms a blur. Then he was just a streak of brown and white, jetting back into the handicap stall at the end of the row.

A gnome.

Holy shit, they *were* real!

Alex gathered herself. "Hey, I just want to know where the manager's office is, okay? Can you help me out?"

Turns out the gnome *could not*. A second later the little man darted to the cleaning cart. Inside it, where Alex hadn't originally noticed, was a little see-saw akin to those things on old-timey railroads. The gnome manned one side of the see-saw and began to pump it up and down. The cart moved off, squeaking rhythmically, its occupant never once glancing at her again.

So, gnomes were not only *real*, they were also *assholes*. Were there any *decent* magical creatures out there?

Alex threw up her hands. "You know what? Screw it." She went back to the genie's kiosk.

When she arrived, it appeared as though the manager had found the genie. The great jinn sat upon his throne, rhinestones glittering, with a stack of paper in his lap. "What villainy is this?"

Alex sat on the counter and swung her legs over. "What's going on, boss?"

The genie stood up and bellowed, "WHAT IS A SOCIAL SECURITY NUMBER AND WHY MUST IT BE PROVIDED?!"

Alex held out a hand. "Can I see that, please?"

The genie thrust the packet into her hands. "They wish to charge me sixteen hundreds of your dollars to remain here! Due with each waxing of the moon, no less!"

The packet was a lease agreement attached to a handbook of Wellspring Mall rules and regulations. Flipping through it, Alex found that there was a segment stapled to the back in a different font and rife with spelling errors that was titled "Rules for Mystical Creatures." Somebody, evidently, had spent the morning typing this up. Alex handed it back. "Welcome to the twenty-first century, dude."

"But this price is outrageous! And the woman did not even tarry to haggle—she thrust it at me as though I were a leper!"

Alex forced a smile at the genie, did her best "calming voice." "Look, it'll be all right."

The genie showed her the leasing agreement, waiting to be

filled out. "Look at this: they ask for my *name*! My true name is not for mortal ears! And here: they want an address! I live in a castle of crystal and fire that floats among the clouds! How do I explain this to them? And then this: a phone number! Also this social security foolishness! How can this be done? What am I to write?"

Alex checked her phone—1:30. According to the contract she'd signed in blood, she was on until "sunset", and she was guessing that was binding because, you know, *in blood* and all. There was no way out of it. She was going to help this genie fill out his lease application. "Lemme see it, okay—I'll take you through it. I got you."

"What does this mean, you *have* me? I *belong* to no one! You said yourself it was illegal this very morn!"

"Jesus Christ, man." Alex rolled her eyes. "Look up some idioms. Take a class or something. I can't spend the whole summer explaining this shit to you."

CHAPTER 4:
APPLICATION

COMMERCIAL LEASE APPLICATION–WELLSPRING MALL

Please provide <u>all</u> the information requested below. Incomplete information can delay the processing of your application. PLEASE PRINT CLEARLY

OCCUPANTS

>   **Company:** *I keep no company save my own*

>   **Address (Main Office):** *A palace of smoke and fire, set among the clouds, where emerald birds sing the ineffable music of Heaven itself*

>   **Sole Prop [X]   Partnership [　]   Corporation [　]**

>   **Year Established:** *I was pressed into service one thousand five hundred years before the birth of your Christ*

>   **Employer ID #:** *For my number, I choose SEVEN*

>   **Number of Employees:** *One*

Type of Business: *I shall sell mortals their most heart-felt desires*

Gross Annual Revenue: *Presumptuous poltroon! The vastness of my treasures are not for mortal eyes to see, nor mortal hands to feel*

CONTACT PERSON

Full Name: *My TRUE NAME is not for you to know!*

Title: *Jinn*

Phone #: *As of this moment, I am reachable by any phone number you desire.*

Fax #: *My mortal servant informs me only a fool still uses a fax machine*

E-mail: *jinnoftheringofkhorad@aol.com*

COMMERCIAL HISTORY

Previous Address: *Imprisoned in the Ring of Khorad, which all men did covet*

Previous Rent: *Enslavement*

Reason for Leaving: *In recent days and for reasons unknown, I found myself liberated from bondage*

FORMER LANDLORD/MORTGAGE COMPANY

Name: *The wretched sorcerer Shulmanu-Ashared, may he dwell in fire forever*

Address: *A crooked tower on the outskirts of ancient*

Nineveh

Phone #: *This mortal is deceased*

BANKING REFERENCE

Name: *I have no need for a mortal to safeguard my infinite wealth*

Address: *I write this only because your instructions were to leave nothing unfinished*

Phone #: *There is obviously no phone number, as this person does not exist*

Account #: *My mortal servant informs me that I would be a fool to provide you with this information, even in the case where it existed, but she also admits that she has little experience in business administration*

SIGNATURE

By signing this document you affirm, under penalty of law, that all information provided is true to the best of your knowledge:

So Sayeth the Jinn Formerly of the Ring of Khorad

Date: *It is Thursday, the twenty-second day of the sixth month, in the Year of Christ two thousand and twenty-three, though I am not responsible if this date does not match the date upon which you peruse this document*

The genie put down his quill pen and blew gently across the application, making the ink dry. He inspected his handiwork with a satisfied grunt and handed it over to Alex. "There— what say you? Shall this satisfy the infernal usurers and petty tyrants that rule this great house?"

Alex looked at the application. She knew what the genie had written—she'd been peppered with questions the whole time he was filling it out—but it was still sort of astounding to see it for real, in her hands. Obviously these answers weren't sufficient. Like, obviously. She looked up at the genie's burning gaze, however, and figured she ought to cut her losses, here. "Yeah, I guess it's fine."

"You *guess*?"

"C'mon, man, you didn't even put your *name* on it."

"I explained about my name!" the genie said.

Alex threw up her hands. "All I'm saying is that this is a weird situation, okay? You see that, right?"

"You feel as though they will refuse me. Is this correct, Alexandria Delmore?"

Alex paused. Okay, so . . . tell the truth or lie? If she told the truth, the genie would get pissed at her or maybe at the mall and he might, well . . . who knows *what* he might do, but it wouldn't be great, whatever it was. Lying, on the other hand, would postpone this freak-out to a time where Alex might not be the closest person. But she also didn't like lying. "I mean, maybe it will, maybe it won't. Only one way to find out, I guess."

The genie seemed to accept this. He handed Alex the application. "Take this to the mistress of this grand bazaar. She is expecting it."

Alex checked her phone—3:30. She clambered over the kiosk counter. "Yeah, okay, sure."

She walked away from the kiosk as fast as she could without making it really obvious she was trying to get away. She hadn't totally anticipated just how *much* she was going to have to be dealing with the genie and his problems on a daily basis. This, like a lot of her other expectations, seemed pretty stupid in retrospect. What did she think this job *would* entail? Did she think the genie was going to hang out in a lamp or something all day?

"Hey!" someone stage-whispered from behind a nearby potted plant. Alex looked to see Frank the mall cop crouching down, his hands tucked into his armpits like he was doing the chicken dance.

"Hey big guy—you okay?" Alex asked.

Frank looked down at his hands and quickly pulled them away from his body. He shuddered all over. "You work for that genie, right?"

"We met, remember?"

The mall cop got up and came closer. "Listen, kid—you know that thing is dangerous, right?"

Alex couldn't exactly disagree, but she also didn't like the idea of agreeing, either, so she just stood there and waited for this guy to get to the point.

"Is that the freak's lease application?" the mall cop said. He reached out for it. "Here—I'll run it down to the office for you."

Alex pulled the papers close to her chest. "No, that's cool. I can get it down there myself."

Frank looked for a second like he was going to yank it out of Alex's hand, but then he backed off. "Listen, you let me know if that genie does anything illegal, okay? Like, really wrong. We all want a safe mall, don't we, kid?"

"Yeah, sure," Alex said. "Ummm . . . which way is the office?"

The mall cop pointed her in the right direction. As Alex walked away, he called after her. "Remember, kid: that freak doesn't belong here! Something like this never ends well, mark my words!"

Alex marked them. She marked them the whole way down the elevator into the basement of the mall.

The basement was a wholly different environment from the one the Wellspring projected above ground. While the mall might have been ailing, it still had spotless floors, bright lighting, and the faintest echo of pleasant music soaring about its towering buttresses. In the bowels of the operation, the world looked quite different.

The cheap fluorescent bulbs down here lacked covers—just bare tubes of flickering light, lining one side of the low-ceilinged corridor. The floor was made up of dusty and cracked tiles in magentas and grays and teals—a pattern probably over thirty years old and never updated. Miscellaneous equipment was left here and there—a stack of folding chairs on a dolly, a couple dusty microphone stands, a helium canister featuring the chipped and faded picture of a clown. Somewhere down the hall, she could hear a prehistoric dot-matrix printer screaming its way across some ream of paper.

Alex stepped off the elevator but didn't want to go down the hall. It was just . . . creepy. But, of course, her alternative was telling the genie to deliver the application himself, which was an obviously bad idea. She tried to put out of her mind all the horror stories her mom told her about sexual deviants and deserted hallways and crept forward, keeping her back to one wall, the application clutched to her chest.

She reached a T-shaped junction. A sign on the wall read

MANAGER'S OFFICE with a helpful arrow pointing her to the left. To the right, she heard a crash.

The hall that way was mostly dark, save for one dim light and a distant exit sign. A vent in the ceiling swung open and a trio of gnomes in tubular white hats rappelled down an extension cord. When they saw Alex, they froze, their eyes glowing green in the partial illumination.

Alex hurried away, toward the manager's office.

Given the size of the mall itself, Alex was expecting something more grandiose for the manager. She found herself standing in the doorway of a tiny square room barely large enough to accommodate a modest desk, the surface of which was dominated by the fat CRT monitor of a primeval computer and the screeching dot-matrix printer, which was running off copies of something in crude, gray typeface.

The walls of the place were covered with bulletin boards and pinned with all kinds of legal notices—employment laws, sexual harassment infographics, and the mugshots of a half dozen convicted sexual predators.

Behind the desk was a petite blonde woman in a bright blue blazer and a lot of glittering jewelry. She was on a phone—an actual landline, plugged into the wall—with one of those handset-expanders that made them easier to pin against the shoulder. This the manager was doing while her lacquered fingernails clacked across the keys of her computer. She held up a finger asking Alex to wait, and so Alex sank into the folding chair across the desk from her that had been provided for presumably this purpose.

After a few seconds, the manager finished her phone call with a "yes, I understand, sir—goodbye!" Her voice was bright and cheery and sharp.

She looked at Alex with her sparkly blue eyes and smiled. "Employee applications get turned in with the manager of the individual stores, honey."

Alex held out the rental application. "I'm not applying. This is . . . uhhh . . . well, this is from the genie."

The smile vanished, as did a lot of the color from her cheeks. "It is?"

"Afraid so."

"It . . . he filled it out?" She reached out with a trembling hand and took the piece of paper.

"Some of those questions don't, you know, exactly apply to him." Alex offered as the manager flipped through.

The manager looked terrified. "Why does he *want* to open a kiosk? Did he tell you?"

The question set Alex back in her chair. Why would a genie need to open a business? For money? What did a genie need money *for*? "Huh. I guess not."

The manager set the application down very carefully on her desk. "Young lady, how well do you know this genie?"

"Ummm . . . this is my first day, sooo . . ."

"Does he seem . . ." she searched for the word, "does he seem *nice*?"

"Not really."

"Well, I have to confess I've been fussing about this all morning. On the phone with the owner, calling our insurance company." She straightened her blazer. "It all seems so . . . *dangerous*."

"I don't think he's actually dangerous," Alex heard herself say. She was surprised she said it.

The manager chuckled. "Honey, creatures like this *are* dangerous. Haven't you seen all those movies? Wishes are *dangerous*, understand? Genies just can't be trusted."

"Don't you have, like, *gnomes* who work here?" Alex asked, gesturing over her shoulder to where she'd come from.

The manager stiffened. "That's different! They're . . . they're very reliable! There's *nothing* wrong with gnomes! Why— what have you heard? Have you been talking to them?"

Alex put up her hands. "Whoa, lady. Whoa."

The manager blushed. "Sorry . . . it's just . . . well, they're *very* good employees and very reliable and this whole mall would be out of business if not for them, but . . . they're a little creepy, honestly." She leaned forward and whispered, "*It seems like they're everywhere!*"

Alex had enough crazy on her plate, so she changed the subject. "So, you won't accept the genie's lease, then?"

She heaved a heavy sigh. "I wish. Turns out the owner, well, he loves stuff like this—he even found the gnomes! He's really excited about it. He thinks it will *help* the mall. Be our own special attraction. But your boss is going to pay double rent, to cover our extra insurance costs. Which is only fair, isn't it?"

"I guess so."

"But I want you to understand something," she said, pointing a finger at Alex. "I'm going to be watching you! If I get one whiff of impropriety from that genie, he's *evicted*, understand?"

The manager stood up. Alex could read her nametag now—Maureen Sturgis. She realized that Sturgis never introduced herself to Alex, nor she to her. Alex thought about rectifying the situation—offering to shake her hand or something—but Sturgis didn't seem like she wanted to offer one. She was wound taut, like a wire ready to break, her eyes wide.

"Okay," Alex said. "I'll tell him."

"Oh God!" she shouted. "Don't *tell* him that! Just . . . just keep it in mind. Do your best."

My best what? "Okay."

Sturgis took a deep breath and closed her eyes. Then the phone rang. She looked down at the caller ID. "Oh! I have to take this. Run along, now! Thanks for bringing this down!"

She sat down and snatched the phone off the hook. The smile was back right away, as though it had never left. "Greg! Thank you *sooo* much for calling back!" She looked over the receiver at Alex and made a shooing motion with her hand.

Alex left. On the way back through the basement, there was no sign of the gnomes. But there was *also* no dust left in the hall whatsoever. Several of the flickering lightbulbs had been replaced, too.

When Alex got back to the kiosk, the genie was on his throne, as usual, chin on his monumental fist. "Did the woman accept my entreaty?" he asked.

"Yeah," said Alex. "I think you're good."

The genie smiled, showing his sharp teeth. "Excellent. Then all is well."

Alex nodded. But she wasn't really sure she agreed.

CHAPTER 5:
THE POWER OF "NO"

It turned out that a glowering jinn in a rhinestone suit on a throne might attract *gawkers*, but it did not attract a lot of customers. No one—not a single person—bought a wish for the first three days Alex was on the job. There were people coming by the kiosk taking pictures all day, but only from a safe distance—say about fifteen feet. If Alex tried to speak to any of them, they quickly fled.

Alex supposed they had been watching the same movies Sturgis had.

Three days. Three long summer days, from nine a.m. to sundown, forced to keep company with a glowering otherworldly being, and Alex hadn't made so much as a nickel. She couldn't decide whether to be outraged or depressed.

It was a Friday afternoon in June when she finally decided to say something about it. "You know, maybe we need a sign or something."

"What do you mean? I am jinn—stories of my powers are prominent in your folklore. What could be clearer?"

"I don't know—a *name* for the business or something. What

did you put on the lease?"

"I did not list a name."

"See? There you go!" She looked away to smile at a man in a business suit going by, but he didn't break stride or even look her direction.

"The businesses in this place all call themselves absurd things. They frequently misspell words and use terrible puns. Some are simply lies." The genie pointed at the Better Body Outlet. "That place sells nothing of the kind. It is a perfumery and nothing more."

Alex snorted. "What, you don't think botanical oils can keep me from getting wrinkles? But what about what all those face-scientists in the ads who are suspiciously women between the ages of twenty-five and thirty?"

The genie frowned at her for a moment. "Oh," he said at last. "You are being sarcastic."

"He can be taught!" Alex said.

"I will not give my business a demeaning name," the genie said. "I demand respect."

"Says the guy in the leisure suit."

The genie grumbled. After a moment, the leisure suit melted away, leaving him shirtless and wearing nothing but a loin-cloth. "Better?"

Alex averted her eyes from his body. "No! Not better, dude. You're going to scare kids!"

The genie crossed his arms.

Alex scanned the people walking by. This didn't make sense—none of it did. "Hey, can't you just, like, *make* people come up and make wishes?"

"No, I cannot," the genie said. "And even if I could, I *would* not. It defeats the purpose, Alexandria Delmore."

"Okay, dude—what *is* the purpose?"

"What?"

Alex gestured to the mall. "Why are you here, man? You can have anything you want, *do* anything you want, and yet you decide to spend all your time at a shitty mall in the suburbs and get hassled by a wise-ass teenager like me. It makes *no* sense."

The genie considered this for a moment, fixing her with his glowing gaze. At length, he looked away. "You would not understand."

"Try me."

"No."

"Then at least wish up some money to pay your rent or something, because this is getting ugly, dude."

"No!"

So much for that.

Alex's next trick was to try the carnival barker approach. She waved at people as they went by. She yelled, "Get your wishes, here! Wishes, cheap cheap cheap! Come be the first in line to realize your wildest fantasies!"

Her verbal broadsides were ignored. One old lady made the sign of the cross as she went by.

"You are demeaning yourself," the genie said.

Alex scowled. "At least I'm *working*, right? What are you contributing to the situation, exactly?"

"You are impatient and impertinent," the genie said. "My product sells itself. We need only wait, and the customer will come to us."

"Any idea if that will be *before* I'm an old lady, or . . ."

"It has been a trifling few days! I once waited for two centuries in a riverbed before my ring was discovered and I was again summoned by a master."

"Dude, your imprisonment in a ring and my job at the mall are *not* comparable situations."

The genie was unimpressed, but he let the subject drop. The hours drew out like days. Her phone ran out of charge and there was no outlet in the kiosk, so all she had left to occupy her was staring at the patterns the floor tiles made and watching her fingernails grow.

Then she saw him: a tall man in a dark tailored suit, walking with a fat briefcase. This guy stuck out because he didn't have that standard, aimless look everybody else had while they ambled around the mall—this guy had a purpose. A target.

The target was them.

Alex straightened her posture in spite of herself. "Heads up," she called back to the genie. The genie gave no sign that he heard her.

Then the guy was right there in front of her. He had salt-and-pepper hair and a strong, clean-shaven chin and his big watch gleamed silver and gold in the Wellspring's diffuse natural light. Alex got a whiff of aftershave from him, and not the cheap shit her male classmates slathered themselves with in the boy's bathroom. The real stuff. From a glass bottle, probably.

"Hi!" Alex said, a little embarrassed at how chipper she sounded. "What can we do for you?"

The man looked through Alex as though she wasn't there. "Excuse me, Mr. Genie?"

The genie looked around as though puzzled at the thought of being addressed. At last, he looked down at the man in the nice suit and fancy watch. "What is it you wish of me?"

"Are there any limits?" the man asked.

"Yes," the genie said.

The man waited for a moment, but when it became clear the genie wasn't going to elaborate, he said, "Will you tell me what they are?"

The genie heaved an enormous sigh. "I may transport one thing to somewhere else. I may alter the form of one thing into another. I may conjure something from nothing or take something are render it non-existent. These are the extent of my powers."

The man nodded slowly. "Can you tell the future?"

"You are a donkey," the genie stated.

"What did you say to me?"

"You ask me what I can do. I tell you. Then you ask if I can do something else," the genie said. "Do you think me a liar? A cheat? Or are you merely stupid?"

The man straightened his tie, but if he was offended, this was the only sign. "I take it you can control the weather."

"Obviously."

"Can you manufacture a drought?"

The genie's whole expression changed. He sat up straighter on his throne, his face somehow even more grave than it had been before. "Yes."

The man nodded. "I will provide you a list of counties in Florida. You will create a drought in those places that will persist for eight weeks. In exchange, I will pay you one million dollars. In cash. Right now." The man reached down and hefted up his suitcase, which he placed on the counter with a *thunk*.

"These counts are your enemies, I take it?" the genie said.

"What?" the man laughed. "No—no, of course not."

"Then why?"

"I decline to tell you. Do we have a deal?" He opened the case and spun it around.

Alex found herself face-to-face with more money than she'd ever laid eyes on in her life. Stacks and stacks of hundred-dollar bills in thick bundles, crisp and clean. What was ten percent of a million? A hundred grand, right? *A hundred THOUSAND dollars!* Alex found that she could barely move. This—this one wish—and everything in her life would be solved. "Holy shit, boss—are you seeing this?"

"Silence!" the genie snapped, looking down at the money. He stroked his smoky beard. "Eight weeks from the moment I agree to this deal?"

"Yes, understood," the man said. "Will there be a record of this transaction?" He glanced at Alex. "I would prefer this be discreet."

"I presume you have the list of counties with you," the genie said.

The man produced a folded piece of paper and held it out to the genie. The genie, however, did not move to take it; it was up to Alex to take the paper and deliver it to the genie's hand.

He unfolded the paper and looked at the names. He looked at them for what seemed a very long time.

Alex and the guy with a million bucks exchanged a brief glance. "Hey . . . uhhh . . . boss? You okay?"

The genie looked up. When he spoke, it was in a weirdly quiet voice. "I . . . decline?"

A beat of total silence. The man with the nice watch just stared at the genie. So did Alex.

The genie, somehow emboldened, sat up straighter. "I decline!"

"WHAT?" Alex shouted at very genie-like volumes.

"Is this some kind of joke?" the man said.

The genie glared down at the man. "Are you deaf as well as stupid? Begone!"

"WHAT?" Alex shouted again. She watched as the man snapped his case closed and spun on his heel.

"No, wait!" Alex shouted after him. "Come back! I . . . I can talk him into it!" She scrambled to get over the counter, to catch up with him. She ran through the crowd, pushing people aside, but the man in his good suit and his nice watch and his giant briefcase of money was gone.

All that money. The solution to all her problems, gone.

She stormed back to the kiosk. "Well, I hope you're fucking satisfied with yourself!" she yelled at the genie as she crawled back over the counter. "Great business sense, you giant *moron!*"

The genie said nothing. He crumpled the little piece of paper in his hand and then lit it aflame. He pondered the ashes in his hand as Alex raged.

"That was our *first* wish! A *million dollars!* You have any idea how much that is? No, no, of *course* you don't!" Alex broke out her phone and tried to use the calculator—her phone was dead. "ARGHH! That's . . . that's like . . . like *forty-thousand* pieces of silver, you giant idiot! That could have changed my life! You know the whole *point* of this stupid kiosk is to *grant* wishes, don't you? Don't you? *Are you even listening?*"

"Are there many such men still abroad in this time?" the genie asked.

Alex's mouth tripped over itself, mid-rant. "Wh-what, you mean like . . . like rich guys?"

"Yes."

"Sure, yeah—plenty. And one of them was just about to drop a *million bucks* just so you could stop some rain in Florida, where everything is so screwed up, they wouldn't even notice anyway!" Alex kicked the wall of the kiosk.

"I have known many such men," the genie said. "I had hoped they were gone. I had hoped your kind had arisen and slain them, for their wishes are seldom kind and never charitable. Indeed, when I saw that the true kings of the world were all but extinct, I had thought my hopes fulfilled. I see now that they no longer wear crowns but are the same men nonetheless."

The genie had a strange, faraway expression. "That was the first wish I have ever declined to grant."

Alex heaved a sigh. "A drought wouldn't have killed anybody, man. Nobody was going to starve."

"I did not know if it was possible, until now," the genie went on.

"Well three freaking cheers for your personal autonomy or whatever." Alex slumped on the counter again. "A *million* bucks. Jesus."

The genie shook his head. "Trust me, Alexandria Delmore," he said. "I know my business."

Alex grunted. "That involve actually making money at some point?"

"Someday," the genie said. "But not today."

Alex sighed. This did not bode well for her long-term employment.

That night, Alex's father made a peace offering in the form of Chinese takeout. He picked it up on his way home from work—a fat brown paper bag, stained with grease and leaking warm, savory smells. It was from Alex's mom's favorite place—Dr.

Chan's. Alex couldn't remember the last time they'd actually ordered from there.

The food was received in all the same spirit as a Soviet embassy during the Nixon administration. Her father solemnly produced carton after carton of her mother's favorites from the big paper bag, announcing each one in turn and setting them on the table in a row: "Peking ravioli. Scallion pancakes. General Tsao's Chicken. Beef and broccoli." Her mother, still in her grocery store uniform, said nothing. Looked at nothing. Her hands were bunched in her lap, her eyes downcast.

Her father stared at her mother, though Alex couldn't read what was behind it. Anger? Pleading? The man was too emotionally stunted to apologize, too proud to admit fault, too dumb to recognize a suicide mission when he saw one. Who knew what he was thinking?

Her mother sat on one side of the table, her father on the other, with Alex in between. Mark had a date, apparently, though Alex didn't buy it—her brother, the grass-stained hick, had never scored a date in his life. No, he knew this was coming and made plans to be somewhere else and hadn't bothered to give *her* the heads-up, the prick. He was probably out doing something stupid with his dumbass buddy Kenny and a case of cheap beer, as he nearly always was.

In any event, Alex was starving. She'd worked a full day on nothing but a bowl of rice cereal and a croissant at the shitty mall café. She reached for the carton of spareribs.

"Wait," her mother said.

"That's right, Lexie," her father said. "Let your mother eat first."

"I'm not eating anything, Charlie."

"These are your favorite things."

"How much did this all cost, Charlie? We don't have the money for you to eat out all the time. You know that."

"I can afford to buy dinner for my family!" her father shouted.

"Oh really? Can you afford to pay the phone bill? Because those late notices would sure love to hear it!"

"You been opening my mail?"

"Charlie, I've been opening your mail for twenty years. This is the first time you've noticed."

Alex's eyes moved back and forth, as at a tennis match. Currently, her mom was winning this particular exchange. Home turf advantage, no doubt.

"Tampering with the mail is a federal crime!" her father said.

"Oh, for fuck's sake!" Alex opened the carton of spareribs and speared out a few and then cracked open the rice.

"Language!" her father snapped.

"Lexie, I don't want you eating this!" her mom said. "Haven't you been listening—it's too expensive!"

"I've got news for you, Mom," Alex said. "You can't *return* Chinese food."

Her father nodded sagely. "Because of the chemicals."

"What the . . . *no*, dad, it has nothing to do with the chemicals. Chinese food doesn't even *have* whatever it is you think it has!"

"Don't yell at your father!" her mother said.

Alex gaped at her. "Really? Don't yell at him? From you? *Really?*"

"How was your day at work, Lexie?" her father asked.

"Okay, that's it—I'm out." Alex tore open a couple cartons and dumped some food on a paper plate and then stood up, the plate sagging in her hands. "You two can continue this without me."

"Lexie!" her mother gasped.

Her father said, "You need to respect your elders, young lady! This kind of behavior is what the liberals want!"

Alex paused by the door. "Dad, the 'liberals' do not goddamned want *any* of this!" She gestured to the tiny kitchen, the pile of unpaid bills, the dirty dishes in the sink no one had gotten around to doing, her sunburned father and her sweaty strung-out mother still in her work apron. "Enjoy your bullshit dinner!" And she left, totally ignoring her father calling "language" after her as she stormed off to her room.

Her room was in the attic. She pulled down the stairs from the ceiling and stomped up. Under the eaves she had a futon, a reading lamp, and stacks of books, mostly for studying for the SAT. Her closet was the portable variety—a frame of cheap aluminum poles inside a canvas exterior. She'd taped posters of her favorite bands on the wall, but in the darkness of the evening they weren't visible except as vague shadows—rockers standing victorious over their screaming fans, skulls and fire, an electric guitar blazing with lightning.

She put the food on top of a milk crate that functioned as an end table and threw herself on the futon. She pressed a pillow to her face and screamed.

She *had* to get out of this place. Had to. She was legitimately going to lose her mind. She screamed a few more times for good measure.

Beneath her, through the floor, she could hear her parents getting into a screaming match of their own. She was pretty sure the food she'd absconded with was the only food being eaten. The rest would be repurposed as projectiles.

She put in her earbuds and turned on some loud, fast-paced music to drown out the noise. She tried to make herself focus on the genie and the day job—her one ticket out of this suburban hell.

She had it all worded out already: *I wish for admission and a full scholarship to NYU in Greenwich Village.* That was it— pretty basic. Not even a big ask, really. Not for a genie, anyway. But she'd never get her opportunity to wish if the genie's *business kept tanking.* She knew the genie must be disappointed, or at least she *thought* she knew—it was hard to differentiate between his various kinds of glowers and scowls. But, like, he hadn't started this thing to suck at it, right? And if things kept going on like this, well . . . no wish. No nothing. A future of mowing grass or making lattes.

She pulled out a piece of notebook paper and decided to list off the things that needed to change if this whole kiosk thing was going to work out.

1. *No signage*
2. *Product unclear (see #1)*
3. *No advertising*
4. *Pricing model impractical*
5. *Genie unfriendly*
6. *You can basically see the genie's balls*

Alex reviewed the list when she was done. "So, everything," she muttered. "Basically everything."

CHAPTER 6:
IT'S ALL ABOUT THE MARKETING

THE NEXT MORNING was Saturday—sunny, hot, and the perfect day for people to go to a big air-conditioned building and buy crap. Today, Alex hoped, was the day they turned some things around.

The genie was wearing a suit—not a leisure suit, but an actual suit. It was off-white and huge and it reminded Alex of vanilla ice cream, but it was a vast improvement. His shirt was open at the collar, revealing the upper regions of his smoky chest hair—gross. Alex chose to work with what she was given. "You look nice."

"It is not my intention to appear friendly," the genie said. "I am supposed to look powerful. I realize now that my previous attire was . . . amusing."

"Believe me," Alex said, "nobody was laughing."

The genie glowered at her. "Attend to your duties!"

Of course, having no distinct duties, Alex just stood there, staring out at the gradually growing crowds of shoppers, all of them mysteriously gaining speed when they came within twenty feet of the kiosk. The genie sat with his head in one hand, looking bored out of his mind.

It was time to put the plan into action. "Hey boss," she said. "Can I have a break?"

The genie sat up. "Lazy wretch! Your labors are only just begun!"

"I've gotta go to the bathroom."

There had been an argument about this once a few days ago. The genie was incredulous at the human need to urinate and insisted on following her to the ladies' room. He also followed her *inside* and waited outside her stall. When he noticed that only women were permitted (the realization really striking home when a lady screamed at him upon entering), the genie appeared to be genuinely embarrassed. Of course, for the genie, embarrassment presented itself as anger.

He was no less angry now. "I forbid it!"

"Fine," she said. "I'll pee in a cup." She put her empty coffee cup on the floor and made as though to squat over it.

The genie recoiled in disgust. "Very well!" the genie said. "Go! But return with haste! We may have need of you!"

"Yeah, right." Alex scrambled over the counter and headed off.

The genie safely out of sight, Alex cruised right by the bathrooms and headed, instead, for the massive, gleaming storefront of ValuDay, its eye-searing green sign dominating that side of the mall and dwarfing every shop in its orbit. Alex didn't know the mall's finances or whatever, but it didn't take a genius to figure out that ValuDay was the only thing holding the Wellspring together. Everybody shopped there, even if they never set foot in the wider mall. It was the largest store by far, dwarfing even the sad little Macy's at the opposite end of the complex.

Alex walked through its wide, automatic doors and maneuvered her way down the broad aisles packed with people in flip-flops buying discount deck furniture and large vats of pre-sweetened iced tea and dog food, and cut through the all-pink "girls" aisle of the toy section until she found herself at the desk of the copy shop the store had sequestered in a distant corner.

The guy behind the counter was wearing glasses, the standard green polo shirt, and the dull expression of a person not allowed to bring their phone onto the floor but also not given anything stimulating to do. "Hey, do you guys do signs?"

It took a moment for the guy's brain to boot-up. He blinked at her. "Sorry, what?"

"Signs? Like, can I get a sign made?"

The guy looked behind him at the cohort of blocky industrial printers, quietly idling. "Uh . . . yeah. How big?"

Alex spread the poster out for the genie. It read BEST WISHES in bright, happy letters and, beneath that, in a sloping calligraphy, said YOUR WISH IS OUR COMMAND! REASONABLE PRICES, SATISFACTION GUARANTEED. All very professional. "Well, what do you think?" Alex asked.

The genie folded his arms. "I cannot guarantee satisfaction. It is impossible."

"Nobody can, but places promise it all the time—trust me, this will get us some business."

"I will not be made a liar!"

"Give people the stuff they wish for and you won't be."

The genie snorted. "Untrue. Human beings wish for things they regret all the time."

"You mean, like, when somebody wins the lottery or something and then they screw up their life? That kind of thing?"

The genie looked at her as if she were stupid. "No, I am thinking of the time my ring was discovered by a fisherman. His first wish was to catch the largest fish in the world. He caught a whale. It killed him."

Alex blinked. "Dude, a whale isn't a fish."

"What?"

"A whale—it's a mammal, like us . . . errr . . . like humans."

The genie's eyes blazed. "It lives in the sea!"

"So?"

"It swims as a fish!"

"Yeah, but it breathes air. You don't think a seal is a fish, do you? An otter?"

The genie's mouth hung open; smoke curled from his nostrils. "What madness is this?"

"Dude, how do you *not* know this? Aren't you all-knowing and all-seeing and stuff?"

"I have *seen* whales!" The genie shouted, loud enough that people nearby paused to stare for a moment before hurrying off. The genie gave no notice. "They *appear* to be extremely large FISH!"

"Dude, *lower* your voice, okay?"

"I am just explaining to you, ignorant mortal, that whales are fish!"

"And I'm explaining to *you*, Mr. Jinn, that the fisherman was probably thinking more along the lines of a big fat tuna."

The genie by this point was leaning over the edge of his throne so that his head was just above Alex's. Alex could see straight up his nose. There was nothing in there—like, nothing. Just darkness and smoke. "Does your nose actually work, or is it just for show?"

The genie slumped back on his throne. "Enough of your insolence. I cannot guarantee the satisfaction of my customers—that is the point."

It was Alex's turn to fold her arms. "You know why people aren't coming over here and making wishes?"

"Because they are cowards?"

"Because you're *scary*, dude."

The genie looked down at his cream suit. "You said I looked nice."

"Wrong kind of nice." Alex pointed to a pair of teenage boys who were taking pictures of the kiosk with their phones from a safe distance. "See those guys? They're not coming over here because they think you're going to grant wishes like the ones you used to grant—stupid, awful, terrible wishes that got people eaten by whales."

She held up the sign. "This sign is supposed to help change that perception. Got it?"

The genie frowned. "What happens if someone comes and wishes for that which is terrible, save they do not realize it? After I grant their wish, they will *not* be satisfied—far from it—and then this sign will have made a liar out of me, which I cannot tolerate."

Alex took a deep breath. "Two things: one, you can tell them ahead of time that the wish is a bad idea—maybe talk them out of it—and, two, *you can just say no, remember?*"

The genie thought about this for a moment. "Just as I did with that knave who wished to starve the state of Florida yesterday eve?"

"Yes, just like you did with that guy who almost paid for my college education. That guy."

"You are angry still?"

"Man, if I could punch you in a way that hurt, you would have *such* a black eye right now."

"Threats, now? From you, whom I employ?"

Alex shook her jacket. "Hear that jingling?"

"No."

It was Alex's turn to yell. "It's because *I haven't gotten paid!*"

The genie sighed. "Very well—I accept your sign. It is done."

The sign was gone—no, the sign was now affixed above the throne. The genie had even added a string of fairy-lights along the edge, blinking cheerily. She'd actually talked him into something! She'd won! For all his faults, the genie was, in the end, susceptible to reason, logic, and a lot of yelling. This summer might not be a failure after all.

About an hour later, they got their second all-time customer. It was Kenny Dufresne, of all people—Alex's brother Mark's idiot best friend. He wandered up to the kiosk at about midmorning, wearing a Velocity Burger uniform and a vacant expression, staring up at the new sign as though trying to sound out the words in his head.

Kenny was tall and lanky with a pronounced Adam's apple and huge hands. Alex had once watched him try to surf on the top of his sister's car as Mark drove it down their street. He had destroyed a mailbox with his face and gotten twenty stitches.

But, God help her, he was cute. "Hi, Kenny!"

Kenny tore his eyes from the sign and from the genie beneath the sign to finally see *her*. It took him a couple seconds to figure out why she knew his name. "Oh! Hey, Alex—I didn't recognize you!"

Alex brushed her hair from her face. "Kenny, I see you literally all the time. I'm not even in a uniform."

Kenny nodded. "Yeah. Right on."

The conversation died. Kenny stood there, Alex waited. Finally, she asked, "Did you want to make a wish?"

Kenny smiled his brainless, two thousand-watt smile. "Oh! Yeah—that'd be awesome. Uhhh . . . how much?"

"That depends on what you want to wish for." Alex gestured to the pricing guide, not that it would be of any use.

Kenny looked at the fat scroll and read the top entry. "A palace of . . . unsurpassed . . . uhhh . . . opulence?" He looked at Alex. "Does that mean it's big?"

"Basically, yeah." Alex found herself grinning as though Kenny had made an intentional joke, not proven himself a moron. "Are you in the market for a palace, Kenny?"

Kenny rubbed the back of his head. "Well . . . I don't have much money, so . . . never mind . . ."

"No wait!" Alex caught his hand before he walked away. "We're open to negotiation."

"We are not," the genie said. His voice was deep and loud— like thunder talking. Kenny took a step back.

"Don't mind him," Alex said. "He's just bad with people. What do you want to wish for?"

"Well . . ."

"C'mon—try us."

Kenny looked around. People were watching them. Some kid had out his phone, filming. "Is it safe?" he asked.

"What? Wishing! Sure it is!" Alex said, looking over her shoulder at the genie, who had not moved, had not uncrossed his arms, and did not look pleased. "It's *totally* safe! Satisfaction guaranteed."

Kenny kept rubbing the back of his head, as though his brain ran on a flywheel. "Okay, so, I don't want to, you know, low-ball you or nothing. So, like, maybe something little."

Alex produced a notebook from beneath the table. "Shoot."

"My boss at Velocity Burger is this prick, Fontana—you know him?"

Alex scowled. "Unfortunately."

"He's been riding my ass. Can you make it so I'm never late for work again or something?"

"You ask me to alter the very sands of time itself?" The genie opened his eyes wide. They blazed like spotlights.

Kenny wilted under the genie's gaze. "Look, man—all I got is twenty dollars. That's it." He dug in his pocket and brought out the sweaty, tattered bill and put it on the table.

The genie considered the piece of paper money on the counter and stroked his smoky beard. "This is barely worth a single piece of silver. For this I could grant you a small boon or curse. Something harmless, but noticeable."

The word "curse" seemed to rattle around Kenny's empty head. "Hey," he said, "I got an idea."

The lunchtime rush at Velocity Burger was the stuff of fast-food nightmares. A line of people six deep and only one operating register, where a middle-aged South American woman bravely fielded the inane requests of a half-insane population in a language not her own. Behind her, the kitchen was a war zone of steam clouds, beeping timers, and the rattle of ticket printers. Sweaty people in aprons bustled to and fro, their faces fused into rictus grins, like people working in the midst of a natural disaster but asked to look perky and fun at the same time.

The basic idea behind Velocity Burger was in the name—velocity. You didn't come to Velocity for a *good* burger, not when there was one of those high-end chains up the street. You didn't come for the ambience. You didn't even come because it was cheap. You came because you were hungry and the food would be in your face in five minutes flat.

So, how do they increase velocity? The fries and the burgers and the milkshakes all cooked or mixed or fried at a steady rate. The customers couldn't be controlled—some dumbass gets to the front of the line and can't decide between a strawberry or a chocolate shake, gets stumped on whipped cream or no whipped cream, and there wasn't a hell of a lot anyone could do about it. Corporate guidelines had thinned out the choice structure of the menu already—no kids meals, only two sizes for everything, no sauce options, and the customers filled up their drinks themselves—and that all meant that the customer was moving through the selection stage of their dining experience as quickly as their brain was capable of.

What was the final variable?

The employees, of course.

You can't make a burger cook faster, but you can improve how fast you put them on the grill, how fast you added toppings, how fast you wrapped them in foil. You can increase the scooping speed at the fry station. You can stay on top of shake production so there's never a shortage. You can ring a customer up fast and correct the first time. You can have somebody on the window who's paying attention to staging and bagging the meals.

That person—that bug on everyone's ass—was Fontana

Russo. Alex had worked fast food at the Bagel Hut, where the Sunday morning rush was intense and Ms. Partagas was out there, helping everybody through. It sucked, but she had felt supported, at least—Partagas was part of the team. Here, in the bowels of this grease-spattered purgatory, Fontana was the slave driver. Alex watched as he clapped his hands behind Felicity—a girl in her year at school—as though cheering her at a track meet. "Gotta give me that velocity, Felicity! Where's my velocity, baby? Chop-chop!"

"Yeah," Kenny said to her as he loped to the counter. "This place sucks."

Fontana spotted him. "Hey man!" he said, holding up a hand to high-five Kenny. "Glad you're back! You're back on fries."

Kenny didn't move. "Still got ten more minutes on my break, boss."

Fontana made himself laugh at what he assumed was a joke. Kenny just stood there, though. "We don't have a break room, Kenny—you get that, right?"

"Yeah," Kenny said. "Right on."

Fontana looked at Kenny and then spotted Alex—he knew something was up. "Well . . . just stay out of the way, okay?"

"Yeah, boss."

Fontana stepped away and threw on his fake smile before leaning on the counter in front of Alex. "Finally ditched the freak, huh? Want me to get you an application?" He waggled his eyebrows.

"Nah, I'm good." Alex pulled out her phone and started filming—for publicity purposes, she told herself. Her stomach was fluttering—would it happen? How long would she have to wait? Would it . . . would it actually *work*?

Fontana was mugging for the camera. "Make sure you get my good side, 'kay baby?" He blew a kiss.

Alex couldn't contain herself. "Oh my God, this is too good."

Fontana beamed and started to flex a bicep while Alex tried to hold in her giggles. And then . . . his expression changed.

He stood up, rigid. Alex heard something *gurgle*, like the last bit of water down a bathtub drain.

"Hey, Fontana?" Alex asked, all innocent. "Everything okay there, babe?"

"Uhhhh . . ." Fontana whirled to run for the bathroom. "MOVE!" he shouted.

Kenny, hands up, let him pass, but Fontana's shout—laced with panic—had caught everyone's attention. All the employees stared. The customers at the front of the line saw it, too. Fontana made it two steps.

His body *shuddered*; some kind of pressure released with the sound of a water balloon popping. A wet spot soaked through the back of his pants. There was a stink, too.

Everyone recoiled, their faces bent with disgust. They could see it. *Everyone* could see it.

Kenny, his face solemn, pulled his phone from his pocket and snapped a picture.

Then Alex started to laugh.

It was magical.

CHAPTER 7:
WORD OF MOUTH

THE VIDEO OF FONTANA crapping his pants turned into a viral sensation when Alex posted it to the internet with the comment "wishes DO come true!" More video of the incident surfaced shortly thereafter, including footage of Kenny making the wish in the first place and also of the immediate aftermath at the burger joint. You got to watch Fontana cursing a blue streak as he tried to open the locked bathroom, yelling for his employees to give him the code, and everybody in the restaurant just kind of standing there, a dumbfounded expression on their faces, as this suntanned young man had a total meltdown. Alex particularly enjoyed the other versions—those set to music, those with goofy sound effects, the memes they generated. They were legit hilarious.

As an advertising strategy, it worked.

After that, the wishes started to trickle in. People were still wary—still clearly afraid of the genie and the power he represented—but the prospect of getting their heart's desire for short money was hard to resist for long. In that first week, ten or twenty people a shift would elbow up to the counter and ask Alex for what they wanted while the genie looked on.

The pricing guide wound up being almost totally useless. People weren't wishing for gleaming palaces or fertile fields and most of the people who were buying didn't have the kind of money for that, anyway. It became a kind of barter system— the wisher would suggest a wish and a price, and then it was between the three of them—Alex, the wisher, and the genie— to hammer out a suitable deal.

Sometimes the process was . . . awkward. This one woman wanted one extra hour of restful sleep a day for the next year; the genie demanded that she tithe him the services of one of her children for one hour a day for the same period.

"What?!" she said. "My kids are little! My eldest is only eight years old!"

"Can this child of eight summers not fetch for me what I demand? Can they not clean my counter or polish my throne? What manner of indolent offspring have you pro- duced, woman?"

"You can't make them work!" she countered. "That's *illegal!*"

The genie turned his fiery gaze on Alex. "Explain!"

Alex thought of all the times her dad had brought her in his truck and had her pulling weeds in some overgrown flower garden. She could hear his voice in her ear right then: *Isn't it fun, honey?* "She's right. Technically."

"Technically?" the genie asked.

"*Technically?!*" the woman scoffed. She turned and walked away, tugging a little girl by the wrist as she went.

Alex wanted to call after her—to apologize—but she was already gone. Her big mouth lost a lot of sales this way. The genie's big mouth lost the rest. He was a complete hard-ass with absolutely no idea what people in this century would put up with.

The one good thing about this was that the genie was utterly unconcerned by any of it. If they offered a fair price, he granted the wish, if not, he just went back to whatever mental headspace he occupied most of the time at the kiosk, staring into nowhere, chin resting heavily on his knuckles. There was no reprimand for Alex driving a customer off. It would have been great if she weren't working on commission. At this rate, and at the prices people were paying, she was barely making minimum wage, and in *silver coins*, which sucked. She tried to make the argument that he could convert her pay into dollars, and he just scoffed.

"Silver is better."

"How?" Alex asked, clanking her jacket pockets together like cymbals. "How is this better?"

"I have learned that the paper bills you revere are fictions— objects that retain their worth only so long as your nation stands. When it collapses, as all nations do, those bills will be worthless."

"Look, boss, if the country collapses, I'm gonna have bigger problems than losing out on the paycheck from my mall sales job. In the meantime, I'd like to buy lunch *today* with money minted *in this century*."

"I will not apologize for paying you in silver, which is a noble currency of ancient and redoubtable value." The genie folded his arms and ignored her arguments from then on out. So, that was that.

Alex didn't think the genie actually *enjoyed* granting wishes very much. He would grant them, sure—fixed a guy's limp with a clap of his hands, made some woman's blouse stain-proof with a snap of the fingers, but afterward there was a moment where the genie looked . . . well . . . looked *sad* sort of. Alex didn't really get it.

But she also wasn't stupid enough to pry.

During downtimes—and there were plenty of them—Alex worked on a three-ring binder she had brought in, featuring the words "Revised Pricing Guide" printed on the front in her jagged, rock-n-roll calligraphy. This was a long-running project that she had taken up—listing off wishes granted and what they cost as a way of developing a better baseline for what things should be priced. It was sort of a little experiment in the free market, happening right there in their little kiosk.

See, the genie's granting of wishes seemed to be without real cost or effort to him. Alex had now seen him do everything from repairing a dented bicycle wheel to letting some colorblind kid see color and all of it had required the slightest gesture on his part. So, labor was effectively free, here—the only thing that mattered was *how much it was worth.*

So, how much *was* a wish worth? The numbers were all over the place. The curing of colorblindness, for instance—which to Alex seemed like a big ask—had cost the wisher only a hundred bucks. One guy wanted to know what his girlfriend's birthday was (that was a weird one) and the genie had charged him twice that. The guy had paid, too.

"Couldn't you have just, like, looked it up on social media or something?" Alex asked.

The guy shook his head. "She'd know, man. She'd just know."

As a result, the prices seemed to follow no clear pattern. She tried making graphs and charts to make sense of the data—nothing really worked. The values of the wishes were wholly idiosyncratic, dependent upon the value to the wisher at the time of the wish. The predictive powers of the guide were proving to be close to zero.

Business was picking up, too. The people who'd seen the poop video and come to see for themselves were now bringing their friends. Their friends were telling their parents. The parents were telling *their* friends. And the more people who approached the genie and walked away pleased, the more people walking by in the mall were likely to get in line.

That's right—they had a *line*. By the second week—closing in on the Fourth of July—it was maybe forty people deep at any one time and getting longer every day.

Alex found herself in an argument every thirty seconds with a stranger. "Do you want my money or not?" some guy in an anime T-shirt yelled. He had wished for the ability to turn water into beer by belching on it.

Alex jerked a thumb at the genie, who had his eyes closed. "Man said five grand."

"I ain't got five grand. I'll pay you a hundo." The guy spread out five wrinkled twenties on the counter—the kind of money you kept balled up in a sock drawer for a rainy day. For a rainy day in an era before credit cards, anyway.

"A hundred dollars for free beer for the rest of your life? What are you, nuts?"

"Maybe if you took a card, then."

"Look at my boss, dude," Alex said. "Does he look like a guy with a bank account? Do you think he's getting credit card statements? Sign says *cash only*." She pointed at the sign she'd recently stuck to the register.

"He's a genie!" the guy yelled. "He can do anything he wants!"

Alex sighed. "Five thousand cash or beat it."

The guy left, calling her nasty names under his breath.

The genie perked up from his mediations. "What did you call her? You! Mortal!"

The guy vanished into the crowd. The genie rose, about to do something terrible, Alex guessed, so she intervened. "Let him go, man—it's fine."

"He called you . . ."

"I *know* what he called me, okay?"

"You accept such indignity?" the genie asked, sitting back down on the throne.

Alex really didn't have it in her for another argument. "Who cares what that jackass thinks?"

She turned back to the counter, only to come face-to-face with her brother Mark. She froze. "Hey sis," he said. "Cool job."

Mark—of course Mark. Kenny, his nicer, dumber other half, had told him, naturally. Why hadn't she thought of this? Dammit! "Oh my God, Mark—you can't tell Dad! Or Mom!" Alex blurted.

Kenney poked his head out from behind her brother, one hand on Mark's shoulder. He waved at her. "Hey, Alex."

Alex pushed a strand of hair behind her ear. "Oh. Hey. How's Velocity Burger?"

"Oh, I was *totally* fired," Kenny said, grinning. Then he threw devil horns with both hands and sung "WORTH IT!" in a high falsetto.

"We want a wish," Mark said.

"Mark, you have to promise not to tell Dad I work here! He'll flip out!"

"Tell you what," Mark said, leaning on the counter, grinning from ear to ear. "You get us a wish on the house, and maybe I'll just forget to mention to Dad *what* you're working for, here."

"It's not like getting an employee discount at the ice cream store, Mark—the boss isn't going to go for it!"

"Ask," Mark said.

Kenny waved at the genie. "Hello, Mr. Genie sir! Good to see you again!" He spoke loudly and slowly, like an idiot might do to a deaf person. "I like your suit!" he gestured to his chest, presumably some kind of mime for "suit."

The genie glared at him. "What is wrong with that one?" he asked Alex. "Has his brain been damaged?"

"Yeah, probably." Alex faced the genie. "This is my brother, Mark. Any chance we could give him a free wish—like, a tiny one, you know?"

The genie peered down at Mark, who gave the genie a confident thumbs up while Kenny threw devil's horns with both hands again and stuck out his tongue. "Presumably they wish to have the sleeves restored to their shirts?" the genie asked.

"I sort of doubt it."

The genie made a face. Alex had gotten better at reading his expressions—this one was an uncomfortable face. "And I am to be paid nothing for this boon?"

"Ummmm . . . you'll be paid in my gratitude?"

"I earn your gratitude with the silver I put in your pockets, and you are less than grateful even for that."

"Because I cannot buy a latte with a freaking silver ingot!"

The genie crossed his arms—Alex was about to lose him. "Please please please, Mr. Jinn? If you don't, then my brother will tell my dad I've been working here and my dad will *freak out*, understand?"

The genie frowned deeply. "You are here against your father's wishes?"

"Yes! Exactly! And if he finds out, you're going to have to find another person to put up with your crap."

The genie seemed unmoved. "You should obey your father. He knows what is best for you."

"He really, really does not, I promise you. He'd say you were a demon who has come to steal my soul or something." In truth, Alex thought her father would say much worse than that, but she was trying to garner sympathy more than indignant rage, here.

The genie was silent for a moment as he came to a decision. "I see. This is easily rectified, then." He turned to face the boys. "What are your names?"

Mark made a whoop of victory and did a combination high-five/chest bump with Kenny. "Let's get this wishing *ON!* My name is Mark Delmore . . . uhhh . . . sir."

"Kenny Dufresne!"

The genie spread his arms wide. "Mark Delmore and Kenny Dufresne, if at this time or in the future you seek to violate Alexandria Delmore's confidence, you shall vomit toads until the next sundown."

There was a clap of thunder that made the whole mall fall silent.

Mark and Kenny gaped at the genie. "What the . . . what the hell, man?"

"It is done," the genie said. "You may go."

"But that's *not* a wish!" Mark said.

"Do you wish to pay me for a wish?" the genie said.

"What? I . . . uhhh . . . no, look . . ."

"THEN BEGONE!" the genie roared.

The boys backed away from the counter. "Not cool, Alex," Mark said.

"Love you! Drive safe!" Alex blew him a kiss and waved.

Mark and Kenney retreated. Alex turned back to the genie. "Thanks! I owe you one!"

"Yes," the genie said. "You do."

The genie removed boils and healed sunburns, he changed hair-color, made the short taller and the tall shorter. He gifted a man with a lawnmower that would not break and a little boy with a balloon that would never pop. He gave a young woman the power to always win at arm-wrestling. He removed another woman's C-section scar and altered or removed at least a half dozen tattoos. The average cost of a wish wound up being about forty dollars, meaning Alex was making an average of four dollars a patron. One day they had served somewhere around a hundred people. It was the most money she'd ever earned in a single day.

On her way out of the mall after sunset, she clanked as the silver coins in her backpack jostled together. She passed by the fountain at the center of the mall, which hadn't worked since she'd been here. A team of gnomes were arrayed on the edge, wearing diving masks and snorkels clearly intended for children. Another gnome was handing out pipe cleaners with a grim expression on his ruddy face, while another group was tying little ropes of braided shoelaces around each gnome's waist. They looked like they were going to war.

Alex stopped to watch. It really did seem like those guys were everywhere. Ever since Ms. Sturgis, the mall manager, had said that, she had been noticing them all over the place, and not only in the mall. She'd seen them running around the oil change place across the street, seen them zipping along beside garbage trucks—you name it. Her father's paranoia had some basis in reality, she had to admit.

She wondered what the gnomes got out of it all. She doubted Sturgis or any of those other places paid them very much—the way Sturgis had talked about it, it seemed like they might not be paid at all. And yet the bathrooms gleamed and the floors were buffed to a mirror shine and all the lights worked and the garbage got taken out and so on. A big place like this had to take them hours to clean, even with their supernatural speed. It baffled Alex why they bothered. Did they even know how badly they had it?

She reached into her backpack and pulled out a silver coin. She placed it on the edge of the fountain. The gnomes froze, staring at her through their little floral and dinosaur-themed diving masks, pipe cleaners in hand. Alex pointed at the coin and smiled. "Just wanted to say thank you, that's all—thought you guys might want a tip, you know?"

They kept staring. Did they speak English or what?

Alex backed away, feeling the eyes of a dozen gnomes on her until the fountain was out of sight. Did the gnomes even *want* money?

She had basically the same question about the genie, come to think of it. If you had unlimited cosmic power, why the hell would you choose to work *retail*, of all things? Alex tried to think of what she would do if she had the genie's magic. There were too many choices to contemplate. None of them involved small business administration.

Outside, her father's truck was there, waiting for her, the engine idling and ancient rock'n roll blasting from the open windows. Mark was in the passenger seat. When she came to the car, he didn't open the door. "How was *work*, Lexie?" he asked, venom dripping from every word.

"Open the door, dick," Alex said.

Kenny Dufresne's head popped out from the middle of the truck's bench seat. "Hey, Alex! Am I in your seat? I'll—"

Alex backed away from the car. "No, that's cool—I'll just ride in the back."

"You better," Mark growled.

"Fuck you, Mark."

"Language!" her father yelled over the music.

Alex stuck out her tongue. She threw her bag into the truck bed and hopped in.

Her own car—*there* was a wish. Her own car, her own place, her own *life*. Just hers and nobody else's. That genie didn't know it, but he was living the dream.

That weekend, as business got better at the mall and her family celebrated the lead-up to the Fourth of July, Alex felt the weight of loneliness more keenly than usual. Each night, her father and Mark and Kenny and a few other friends lit off fireworks in the driveway and drank beers, daring each other to new heights of stupidity. Her mom picked up extra shifts at the grocery store and went out at night with Alex's aunts. And Alex? She sat in her stuffy room, her silver coins lined up on her bed, and saw nobody.

The few friends she'd had were a year or two ahead of her and were now at colleges scattered all over the country. They'd escaped, just like she wanted to. She was happy for them. But they were gone. There was the occasional text conversation.

She saw their stuff on social media—taking pictures of their dorm room or this or that party or whatever. Did they really care, though? She kinda doubted it. The fact that none of them had come home for the summer sort of clinched it, right? She wanted to be mad, but why? She was planning to do the same exact thing. Why come back to hicksville if you could live in Chicago or Boston or, hell, *Pittsburgh*.

The kids in *her* year? They were all the same stupid cookie-cutter version of white suburban boring. They went to high school football games and ran youth activities at church. They had promise rings and went "steady" and drove *cars*. The pandemic had proven she had nothing in common with these people. She knew it; they knew it. She had only run for school treasurer because she needed it for her college applications and knew nobody ever wanted it (do math? For *fun*?). Mr. Dodgson, her math teacher, was just delighted he didn't have to do it himself. She wasn't popular, she was just . . . there. Standing on the outside, looking in.

When she watched Mark and Kenny wrestling on the front lawn, laughing and laughing and *laughing*, she wondered if maybe she was wrong. Maybe it was better to be part of the group. Mark and Kenny were like brothers, able to communicate without speaking, sometimes. They were always pushing each other and giving each other headlocks and smacking each other in the groin—a kind of weird closeness that they seemed to feed on. Even Mark and her *dad* were close in a way she had never been—with either of her parents—for years, it seemed. He seemed to bask in her father's attention and craved his approval. He was like a little kid.

It was pathetic, of course—young man of nineteen years, trotting in his deadbeat father's wake like he was a six-year-old—but also . . . sweet? Alex didn't know. She didn't know why Mark did it. Didn't know what he got out of it, other than stitches when he inevitably tried something like skateboarding off the roof into a kiddie pool.

No, her job was the only thing that mattered. Making that money so she could get out of here and start over. Start over among way cooler people who sometimes read books and maybe even spoke more than one language. People who were the exact opposite of all the people she knew in this stupid little town.

Which meant, of course, that they would be just like her.

CHAPTER 8:
SATISFACTION GUARANTEED

ALEX'S NEXT DAY at work was the actual Fourth of July, and it was legit nuts. When her father pulled into the parking lot to drop her off—not even late—there was already a line of people stretching all the way out the door of the mall. "What the hell's all that about?" her father asked.

Alex, squeezed between her father and her brother, tried to remain casual. "I dunno, maybe there's some kind of celebrity, signing autographs today?" She knew her dad, who hated celebrities as a rule (lazy, liberal, good-for-nothings, never worked a day in their lives, etc.), would recoil from the idea of standing in line to have one of those "soft pinkos" sign a picture of their own face.

"I heard they got a genie there now," Mark said. "Granting wishes."

Her dad stopped the truck short. "What? For real?"

Alex gave her brother her bitterest glare. "I'm sure it's all hype. Some kind of scam."

Strategic error—she knew the second "scam" passed her lips. There wasn't a scam on this planet that Charlie Delmore wouldn't be a part of if the price was right. Instead of dropping Alex at the curb, her dad swung around and stopped the truck in a handicapped parking spot near the entrance. "Lexie, you know anything about this genie?"

"Yeah, Lex," Mark said, his face impassive. *"Do you?"*

Lexie mouthed the words "fuck you" to her brother. "I haven't heard anything, Dad—the cell phone place is on the second floor, kinda out of the way, you know? It's . . . uhhh . . . quiet."

Her dad shifted the truck into park. "Well, why don't we check it out."

Alex could practically *hear* her brother's gloating grin. "Oh, come on, Dad—look at the line! It'll take hours. Don't you have work? You can't afford to lose any more clients, can you?"

But Charlie Delmore was too far gone. He has this crazed look on his face—something distinct from other crazed looks Alex had become accustomed to over the course of her life. No, this time her dad looked . . . desperate? Could that be it? He opened the door and stepped out. "No work a wish can't fix, right?"

"What would you even wish for?" Alex asked, sliding out after him. The fear of her father uncovering her job was temporarily muted beneath a sudden, terrible curiosity. "No more gnomes? A new truck?"

Her dad blinked, and that raw desperation she had glimpsed was gone, buried beneath his usual brusqueness. "You get on to work, Alex. Don't you worry about a thing."

Alex backed away, uncertain.

Mark grinned at her. "Yeah, Alex—have a *nice* day."

Her stomach fluttering like a leaf, Alex turned and headed toward the mall entrance, while her dad and Mark journeyed to the distant end of the massive line.

As she got closer, Alex got a better look at the horde of customers she was about to confront. They—every single one of them—looked like they were barely in control of themselves, like teenage girls at a pop idol concert.

"Ummm . . . excuse me?" Alex said, trying to elbow her way past the mob and get inside.

A woman confronted her, hands on her hips. "Oh hell no! I *know* you are not thinking of cutting *this* line, Little Miss Punk!"

Alex didn't want to ask, because she knew, but she asked anyway. "Excuse me, but what is this line for?"

"Wishes!" The woman's eyes gleamed with a kind of frantic greed that made Alex take a step back. "I took out a home equity loan last week. Wait until you *see* what I do with that much money!"

A home equity loan! "What . . . what *will* you do?"

"I'm going to marry Chris Hemsworth!" The woman hopped up and down, clutching a bulging purse that Alex guessed was full of cash.

"Oh my God," Alex said.

Another woman a little ways back poked her head out of the line. "Hey, *I* was going to wish that!"

The first woman made an exaggerated shrug. "Too bad, so sad—I'm in line first!"

The second woman laughed. "Yeah, but I'm wishing *last*, so good luck with that!"

Alex looked for a way to slip past the first woman and get inside.

The good news was that first woman seemed to have forgotten that Alex existed. She brandished her purse at the other woman. "Oh yeah, well, *I'm* paying twenty-five thousand *cash!* Beat that!"

"Well maybe *I'll* just wish you were never born—how about them apples, huh?"

The two of them were out of line now, yelling at each other from about five paces apart. The other people in line were doing their best to ignore what was happening. One of them was filming the interaction on his phone.

Alex stopped at the doorway and turned. "You two *do* know that Chris Hemsworth is already married, right?"

The two women looked at Alex as though she had just belched. The first one spoke slowly, like to an idiot: "That's why it's a *wish*, honey."

Alex was speaking with a lunatic, so rather than continue, she just went inside.

The line seemed endless—people carting suitcases of cash, jars of change, and one guy and his maybe seven-year-old son had their arms full of gold bars. An old woman pushing an oxygen tank kept asking, "Do you think he'll take a check? He must take a check, right? All I have is checks."

When Alex finally found her way to the front of the line— the kiosk—she found the genie glowering on his throne, clawed fingers tapping on the armrests. Someone near the front of the line had his eyes fixed on his watch. "One minute to 9:00 a.m.!" he yelled back at the line behind him. The call was echoed backward.

Alex crawled over the counter and looked up at the genie. "Morning, boss." She jerked a thumb at the enormous line. "You ready for this?"

The genie motioned to the first wisher. "Let us begin."

The first person in line was Fontana Russo, a fake smile pinned to his face. "Hey there, friends—busy day, eh?"

"Hey there, Fontana," Alex said. "New pants?"

Fontana's saccharine expression crumpled a bit, but he made a brave recovery. He leaned on the counter, pushing his Velocity Burger visor back on his head, and winked at her. "Look, I know you two did me pretty dirty the other day, but I want you both to know I don't blame you—you were getting your business off the ground, any means necessary. I respect the hustle. That's why I'm here—I'm gonna make you two an offer you can't refuse."

The genie declined to react, so it was left to Alex. She rolled her eyes. "You gonna make a wish, or what?"

"Sure, sure—about that . . ." Fontana pulled out his phone, on which he opened up some kind of memo. "This is kind of a complicated one—you wanna take notes?"

Alex snorted. "You serious, right now?"

"Okay: I want the sum total of all knowledge uploaded into my brain *and* the ability to handle all that information without going insane. In exchange I'll give you ten percent of my net earnings for life." Fontana looked up from his phone. "Whaddya say?"

Alex looked over her shoulder. "Boss?"

The genie looked down, acknowledging Fontana's presence for the first time. "You want a different brain."

"No, *my* brain, just with all the knowledge in the universe inside it."

"And the ability to handle it and *not* go insane. Key part, there." Alex added, stifling a laugh.

"Oh, yeah—that too." Fontana grinned and held out a fist. "Thanks babe. Bump it out?"

Alex didn't move. "Are you kidding?"

"That would mean a different brain," the genie said. "You would become a different person."

"That's not the deal," Fontana said.

"Why do you not just attend a school and learn from the masters there?"

"Grad school is a waste of money and time," Fontana said. "This cuts to the chase—I want to know everything. Once I know everything, I'll be rich, and you'll get a cut. That's a fair price."

The genie shook his head. "Wealth is not earned by the most knowledgeable. It is amassed by the most ruthless. This is known."

"Okay, okay." Fontana reached into his pocket and produced a money clip. "How much you need as a down payment?" He slid out a few twenty-dollar bills.

The genie barely hesitated. "No."

Fontana had laid three hundred dollars on the counter and was still going. "More where this came from, my man."

"I said no," the genie said again.

Fontana just kept on laying out money until there were sixteen hundred-dollar bills—crisp and fresh from the bank—fanned out in a neat semi-circle on the counter. "I don't think you realize what a deal this is, Big G. You do this, and I'll be worth millions in five years. I'll make my first billion in ten. The money here is *incalculable,* you get me? This is just a down payment."

The genie fixed his burning glare on the man in the burger uniform: "You could offer me all the riches of the Nile, Fontana Russo, and still I would refuse, for it is not your money I find repellent."

Fontana stiffened. He looked at Alex. "He serious?"

"Take a walk, jerk." Alex said.

Fontana forced a chuckle. "You'll be sorry about this. Both of you will." He swept his money up with one hand.

Alex pointed to the nigh-endless line behind him. "I doubt it."

Two hours and at least a hundred wishers later, and the genie's kiosk looked like a treasure pile from a pirate movie. Stacks of dollar bills weighted down by *objet d'art*. There were paintings, piles of silver coins, briefcases of cash. The genie had turned down about as many wishes as he'd granted, and still they came.

Her father, if he was even still in the line, was so far back Alex hadn't so much as caught a glimpse. She still didn't know what she'd do or say when he appeared. She was too busy, though, to make a plan or even think much about it.

She was in the middle of probably the fortieth fight of the day, this time with a guy who had a suitcase full of gold watches. Her argument against this guy's wish was summarized pretty simply: "Because that's *genocide*, you asshole!"

The customer—a man in a torn T-shirt and jeans—yelled back at her. "If I can't get rid of the fucking Dutch, then WHAT IS EVEN THE POINT OF A GENIE?"

"Those timepieces are forgeries," the genie announced.

"They are not! Them's authentic Rolex! My dead uncle left them to me!"

"And you want to trade them to nuke Dutch people?" Alex said. "What is *wrong* with you?"

"It's my treasure. I can do what I want." The customer addressed the genie. "Look, big man—we gotta deal or not?"

The genie looked down at him, his eyes blazing. "No. Begone."

"What!?"

"Begone, or I shall banish you to these Nether-lands forevermore, so that you forget the sun's face and live as a worm, squirming in the earth."

The customer took his suitcase and backed off, grumbling to himself.

"Dude," Alex said to the genie, "the Netherlands aren't *literally* underground. How do you not know this?"

A woman barged to the front of the line and cleared her throat. "Excuse me?"

"Back of the line assho—" Alex began, but then caught herself—it was Maureen Sturgis, the mall manager. "Oh, shit—my bad. Hey."

"The rent has been paid in full, oh Mistress of the Bazaar. Why do you come?" said the genie.

"What *exactly* is going on here?" Sturgis said.

The genie gestured to the huge line. "I am pursuing my trade. What else?"

"Excuse me?" The next person in line—a teenager—raised her hand as though in school. "I'm next, right?"

"My supplicants are many, so make your business brief, woman," the genie said.

"I'm concerned there might be something illegal going on here," Sturgis said.

"I have violated no law I know of," the genie said.

"That he knows of being the operative term, there," Alex said.

Sturgis crossed her arms. "And just what is *that* supposed to mean?"

Oops—Alex waved her hands, "No, no—it's cool. I've been keeping an eye on him."

"Yes," the genie said. "Alexandria has been instrumental

in familiarizing me with the customs and statutes of your culture."

Sturgis frowned. "I can think of several reasons why a teenage girl shouldn't be your legal counsel, but let's leave that aside for a minute. What about all this money? Do you have any security arrangements?"

The genie laughed, making his eyes blaze and showing his fearsome teeth. "What manner of fool would steal from me, a jinn of great power and esteem? Any thief so bold would die ten thousand deaths in the burning pits of Gehenna!"

Alex noted Sturgis's panicked expression. "Bad turn of phrase there, boss."

Sturgis shook her head. "You need to shut down. You need to shut down *right now!*"

"Oh, come on, Ms. Sturgis! It's a holiday! We're making bank, here!"

The girl at the front of the line raised her hand again. "If you're gonna close, can you just do my wish real quick, okay?"

"What are you wishing for?" Sturgis asked.

The girl slid the shoulder of her T-shirt aside to reveal livid red flesh. "I got this killer sunburn yesterday at the pool, right? But me and my friends are supposed to go to the beach tomorrow, so, like, could you maybe get rid of the sunburn?"

"What do you offer in exchange?" the genie asked.

"I've got fifty bucks and my mom's old cell phone?" The girl held out the money and a dinged-up smartphone with a cracked screen.

"I've no need of a telephone. I will take the money," the genie said.

Alex took the cash. The genie clapped his hands softly together. "It is done."

The girl stiffened, eyes wide with shock, then poked gingerly at her shoulder and back. "Oh my . . . oh my GOD! It worked! It's totally gone!"

Sturgis stared at the girl in shock. "Really? He really healed it? Totally?"

The girl slid her T-shirt aside to show her shoulder again. The sunburn was gone.

Sturgis faced the genie. "And this isn't some kind of trick? Her sunburn won't come back later today or anything? She doesn't owe, like, her first born?"

The genie glared at her with his burning eyes. "What manner of villain do you take me for? And what possible use would I have for a child?"

Alex chuckled. "You did ask that one lady to have her kid dust the kiosk and get you drinks." When Sturgis and the genie both stared at her, she winced. "Sorry, sorry—shutting up now."

"I can't have you sitting here, in the middle of my mall, *warping reality*, Mr. Genie. It's . . . it's . . . well, it's going to cause problems."

"Oh, come on, Ms. Sturgis!" Alex said. "We've been at it two weeks and nothing bad has happened yet! He'll be good, I promise! We won't do anything crazy!"

"Like give away my parking spot?" Sturgis asked.

"It was a fair price," the genie said. "What matter is it if you must leave your vehicle six more paces from the door? Are you infirm?"

Alex searched her memory for the wish in question—right, some guy named Barney. "Dude," Alex said to the genie, "you gave that jerk *her* parking spot? What the hell, man?"

The genie was unmoved. "Am I beholden to you, my employee? Must I live by your decree, you whose services I purchase with pay? Have I misunderstood something in the title 'boss?'"

"See," Sturgis said, pointing at the genie and talking to Alex. "This is what I'm talking about. He doesn't know. He's going to mess up, and people are going to get hurt."

"For over *three thousand years* did I grant the wishes of all mortals, from mighty kings to lowly lepers, and never once was I accused of 'messing up,' as you put it! The *very notion* is an affront to my power!" The genie stood up from his throne. Everyone in the line took a big step back. Even Alex felt the bottom drop out of her stomach when she saw him at his full height.

"Hey, big guy," Alex said, back pressed against the counter. "Let's take it down a notch, okay? You did get that one dude eaten by a whale, remember?"

"What must I do to prove myself to you, Maureen Sturgis, mistress of the Wellspring Mall?" the genie said, stepping down off his throne and phasing through the counter like smoke. "Ask your boon and see it granted!"

Sturgis looked like she was tempted—just for a moment— but she clenched her fists and shook her head again. "The mall is being sued—sued because of *your* actions, Mr. Genie."

"Sued?" Alex said. "By who?"

Sturgis glanced at the crowd of people behind them— their argument had amassed quite an audience. "We'll meet tomorrow—*privately*—to discuss that and the rules for your continued tenancy."

The genie folded his arms. "You are certain?"

Sturgis took a deep breath. "Yes."

Those at the front of the line began to jeer at Sturgis. "You *bitch!*" one shouted. "I've been waiting two hours!"

"Tell all these people to disperse," Sturgis said, turning away from the crowd.

"No need," the genie said.

The sound of the crowd stopped abruptly. Alex looked up and Sturgis spun around. The mall concourse was empty, with only the fluttering of a single piece of paper indicating there had been people there at all. The paper slid to Sturgis's feet and she picked it up. Alex could read it over her shoulder. "*Wish list*," it said. The top one was "*Make Stacy Conover kiss me.*"

"Wh-where did they go?" Sturgis gasped. "What did you *do*?"

Alex also gaped at the sudden, echoing silence. "Oh my God! You didn't . . . you didn't *disintegrate* them, did you?" Her dad! Mark! *Oh god oh god oh god!*

"Of course not! What manner of butcher do you take me for?" The genie returned to his throne. "I returned them to their homes, of course."

Alex deflated with relief. "Oh thank God!"

Sturgis blinked at him. "But . . . but what about all their *cars*? You know, *in the parking lot*?"

"Oh . . . good point," Alex said, and looked at her boss.

The genie frowned as he sat down. "Hmmm . . . I did not think of that. Is there any way of knowing which automobiles belonged to whom?"

Alex shrugged. "A license plate reader, I guess? Like the ones cops have?"

"Just . . . just *fix* it, will you?" With an exasperated sigh, Sturgis turned and left. The mall, now eerily empty, echoed with the sound of her heels clicking on the floor.

* * *

The genie's powers did not allow him to instantly transport home all the cars that belonged to the people he'd transported out of the mall. For one thing, with the exception of her dad's truck, he and Alex didn't actually know *which* cars belonged to people who had been in line and which cars belonged to people who were at the mall for other reasons. So, once the truck was returned (complete with parking ticket for parking in a handicap zone) Alex and the genie spent the afternoon of the Fourth of July walking around the parking lot in the summer heat with a license plate reader the genie had conjured up out of nothing and were scanning the cars to see if they could figure it out themselves. The relief of Alex's secret being safe aside, it was not going well.

Alex showed her phone to the genie, with the driver's license picture of some guy named "Jesus Picardo," who drove a beat-up old Jeep. "Recognize this guy?"

"No." The genie stood there, his arms folded, his expression its usual contemptuous self. "There were hundreds of people who waited to see me this morning—I cannot possibly be expected to know all of their faces."

"Aren't you genies all-powerful or something?" Alex asked as she scanned the next car in the line. It was boiling hot out here, the black asphalt sizzling like a griddle.

"I am all-powerful, not all-knowing or all-seeing."

Alex was regretting her jeans and her tank top was sodden with sweat. Much more of this and *she* was going to need to cough up fifty bucks to wish away a sunburn. "Then how did you know how to make a license plate reader?"

"I did not." The genie didn't seem troubled by the heat at all. This made sense, as he was pretty much made out of fire.

Alex wanted to scream. They had been making *real money*

today. Hand over fist. People couldn't shovel it at them fast enough! Ten percent of the cash alone ought to come up to a couple thousand dollars, at least. Never mind the value of those statues and paintings and stuff! When they finally got down to accounting for her share, she wouldn't be surprised if there was a year's tuition in that pile. They were on a roll!

They had barely gotten started and then BAM—it was over. Instead, here she was, being fried like an egg and talking to a mythical being who reminded her of an angry track coach. "How can you make a license plate reader without knowing how to make one? That makes no sense."

The genie didn't answer. Though he wasn't hot, he was pretty clearly irritated at their chore, too. He was almost sulking.

Alex scanned another license plate and held up another face—an old woman with the absurd name of Breanna Whol-fan. "Recognize her?"

"Yes. She attempted to cut the line and demanded I give her husband painful boils on his backside. You sent her to the back."

Alex nodded, remembering. "Oh right. She wanted to pay with two pounds of fudge—I remember now."

The genie snapped his fingers and the car vanished.

"Like that, right there—how do you even know where her address *is*? I just showed it to you and I'm betting you've never been there."

"No, I have not."

"Then how can you wish her car back there if you aren't all-knowing or all-seeing? Come to think of it, how can you make it so my brother pukes every time he tries to snitch on me? How do you even know if he's snitching?"

The genie scowled more than usual. "Why are you pestering

me with these questions? What good will explaining my power to you do?"

Alex scanned the next car and held up the name, address, and picture of the next car owner. "This guy?"

"No."

They moved to the next row.

"The good it will do is I will have a better idea of what you can do and I'll be able to babysit you better."

"Babysit!"

Alex wiped sweat off her forehead. "Poor choice of words, okay? But look, Sturgis just shut us down because she thinks you're gonna do some crazy shit and, let's be honest, some crazy shit *did* just go down." She gestured to the parking lot. "Hence our current predicament, right?"

"Hmmm . . ." the genie said. "I think you are simply fabricating this excuse so you may pry into matters beyond your ken."

Alex flapped her shirt from the bottom to try and get some air in there. "Can't you make it cloudy or something? Cool it off a dozen degrees or so?"

"No."

"I know you can control the weather, dude—rains over one's fields, right? C'mon—just give me this one freebie."

"I said no!"

The parking lot was a desert of steel and tar around them, with no relief in sight. Alex relented. "Fine, I'll pay for it. Advance me the cost of one cool breeze and a nice fat rain cloud."

"This would conflict with the wish of the man who paid me two hundred and fifty dollars to ensure that his game of soft balls would not be rained upon today."

"Can't you just make it rain *exactly* here?"

"You are being lazy and frivolous, and I am displeased. Focus on our task, Alexandria Delmore."

Alex tossed the license plate reader at his feet. "Then finish this yourself, dude. I'm taking my lunch break." She started back toward the mall, her mind conjuring up images of an ice-cold drink with whipped cream and chocolate that could only loosely be considered a "coffee."

The genie called after her. "Stop! I require you to operate this infernal device, else my misdeeds will go unresolved!"

Alex turned around, still walking backward. "You don't own me! You get that, right? This is a *job*. I can stay or go as I please—hell, it was even in the contract! I'm a free being, and I'm using that freedom to not die of goddamned heat stroke!"

This brought the genie up short, "I . . . I . . . but I require your *assistance!*" He waved the license plate reader at her.

"Just use it yourself! You *created* the thing, so *use* it! What do you need me for?"

"I . . ." the genie opened his mouth, closed it. His eyes blazed. "Return this instant, or I shall name you oathbreaker and shall rescind the curse I laid upon your brother and his companion!"

Alex stopped walking. "You can't do that! You do that and my parents will make me quit, and where will that put you, huh? You can't run that place without me and you *know* it!"

The genie clapped his hands and—FOOM—Alex found herself standing in front of the genie, the license plate reader in her hands again. She threw it down and ran away.

FOOM! She was back, again with the reader. She threw it at the genie this time and took off again.

"Stop this!" the genie roared.

FOOM! Alex was back, but now she was chained by the ankle to a huge iron ball. "Jerk, you get this off me or I'll tell my dad anyway!"

"And is your father a wizard?"

"No, he just owns a ton of guns!" Alex yanked at the chain.

"Ha! Mortal weaponry is of no use against me! I am smokeless fire! I am infused with the power of God! I am—"

Alex kicked him in the groin with her free leg. Her foot just sort of . . . passed through where he ought to be and she lost her balance. She fell butt-first on the asphalt, which was hot enough to singe her palms. "Dammit! You stupid asshole! Let me go!"

The genie crouched. "Why are you behaving this way? Are you drunk? Cursed? Suffering from your monthly blood?"

"Oh, screw you." Alex staggered to her feet, the ball and chain jingling as she did so. "I'm hot and I'm tired and this *whole thing* is stupid and the manager just basically closed us down, so I'm not getting any more of your stupid silver coins, which I *can't spend anyway* because it's the twenty-first century and that's not how any of this works and I just . . . I just *don't* understand why, if you can do anything, you can't just *fix* things for once. Just *do it*. Jesus, why are you such an asshole?"

The genie frowned, but then he was always frowning. There was something extra to this frown, though—that same sadness she'd seen glimpses of before, some sort of . . . *weight*. It was as though she could see his age for the first time—he was thousands of years old, she realized. He was *tired*.

The genie waved his hand and the ball and chain disappeared. "Wish for refreshment," he said.

Alex wiped tears from the corners of her eyes. "I wish for refreshment."

The genie held out his hand and a tall, frosty cup of Alex's favorite frozen coffee concoction was there, complete with whipped cream and chocolate drizzle. "How . . . how did you know?"

"My powers are not mine alone, Alexandria Delmore. When I conjure a thing, I am . . ." he searched for the words. "I am making a *connection* between the power of God and the dreams of men. Or women. Or people. You receive what you desire. I make it possible, but the desire is your own."

Alex took the frozen coffee and took a sip. It was pure, icy bliss. "So . . . this came from me?"

"In a manner of speaking. You wished it. I granted it. The power requires two wills to manifest."

Alex gestured to her ankle. "Then what about the ball and chain?"

The genie shrugged. "It also works the other way. That which you loathe or fear or hate—that which you expressly *do not* wish—I can make that, too."

"What about your palace of crystal in the clouds or whatever? Who wished for that?"

"That?" The genie's massive shoulders sagged a little. "It does not exist."

Alex nearly choked on her coffee. "What? What do you mean? Where do you *live*?"

"Everywhere. Nowhere. I am smokeless fire—I exist as dreams made real. I need no sleep, no rest. What need have I, in the end, for a home?"

"Everybody needs a home, are you kidding?" Alex gaped at him. "This whole time you've just been, what, floating down the shoulder of the interstate like a hot breeze? You're *homeless*?"

"It is as I said." The genie turned away from Alex. "You are right. This task is fruitless. Let us return to my business."

They headed back inside. Well, more accurately, *Alex* headed back inside. The genie just disappeared and, she presumed, would meet her back at the kiosk. She took her time walking, savoring the air-conditioning of the mall while she turned over the new things she'd learned.

The fact that the genie had no fantastical palace somewhere in the clouds changed a lot about how she saw her employer. For one thing, he became less intimidating. His arrogant manner didn't seem so much like the disdain of some superior being, looking down its nose at ant-like mortals. She started thinking of it as bluster—he was talking himself up. The genie had been a *slave* for ages and ages. He had spent an eternity groveling at the feet of whatever jerk picked up that ring he had been trapped inside—who could blame him if he swerved hard the other direction? If anything, she suspected the genie didn't know what he was doing with himself any better than Alex did.

At the kiosk, the genie was already there with a giant strong box floating nearby, its lid open. The genie was throwing all the treasures of the morning rush into them—cash, gold, jewelry, and so on. "Hey," Alex said as she came up to the counter. "There's a lot of money here. Maybe you could start renting an apartment or something?"

"No. I will not serve any lord."

"Lord? Like . . . *land*lord?" When the genie looked at her quizzically, Alex just threw up her hands. "You know what, forget it. What do you need me to do?"

"Nothing. Cease your ceaseless prattle, that is all."

So Alex pushed herself up on the counter and sat there, legs swinging, and scrolled her phone. She had set up social media accounts for the genie's business, and she was looking at photos of all kinds of crazed people excited about the weird things they wished for. A lot of pissed off people, too, complaining they had been teleported home without consent. One post by a wisher, marked "Adult Content," she clicked on out of perverse curiosity. "Oh, gross!" She threw her phone down.

The genie grunted, though the meaning of the grunt was obscure. He was stewing over something, that much was clear. The lawsuit, maybe? The loss of all that business?

"You think you can convince the manager to let us re-open tomorrow?" she asked. "That was a good crowd today, you know? She can't want to turn away business from this dump."

The genie did not respond, but seemed to throw the stacks of money into the chest with greater ferocity than he had a moment before.

"Excuse me?" a young woman's voice, fragile and hollow, interrupted them. It was a rail-thin teenage girl—maybe Alex's age, maybe a bit older—with stringy blonde hair and a wrinkled T-shirt standing in front of the kiosk. Her eyes were bloodshot, with deep rings beneath them. She clutched her purse tightly to her chest. "I need a wish granted."

"We're closed for the day, sorry," Alex said.

"You don't understand," the girl said, taking Alex's hand and squeezing so tight it hurt. Her fingers were bony and hard. "I *need* this. I need it. Please?"

Alex tried to retrieve her hand but failed. "Boss?"

The genie turned. "You were in line earlier, were you not? You returned, even after being banished from my presence—why?"

"I need help." The girl shivered, her voice verging on tears.

The genie looked at her long and hard. "I cannot do what you wish."

"You know what she wants?" Alex looked at the genie and then at the girl. "What do you want?"

The woman smiled weakly at the genie. "I'll pay anything. Anything."

The genie folded his arms. "No."

"What?" Alex glared at him. "Why not?"

Tears streaked across the girl's cheeks. "Please, sir! Please! Just this once, and you'll never see me again. It will fix everything! I'll be better!"

"This I will not do."

The girl burst into full-on sobs, her sharp collarbones shaking beneath her shirt. People passing the kiosk stared at her.

Alex, at last, recovered her hand from the girl's death grip. "She just wants to feel better, Jesus! Just do it! The manager isn't around, neither is that mall cop—what's the big deal?"

The genie didn't budge. "I can refuse any wish I desire, yes? It is my right to decline!"

"Yeah, but that's for assholes like Fontana and their asshole wishes. This girl just wants a night's sleep, you know?" Alex said. "Christ, man—look at her. She's sick."

"She does not realize what she asks. Neither do you," the genie said.

"You know, would it kill you to actually *help* someone at some point? I get that you're trying to, I dunno, make your way in the world or whatever, but people are supposed to *help each other*, understand? You can do that, man! Why don't you?"

The genie heaved a heavy sigh. "Very well." He faced the girl. "I will grant your wish, but you will provide me with no payment. Do you understand?"

"Yes!" the girl said through her choked moans. "Yes yes!"

"Ask."

The girl gradually got control of herself. She squared her bony shoulders. "I wish to lose fifteen pounds."

Alex stiffened. "Oh. Oh my God."

"It is done," the genie said.

Alex watched as the girl *withered* in front of her. Her cheeks became more sunken, her collarbones more pronounced. The slight musculature of her arms and legs thinned.

The girl's miserable expression lessened and then vanished altogether in a few seconds. She drew herself out of her slouch and took a long breath. "Oh . . . I feel it . . . it worked!"

"Then you are satisfied?" the genie asked.

"Yes!" The girl whipped out a roll of twenty-dollar bills. "Take this, I insist."

"Never," the genie said. "Begone. Never return."

The girl looked somewhat shocked, but she turned and left, laughing to herself. Laughing long and hard. Hysterically, even. Alex couldn't believe she had the strength to walk away at all.

"What the hell?" Alex said. A shudder ran down her spine and into her feet. "What the actual, dude?"

"In less than a day's time, I expect she shall return," the genie said. "For her affliction, there is no end. I could see it."

"Then why did you *do* it?"

"Because she wished it. Because *you* wished it. Because granting wishes is all I know how to do! You mortals . . . you never know what you really want." The genie closed his eyes. "Do you know that there is one wish oft asked of me that I did not include there." He gestured toward the pricing guide.

"What is it?"

"Across ages and regions, in times distant and near, there is always someone who wishes for me to restore their deceased loved ones to life, only to be horrified when I actually do what they ask."

Alex's mouth fell open. "Holy shit—you actually did that?"

The genie looked down at his hands. "Scores of times."

"What the fuck, man? How did you *think* that would turn out?"

"It wasn't up to me!" the genie roared. "They were my masters! They *demanded* it of me, and so I obeyed. I restored their relative's body, even created a facsimile of their mind, but what power have I to restore a soul to an empty husk? What power have I over how they react to such a thing, knocking upon their door?"

Alex tried to imagine it. She'd heard stories like this— around campfires and stuff, when her dad had a couple beers in him and felt like scaring his kids to death—but she hadn't really thought of the *reality* of such a thing. What that would do to a person, afterward. "That must have been . . . uhhh . . . pretty bad, huh?"

"And even when I tell them what they ask is madness, even when I say it is beyond my power—do they listen? No. Never. They are like you, like her, like all of you. So desperate to claim that which they do not have, that they are blind to the cost."

The genie hung his head. Alex thought about hugging him or something, but the idea seemed so immediately absurd that she stopped herself. "I'm . . . I'm sorry, boss. I don't know what to say."

"Never in three thousand years did I meet a person who was content. And now? Matters are worse." The genie opened his eyes, and once again there was that weight—that incredible, palpable sadness. Alex realized she had misunderstood something. The genie was not sad because he was homeless. He was sad because, after thousands of years, the world remained broken, and no amount of wishing would ever fix it.

"I will see you tomorrow, Alexandria Delmore. Go. Celebrate your nation's independence from the whims of a king. It is a greater gift than you know."

CHAPTER 9:
A PLAGUE OF TOADS

ALEX HAD TO *WALK* HOME because work ended early and her dad wasn't answering his phone and her mom was at work and didn't have her phone *on* her and of course she wasn't allowed to ride her moped to work (which was ridiculous), so . . . walking. Which was a couple miles. Maybe an hour walk. In July.

Once you got off the state highways, with their sketchy shoulders full of junk and their cars whipping by at a million miles an hour and turned down the little streets and winding roads of her town, it all looked like paradise. The manicured lawns and the automatic sprinklers. The dogs barking in the backyards. The shiny cars in the driveways and the kids playing street hockey. The smell of people grilling burgers and the American flags flying from every porch. Everything seemed safe and secure and in place. Summer, with that lazy heat, had relaxed the hard corners of the world and painted over the cracks with the golden rays of sunlight.

Alex knew better than to buy into the myth. That huge

line of people in the mall this morning wasn't a coincidence. That lady hadn't cooked up two pounds of fudge to give her husband hemorrhoids because *all was well*. Shit was bent sideways in this town, only nobody wanted anybody else to know it.

She thought of her father this morning. That desperate look in his eyes. That deep, simmering terror.

She only wished she knew exactly what the root of the problem *was*.

She got home in the late afternoon and, *of course*, there was some kind of drama. Everybody else was hiding their bullshit— the Delmores? The Delmores flew it from the flagpole. She saw her dad's pickup in the driveway, parked at a severe angle. There was a tire tread across the front lawn and the mailbox was knocked flat, giving Alex some idea of how accurately the genie had teleported it home, or maybe how her father had reacted to it appearing.

But the truck was still *running*. Her father had gone some-where, come back in a rush. The doors were open. Something was *wrong*. Alex hurried closer. "Dad? Mark?"

She looked inside. Looking back at her were about fifty toads, lined up on the dashboard along with the Jesus figu-rine and the cartoon characters. They chirped at her, blinking their bugged-out eyes in curiosity.

"Oh no."

BOOM!

Alex's heart stopped for a moment—had the house exploded? No. Her brain caught up—shotgun. That was a shotgun blast.

"Oh SHIT!"

Alex went around to the backyard, pressing her back to the garage so as not to startle an agitated Charlie Delmore with a firearm. She heard him yell. "Hold it in, boy! Hoooold it!"

A squadron of toads hopped around the corner of the garage, trying to make an escape. There was another huge boom and about half of them blew apart into red and orange chunks. The others kept hopping.

"Dad!" Alex yelled, waving her hand around the edge of the garage. "It's Alex! Don't shoot!"

She heard a retching sound—that would be Mark—and then a sound like a wet towel slapping on a pool deck. Alex noticed now for the first time the sound of toads—hundreds of toads—singing their high-pitched little songs. She had assumed it was birds.

"Lexie!" her father yelled. "Get over here, and don't touch those frogs! They're cursed!"

Alex came around the garage to find their usually well-kept backyard the scene of a battle, with Mark at its center. Mark, who looked pale and drawn and clammy, was clutching his stomach with one hand and an industrial-sized crucifix with the other—probably the cross her father had kept in his closet ever since her mother had made him take it down from over their bed a couple years back. Mark was sitting next to a plastic kiddie pool full of toads and the mashed corpses of toads—just a giant, blue basin of goo and slime and wriggling little creatures. Next to it, discarded, was a sledgehammer encrusted in toad guts. Around the yard were little craters where the shotgun had been employed—Alex realized she had been hearing it for a few blocks and assumed it was fireworks. It had not been.

A stream of amphibious refugees were fanning out in all directions, squeezing through the chain-link fence between them and their neighbor, hopping into the woods at the rear of their property, or making a break for the garage, as that last group had.

A reconstruction of events was pretty clear: her brother, the jerk, had tried to snitch, the curse had kicked in, and her father was losing a battle against the forces of toad-dom.

"Lexie . . . you . . . you . . ." Mark panted. "You bit . . ." But before he could finish the word, he convulsed and another dozen toads wriggled out of his mouth.

Her dad grabbed her by the arm and dragged her over by him, standing guard by the edge of the patio. He fumbled in a box of shotgun ammunition for more cartridges. "Look out! Look out!"

Alex was pretty sure the toads were just toads, but her father was acting as though they were going to eat him whole, like amphibious piranha. When they hopped toward him, he yelped a little and smashed them frantically with the butt of his gun. He had blood and guts all over his jeans and shirt. Even his face was speckled with toad-bits. "Gross, Dad! Chill, okay!"

"Your brother's been *cursed*, Lexie! I sure as hell *won't* calm down." He yelled at Mark. "The Lord's Prayer, Mark! Recite the Lord's Prayer again!"

"Our F-father who . . . who art in . . . i-in . . ." Mark vomited, this time for a solid four seconds. One little toad crawled out of his nose and took to the lawn.

Her father was frantic. "In the pool, Mark! In the pool! Jesus!"

Alex stood back, folded her arms, and gave her brother a hard look.

Mark raised one trembling hand and extended his middle finger in her direction. A toad hopped off his shoulder.

Her father emptied another magazine of shotgun shells at the yard full of magic toads, obliterating maybe a hundred of them. There were at least ten times that many remaining. He was also blowing giant chunks out of the lawn.

"So . . ." Alex said, trying to sound conversational as her father was re-loading. "How'd this happen?"

"It's them *gnomes!*" her father said, his eyes red with hate. "They cursed my son! They cursed him because they want my business to fail! Unnatural bastards!"

"Yeah, I'm guessing that's not it, Dad. Mark just isn't that important."

Mark, over their father's shoulder, gave her the finger again as he puked up another thirty creatures.

"Well what else *could* it be? Think one of the neighbors is a witch?" He looked suspiciously over the fence into the next yard. There was Mrs. Phoung on her phone. When she saw she was spotted, she ran inside.

"Dad, do you think maybe you could put the gun down? I think she just called the cops."

"What, a man can't defend his home anymore?"

"Dad, they're tiny little toads, not terrorists."

"Screw you, Lexie!" Mark managed between convulsions.

"That's the spirit!" Alex called back. "Only a few hours until sundown. You can make it! I believe in you!"

Their father was crushing toads with the butt of his shotgun again. "This isn't natural! These aren't natural frogs!"

Alex put a hand gently on her father's arm. "Dad, I think maybe we should calm down, don't you? You are covered in toad guts. Mom is going to freak if she comes home and sees all this, right?"

"But . . . but Mark . . ."

"Mark is just puking toads. It's just toads. Normal, regular toads. He and Kenny probably dared each other to eat toad eggs or something."

Her father grabbed her arm right back. "You can't trust them gnomes, Lexie! Those toads could be anything! *Anything*, you hear me?"

"Dad, I've got this, okay?" Alex steered him toward the house. "Go get cleaned up and I'll handle this for a while."

"But—"

"If he gets any worse, we'll take him to the hospital. Which is where he should have gone in the first place—I'm sure they've got people who handle stuff like this."

Her father, trembling and numb, let himself be guided through the back door. Alex managed to disentangle the gun from him and place it gently on the ground before he went in. "Take a shower. Drink a beer. You've had a long day."

The door closed. She wedged a patio chair under the screen door handle to keep it shut and then turned around. "Three days. You couldn't wait *three days* before you went narc on me, could you, Mark?"

"F-fuck . . . y . . ." Mark puked toads again—just a little one this time. Four or five little hoppers leapt off his chin and dove into the bloody horror-show that was the kiddie pool.

"No no no—fuck *you*, Mark! You suck, and I hope you enjoy the taste of frog, you back-stabbing asshole. You brought this on yourself!"

"He . . . he just asked . . . what . . . what your job was like . . . th-that's . . . that's . . ." Mark turned around and covered his mouth. He spat a few times. The choir of toads chirping in the dying light intensified. He gasped for air and continued,

"What'd you have him *curse* me for! That's not cool!"

"I didn't *have* him curse you—he just did it. And he did it because he knew you couldn't keep your mouth shut. And what was the big idea trying to put the hustle on a genie, anyway? How stupid is that? You're lucky you just wound up with this. I saw him turn a guy into a cockatoo once and I'm pretty sure the guy has some kind of complex now."

"I wasn't *trying* to tell him, Lex!" Mark belched and a fat toad—twice the size of the others—flew out of his mouth. Alex had to duck. "He *asked what your job was like*! What was I supposed to do? Lie?"

"Yes, Mark—you were *supposed to lie.* Tell him I sold cell phones or khakis or something."

Mark shook his head. He hiccupped, and it sounded suspiciously like a ribbit.

Alex came over and helped him up and over to the picnic table—a table now filled with buckshot, unfortunately, and covered in singing toads. Mark puked again, adding to their number. "What are you going to tell Dad?"

"About what?"

"About me."

"I'm not telling him shit—*you* make up your own lie."

Mark shrugged. "I'm just gonna tell him the genie did it!"

"Mark!"

"How else am I gonna explain this? Dad freaked out so bad he nearly crashed the car. He was talking about taking a blowtorch to the Houlihan's hedges to 'smoke out the leprechauns.' They're one of our best clients, Lex!"

"If you tell him it was the genie, then Dad will go *after* the genie. He'll bring a gun to the mall, Mark. *Again.* He will bring a gun to the mall *again.*"

They were quiet for a moment. Around them, the thousand toads were a chorus to the coming dusk. Alex reflected that they probably wouldn't have to worry about mosquitos in the backyard for a while.

Mark puked a few more times, adding to the throng. "Toads taste terrible," he said.

"I bet."

"You gotta tell him, Lex. You gotta tell both of them. Keeping stuff—you know, *important* stuff—from them . . . it, well, it'll eat you up inside. Trust me."

Alex frowned. "What big dark secrets are *you* keeping? You harboring a secret love for the poetry of Adrienne Rich?"

"Fuck you, Alex. You gotta tell 'em."

Alex's stomach sank. "Why?"

"Because they're gonna find out. Not from me—no way—but they'll find out eventually. Someday Dad will wanna visit you himself. You might end up on the news. One of our neighbors might go. They're gonna find out. Your genie can't curse them all."

"Mark, if I tell them, they'll make me quit."

Mark snorted. A tiny little toad slipped out of his right nostril. "What, you telling me you love this job that much? C'mon—that genie is a jerk."

"He's not a jerk. And Mark, the money is good and . . . and . . ."

"And you want to make a wish." Mark nodded. He pawed his pockets until he found his vape pen. "You want to wish yourself outta here—I get it. Don't we all."

Alex arched an eyebrow at her older brother. "Why are you acting so weird? You have ambitions to be a beer-guzzling townie in some other town?"

"You know what? I was right the first time. Screw you, Alex!" He stood but had to pause to spit up another seven or eight toads. "You suck." He took a long drag on his vape pen and exhaled. The air smelled like cinnamon and toad blood. He stormed into the house.

At least he had called her Alex.

Progress, you know?

The cops showed up well after sundown, so the torrent of toad-vomit had ceased, but they did arrive in time to meet Alex's mom, just getting home from work in her dented old Toyota hatchback. She emerged from the car with a resigned expression. "What did he do this time?" she asked the officers at the front door.

Alex was sitting on the couch, still trying to act like this whole debacle had nothing to do with her. Mark was in his room, sleeping off the ordeal of repopulating the amphibian portion of the local biosphere.

"I defended my home!" her dad yelled at the cops, but he was handing over his firearms license for inspection like a respectable adult instead of getting maced in their front hall and breaking a lamp as he thrashed around. Alex hoped this indicated some degree of growth, but she doubted it. He was probably still too rattled by the toad-splosion to muster up enough *energy* to get maced by the police.

The cops were on a first-name basis with her dad. They were all laughing, "Sure, Charlie, sure—cursed frogs, you said? Look, we got a goblin on call who helps us out with this stuff. Want us to get him?"

Rosalind Delmore, still clutching her purse in both hands, still in the doorway, wasn't yet satisfied. "Someone explain to me what checking my idiot husband's gun license has to do with cursed frogs. Is Mark okay?"

"I'm fine, too, in case you were wondering," Alex said, scrolling her phone.

"I *know* you're fine, Lexie," her mom said. "In this house, your father gets arrested, your brother goes to the emergency room, and you talk back. Where is Mark? Everybody stop staring at me and *talk*!"

The story of the toads and the shotgun (and the sad fate of both the picnic table and the kiddie pool) were related to Alex's mom in fits and spurts by a mixture of the police, her father, and Alex. No one gave any indication that they suspected Alex of anything, but she got the sense about halfway through the story that it was *her* that was in trouble, here. Something about how her mom got very still and very quiet as they got to the part about Alex coaxing her dad to give up the shotgun and go inside. She looked at Alex then with a closed expression—narrowed eyes, pursed lips—that told her "I know you're lying."

No one else picked up on it. Least of all the cops. "Well, we're going to let you off with a warning, Charlie. You know better than to go firing off a shotgun in a thickly settled area— it isn't safe."

"I thought this was a free country." Her dad grumbled under his breath, but his heart wasn't in it. He knew he'd screwed up. There was a whole backyard full of dead toads to prove it.

The cops left with a tip of their hats to Rosalind. Her father didn't make eye contact with either of them. He just got a plastic trash bag from under the sink and said, "Well, I'm gonna clean up a bit," and went out the back door, leaving Alex alone with her mom.

Her mother sat on the edge of the duct-taped recliner across from her and said, "Well?"

"Well what?" Alex said.

"I know you, Alexandria, and I know you had something to do with this, and I need you to tell me what it is. Now."

Alex sat up on the couch. "*I* didn't do anything."

"Now I *know* you know more about this, because that was a pretty clear dodge, young lady. Now: tell me what you're doing at that mall."

Alex blinked. How did she . . . how could she . . .

Rosalind did the mind-reading thing again. "I'm your mother, Lexie, and I might not be at my best right now, but I'll always know when my little girl isn't telling me something. Or maybe it's not the mall, but then it means you're either pregnant or addicted to drugs, so which is it?"

"Oh my God, Mom, I am *not* pregnant."

"Drugs?"

"Do you want to inspect my arms for needle tracks or something?"

"Then it's the mall. *Spill it*, Lexie."

Alex closed her eyes. "Mom, you *can't* tell Dad! He'll freak out."

"He already *has* freaked out, honey. He blew up our picnic table and shot holes in our lawn and ruined a kiddie pool. Tell me."

Mark was right, she thought. *They found out anyway.* "I've been working for a genie."

Rosalind gasped and put her hand over her mouth. "The

one at the Wellspring Mall? The one on the news?"

"The one on the *what*?"

"It was on the radio on the way home. A genie granting wishes at the mall is getting sued."

"Do they know by who?" Alex picked up her phone, thumbs primed to google.

Her mother snapped her fingers over the phone. "Alex, tell me about this job. What do you do for the genie? He hasn't made you part of his . . . you know . . ."

"His what?"

"His *harem*?" This last word she whispered.

Alex burst out laughing. "Oh my God, you *didn't* just ask me that!"

"I'm being serious! I understand those genies have . . . you know . . . *ways*."

"Mom, I run the cash register. You know, for the wishes? And I'm pretty sure what you just said is racist."

Rosalind waved away the accusation. "Working for one of those *things* is dangerous, Lexie. You know this. We raised you better than that!"

Alex felt a spike of anger, but she kept a handle on it. "He is *not* a 'thing,' and my job is fine. I made, like, thousands of dollars today. I made it helping people."

"And what about your poor brother?"

Yeah, sure—*poor* Mark. "He tried to *blackmail* me, Mom. He wanted a free wish or he was gonna tell Dad. So the genie . . . you know . . . *dealt* with it. I didn't ask him to, either. He just did it. Mark will be fine."

A look of horror encompassed her mother's face. "Your brother was *cursed* by a *genie*, Lexie! The poor guy has *enough* on his plate without you . . ."

"Plate? What does *Mark* have on his plate besides screwing around with Kenny and getting drunk?"

Her mom shook her head, abruptly changing tactics. "I don't like this job and I don't care how much money you are getting paid!"

Alex stood up. "Oh yeah, well *I* care. The amount of money I'm getting is enough to pay the cell phone bill, how about that? Do you care now? What if I wished you up a new car? Paid off the house? Would you still *not* care about how much money I'm being paid?"

"Fine—where is this money?" Her mother put out her hand. "Show it to me."

Alex's stomach clenched. She thought of the bag of silver coins in her closet upstairs. "Well . . . that part's a little complicated. I have to go the bank and . . ."

"Lexie, you need to quit that job, do you hear me? It is dangerous and I don't like it and you need to quit."

Alex left the living room and went through the kitchen. Her mother followed.

"Don't you walk away from me, young lady!"

"I'm not quitting, Mom! No way!"

"I'll tell your father!"

Alex rounded on her. "Oh, are you two speaking again? Did I miss something?"

"Lexie, the problems between me and your father aren't relevant. You need to—"

Alex pulled down the stairs to her room. "What, am I the only person in this family who doesn't get to live a screwed-up life, then? Mark is a burn-out, Dad's insane, *you've* given up on pretty much everything—I think it's my turn to act irresponsibly, don't you?"

Rosalind blinked at the assault. She had to take a moment to compose herself. "Lexie, that is *not* fair!"

But Alex was already up the attic stairs and was pulling them up after her.

CHAPTER 10:
REVISED BUSINESS MODEL

A NIGHT OF GOOGLING gave Alex the details: the genie was being sued by the "young victim of the genie's first granted wish in the area" for civil assault, since the DA apparently declined to issue a warrant for the genie's arrest, for various complicated legal reasons surrounding the status of mythical creatures under US law. It was large enough news that it made it to some talking heads on cable news and a few syndicated opinion columns.

There was a lot of talk, generally, about the *existence* of the genie. What was it, really? Was it a hoax? If not, what did that *mean* for society or the world at large? One guy—some puffy, bloviating jerk whose voice Alex vaguely recognized from one of her dad's favorite AM talk radio programs, ranted on and on about how "this *thing* could unbalance our entire system! Our entire way of life! Something must be done!"

And it wasn't *just* the genie. Alex spent the night scrolling through the hysterical hellfire that was on some of the larger, more unhinged social media sites and saw accounts of weird creatures popping up here and there everywhere. Trolls in state forests. Vampires on Long Island. Dragons in Africa. And gnomes—gnomes *everywhere*. "They're stealing our jobs," people shrieked into the digital abyss. "We're obsolete, I tell you! It's *us* or *them!*"

It all made Alex concerned about how tomorrow morning's meeting would go.

What also made her concerned was the status of the rest of her family. Her father spent all morning hosing down the yard, Mark and her mother weren't speaking to her, and nobody had suggested giving her a ride to work. So, she took the moped—something she ordinarily would have preferred, but the idea that everyone was tacitly upset with her made it notably less fun.

So, to the meeting at the mall she went with butterflies in her stomach and an absolute, ironclad desire not to mess this up.

Ms. Sturgis sat across from Alex and the genie at a table in the food court right next to a large potted plant that provided a degree of ostensible "privacy." This was assuming eavesdroppers would be considerate enough to attempt to spy on the proceedings from that one, specific direction. In every other direction, employees of various stores and a few people Alex assumed were journalists were loitering at a fairly uniform distance away, all of them making sure to look *deeply engaged* in whatever was happening on their phones and not, you know, *obviously eavesdropping*.

"I've been reviewing the wishes you've granted over the past few days." Sturgis produced Alex's hand-made pricing guide and flipped it open.

"None of those are illegal!" Alex blurted out.

Sturgis looked up at her over her glasses. "There is a difference between legality and propriety, Ms. Delmore. None of these might be illegal, but many of them are *inappropriate*."

"Like what?"

The genie held up a hand. "I shall speak for myself, Alexandria Delmore." He glared at the mall manager. "Like what?"

"What about this, on page two: The ability to squirt silly string out your nose?"

Alex shrugged. "What's the big deal?"

"Indeed," the genie added. "I was given to believe the string is only *silly*, not malevolent."

"Do you know how much silly string my employees found in the parking lot?"

"I do not," the genie said.

"That was a rhetorical question," Sturgis said.

The genie frowned. "No, it was not. That is not what a rhetorical question is."

"On page five," Sturgis went on, "the ability to see through walls. This is *obviously* a privacy concern."

Alex nodded. "Yeah, I thought that guy seemed sketchy."

"What is wrong with seeing through walls?" the genie asked. "*Windows* allow one to see through walls. Are you to tell me *windows* are inappropriate?"

"In the girls' locker room?" Sturgis said. "Yes! I should say so!"

"Oh, gross," Alex said. "I didn't even think of that."

"See?" Sturgis tapped the pricing guide with one manicured finger. "This is my point! This book is *full* of extremely borderline desires. One person here wanted to be able to change into a car!"

"Oh, we didn't grant that," Alex said.

"*I* did not grant it. I asked for ten thousand dollars and he could not pay."

"According to your records, this individual was a minor!

He was only fourteen! *He is not permitted to drive!*"

The genie and Alex exchanged glances. "But he would *be* the car," the genie said. "How would he be able to drive?"

Sturgis stopped. "Isn't that . . . isn't that *obviously* what he wanted to be able to do?"

"Uhhhh," Alex pursed her lips. "Honestly, I just assumed the kid had a thing for Corvettes."

The genie nodded. "Had the wish been granted, he would not have been able to pilot himself around. Cars cannot drive themselves, as I understand it."

"Well, *some* can, I guess," Alex said.

"What?! You never said this!" the genie looked down at her. He was barely able to fit behind the table on the little plastic chair as it was. The act of twisting his torso to one side caused the table to crack.

"Dude, it is *impossible* for me to explain *absolutely everything* about the modern world!"

"Enough!" Sturgis held up her hands. "You two are exposing yourselves to civil liability and, by extension, you have exposed *the mall* to liability. Do you understand?"

"No," said the genie.

Alex hung her head. "Look, I'll explain it to you later, okay? It's a court thing. It's why you're getting sued."

"We *all* are being sued." Sturgis pulled a piece of paper out of a briefcase and laid it on the table. The heading indicated it was from some law firm.

Alex skimmed it—it was the thing from the news, all right. "We didn't assault anyone!"

"Yes, you did," Sturgis said. "When you made this young man—a Fontana Russo—soil himself at work, that constitutes assault. Or at least his lawyers think so."

"That little shit!" Alex said.

"No, it was substantial. I made certain of it," the genie said.

Sturgis rubbed her temples with her middle fingers. "Look, I've spoken with the mall's lawyer, and they don't have a case—there is no way they could effectively prove that the genie made him . . . you know. At least not reliably. And anyway, suing mythological creatures is a . . . well . . . a *tricky* area of the law, apparently. *The point is*, though, that you two need to clean up your act before you do something that *does* result in a legally actionable case. We *cannot* afford a serious lawsuit!" Sturgis motioned to the food court and the mall at large. "I am keeping this place going *by a string*, understand? If you want to keep this job and *you*," she pointed at the genie, "want to keep running this business for some reason, then *get things under control*. No more selling supernatural powers or weird curses or anything."

Alex snorted. "Then what are people gonna wish for?"

Sturgis threw up her hands. "I don't know—discount sneakers. A new watch. A gift certificate to the movies—you know, *normal stuff.*"

"These do not seem to be great uses of my power," the genie said. "You would reduce me to a mere peddler of trinkets."

"Okay, fine, but you know what trinkets don't do?" Sturgis waived the legal letter at him. "They don't draw lawsuits. So, if you want to work here, then limit your business to selling the kind of things people buy *at the mall*. Got it?"

The genie's nod was solemn. "It shall be so."

* * *

By the time Alex made it back to the Best Wishes kiosk, the line already stretched halfway back to the food court.

The genie had taken his place upon the throne but was ignoring his first customer of the day—some old guy in pleated golf pants and boat shoes. Alex hopped up on the counter and slid inside.

There, sitting next to the cash register, was a single silver coin, just like the ones the genie conjured to pay her. She picked it up. "Hey, where did this come from?"

The genie looked down. "It was here when I arrived. You must have neglected to bring it with you when last you were paid."

Alex was certain *that* hadn't happened. The stupid silver coins might be a pain in the ass, but she wasn't in the business of throwing money away. Well, except that once, to the gnomes.

That was it—the gnomes. "Huh," she muttered. "Little jerks returned my tip."

"Alexandria, are you here to work?" the genie asked.

"What? Oh, yeah—sorry boss. I'm here."

The genie pointed to the first customer. "Good, because we have much business to attend to. Begin."

Alex looked up at the old guy in the pleated pants. "Welcome to Best Wishes. What'll it be?"

"I want you to make my wife a blonde." He considered for a moment. "A *natural* blonde."

Alex groaned. "It is too early for this shit."

"What?" the guy said. "I think she'll be happier that way."

The genie stroked his beard of smoke. "Is this a thing that, as the Mistress of the Bazaar indicated, might be purchased in this marketplace?"

Alex shook her head. "Nope."

"So what?" the guy said. He pulled out a roll of twenties in a rubber band. A thick roll. "I can pay!"

"Your wealth is of no consequence to me," the genie said. "Begone!"

"Hey now," the guy stabbed the countertop with his index finger. "You gave my friend Max Dentworth a full head of hair yesterday, so I know you can do this. What's the problem?"

"Look, dude, even skipping past the part where you're doing this *without your wife consenting to it*—which is super creepy and not okay, by the way—we can't grant supernatural . . . uhhh . . . blessings and curses and stuff anymore for legal reasons. So, if you want a bottle of hair dye or something, we can do it for you, but otherwise . . ." Alex shrugged. "Tough luck."

The guy was pissed, but he left when the genie gave him an ugly look.

Something similar happened to the next person, who wanted to change their eye color. Same with the next person, who wanted a never-ending coffee cup. The third wanted a fuzzy tail, like a cat—also no. Word rippled backward through the big line, and a lot of insults and bitter looks were thrown their way. Most of them were aimed at Alex herself.

"Well, can you at least give me a *vacation* in Bermuda?" the next guy said, after having his desire for a magic door that opened to a Caribbean beach was denied. "That's something you can buy, right?"

The genie looked to Alex. "Is it?"

"There's a travel agent on the second floor down by Valu-Day, so . . . yeah, I guess so." Alex said. She looked back at the guy. "Give us the deets on your vacation, man."

Alex was expecting some kind of delay, but the guy just started talking "Ten nights at the Rosewood Bermuda, a royal suite, unlimited minibar and . . . uhh . . . a direct flight, please."

Alex looked over her shoulder. "Well?"

"How much?" the genie asked the guy.

"A thousand bucks?" The man put a shoebox on the counter and dug out a crisp stack of bills. "How about that?"

"Done," the genie said. "Your reservations are made."

The man yelled "YES!" loud enough to echo. He paid his money and got out of there.

"Dude," Alex said when he had gone, "I think we just sold that guy a *crazy* cheap vacation."

The genie shrugged. "What business is that of mine?"

That interaction was the rare success, though. Most people were not so accommodating—they came to the genie to have the impossible happen, not to save money. Business was poor, the customers were angry. Inside an hour or two, they were once again alone in the middle of the mall concourse.

"Great," Alex said. "Just great."

"You are a mercurial creature, Alexandria Delmore," the genie said. "Yesterday you were fearful at the size and intensity of your labors. Now you are upset that your labors are slight. How do you explain this?"

"I just think there should be some way for me to earn steady money without being miserable, that's all." Alex sighed. "Is that too much to ask? If I wished for that, could you grant it?"

The genie considered this. "There are ways, I suppose. But labor is enriching, Alexandria Delmore. It is not to be cast aside so lightly."

"Oh yeah, is that why you decided to get a job after being a slave for a billion years or whatever?"

The genie nodded. "Yes. It is."

"What? You're *serious?*"

"Of course! Why would I lie about such a thing?"

"You mean to tell me that you were forced to take orders from any asshole who polished that old ring since, like, before the pyramids were built and then, when you were finally free, you were like 'damn, I need to get a job?'"

"Yes."

"You're insane."

"I am not."

"Why didn't you take a vacation? Explore time and space or whatever? Who the hell *voluntarily* chooses a life in retail?"

"Because, as I said, labor is inherently enriching."

Alex rolled her eyes. Like hell it was. Tell that to her dad. Her mom. Her brother. Alex literally didn't know *anyone* whose labor made them feel enriched. It just made them tired and sore and bitter at the world and, at the end of the day, the money they earned was only barely enough to keep them off the street. Enriched? Gimmie a break.

"I'm gonna take a walk, okay?" Alex said, hopping over the counter. By this point, the genie was used to her breaks—he didn't say anything as she left.

The genie was right about one thing: labor was enriching insofar as it earned her money. And no labor meant no money, which meant no wish. For all its limitations, her revised pricing guide had given her some idea of what she could get a full ride to NYU for from the genie, and it was still somewhere in the neighborhood of fifteen thousand dollars. She had nowhere near that much, or at least she didn't think she did—it was hard to tell, with the silver and all. She made another mental note to go to a bank that exchanged silver coins.

Short term, though, she was still the person who had to fix the genie's business if it was going to go anywhere. The interaction with the Bermuda guy had gotten her thinking: miracles were great and all, but she suspected there was a lot of stuff that people would wish for that wasn't all that magical at all. The price just had to be right.

She breezed through the doors of ValuDay again and there was Kenny, of all people, waiting to greet her. "New job, huh?"

Kenny raised a hand, waved, and said, "Hey, Alex, I'm sorry about the other day!"

Alex stopped mid-stride. "Wait, what?"

Kenny scuffed his feet on the floor and put his hands in his pockets. "I'm sorry, that's all. It wasn't cool of Mark to try to force you to give us free wishes. I didn't know he was gonna do that, okay? I . . . I wouldn't do that. We, like, had a whole fight about it."

Alex felt herself starting to blush and immediately hated her capillaries. Him? Fighting over *her*? "Yeah . . . okay, thanks Kenny. No hard feelings, all right?"

He smiled brightly. It was beautiful. "Yeah, sure! Right on!"

Alex got the hell out of there and went to make another sign.

When she got back, she mounted it right on the cash register: SPECIAL: BRING US ANY AD PRICE, AND WE'LL BEAT IT BY 50%, GUARANTEED!

The genie looked at it. "This seems . . . crass."

"Welcome to retail," Alex said.

Within two hours, the giant line was back. This time, though, it was a different clientele. For one thing, it was primarily female. For another, there was a sort of desperate look in most of their eyes—not the gleam of greed Alex had seen in the old wish customers, who had come seeking forbidden or impossible things, but instead the hollow look of people at the end of their rope.

A woman with a baby in a snuggly and a toddler yanking on her hand slapped a paper ValuDay circular on the counter. It was advertising baby formula and diapers. "Can you beat this price?"

Alex nodded. "Of course. We'll give it to you for half."

The woman visibly relaxed. "Can I hug you, too?"

Alex couldn't help but grin. "That part's extra."

They shared a laugh. The woman bought two huge canisters of formula and a massive pack of diapers; the genie even conjured a shopping cart to take them away in.

They sold a little bit of everything that day: shoes, groceries, clothing, pet food, toys—you name it, the genie conjured it with a blink and Alex took the cash. The sums weren't individually very large, but business was non-stop. Another few hours of selling designer handbags and cheap ibuprofen and discount washing machines, ground down her mood until she was just tired, all the way through, from the roots of her hair to the soles of her shoes.

Toward the end of the shift, one woman—someone Alex had noted hanging back in the constant crowd of onlookers for an hour or so—finally approached the counter with a little slip of paper in her hand and a little boy with glasses in tow. She placed the paper on the counter. "Can you . . . can you fill this prescription?"

"I . . . uhhh . . ." Alex looked down.

The script was for some kind of anticancer drug. An anticancer drug dosed for *children*.

"Oh God!" Alex blurted aloud. She looked up at the woman and met her eyes. She was probably pretty young, but with sharp lines of stress creasing her forehead and around her eyes. She looked like she was about to cry.

"Please?" was all the woman said.

"What is it?" the genie asked.

"Medicine," Alex said, turning back toward him. "This woman wants medicine."

"How much does this medicine usually cost?"

Alex looked back at the woman, who said, "About six thousand dollars for a month's supply, sir."

This got the genie's attention. "That is . . . two hundred forty pieces of silver or so. A month's supply? You pay this *every month*?"

"I can't. I try, but I can't."

"Mommy?" The little boy yanked on her hand. "Can we go?"

The genie scowled down at the woman, thinking. He came to a decision. "Two thousand dollars. A bargain, yes?"

The woman nodded rapidly. "Yes! Yes, very much so! Thank you!"

Alex held up a hand to block her purse from making it to the counter. "Hold on, hold on," she looked at the genie. "Dude, just cure the cancer."

The genie shook his head. "This was not our arrangement with Madam Sturgis."

"Man, to hell with Sturgis!" Alex yelled. "This lady can't afford two thousand bucks every month! Jesus!"

"Very well, five hundred," the genie said.

"No, you aren't getting it," Alex said.

The woman pulled out a fat stack of cash. "I'll take four months! Are you sure it is safe? Pure?"

The genie nodded. "Your child will be safe, woman. This I

swear to you." Twelve vials of the drug appeared on the counter. The woman scooped them into her purse with trembling hands and made her hasty exit. They all left that way—every one of them terrified that what they had just been given could be taken away.

Alex glared at the genie. "You could have cured that kid."

"Yes, but I promised that I wouldn't."

"That's a bullshit promise, dude."

The genie gave her a fiery glare. "There is no such thing. My word is all I have, Alexandria Delmore. It is my most sacred bond. Madam Sturgis is correct—what know I about the vagaries of your mortal lives? Have I not spent eons granting the fondest wishes of men only to see them destroyed and despondent in the end? How can I know that curing the child's affliction would not be a curse in disguise? Verily, I cannot know this. It is true that I find this . . . this common *peddling* of trifles to be a tedious waste of my power, but I have no choice. I do what I promise, for no other recourse seems wise. As I gave my word to that woman and as I gave my word to Maureen Sturgis—all are clad in iron. That which I promise, I shall do."

Alex shook her head, too tired to argue. "Great—so glad you still have your pride or whatever."

"It is not pride," the genie said. "It is prudence, hard-earned."

That evening, as she rode home on her sputtering moped, she found she couldn't get that mother's desperate look out of her head. The same look she'd seen on customers throughout the day. The same look she'd seen on her father. *All* of them were desperate, she realized. No, all of *us*. They were desperate because the world was set up to extract everything it could from people—their time, their labor, their *life*—just so other people could live in comfort. Ironically, ninety percent of the money they'd made today had gone straight to the genie, and he *wasn't even happy about it*. All that mattered to him was respect.

Alex wondered whether that was a good or a bad thing. Was her boss doing good or evil in the world? She didn't know. All she was sure about was that it shouldn't have to be this way. But if wishes couldn't fix the world, what could?

CHAPTER 11:
MAKING CHANGE

ALEX'S NEXT PAYDAY was legit insane—all the money from the Fourth of July was coming to her, as well as their newest adventures in low-end retail. Whereas most of the time she was drawing a handful of silver coins, this time she was looking at an eight-pound sack. It barely fit inside her knapsack. She was no expert, but she thought this meant real money. Thousands of dollars, at least.

The genie was shoveling the cash from the register into that same magical treasure chest he summoned every evening at close. A few aimless customers and employees just off-shift gawked as they ambled by, headed for the exits. A twenty-dollar bill slipped from the genie's grasp and fluttered in front of a kid from SpeedJava. They paused, looked down. They thought about it.

The genie snapped his fingers and the twenty flew back to his hands as though attached to a string. He glared at the kid until they fled the opposite direction.

"What do you do with all that money, anyway?" Alex asked.

"What do you mean?" the genie grumbled. He'd been in

a bad mood all day. It wasn't just that conjuring up designer sneakers at discount prices was *not* his definition of worth-while employment—*join the club*, Alex thought—but he'd been snarling at everyone ever since that kid with cancer came by the other day.

"Like, do you even have things to buy? Do you play the stock market? What?"

"The purpose of wealth is not to spend it, Alexandria Del-more. The purpose of wealth is to demonstrate your worth."

"You trying to say being rich makes you a good person?" Alex arched an eyebrow at him.

The genie snorted. "No. Wealth indicates your labor is of value to society. These treasures tell me that my contributions to society are positive and useful. I am alarmed you do not know this—this is the basis of your entire civilization, is it not?"

She got the sense that he was talking to himself as much as to her. Justifying things the same way he justified not curing that kid's cancer, the jerk. "I sure hope it isn't," Alex said.

The genie threw up his hands. "Then you are ignorant and insolent, as always. Your labors are complete this day—the sun has set. Begone!"

Alex be-went. She wandered out of the mall, taking the same route as always. This evening, the fountain was partially working, the water rumbling happily. A couple gnomes were there again, dressed in little lab coats and testing the chlorine levels by sucking up the water with eyedroppers and squirting it on the chest of a shirtless third gnome and seeing if it burned. It did—he screamed as smoke and blisters rose from his pale skin. The sound was high pitched, like the kind of sound she imagined a squirrel might make if it stubbed its toe.

She stopped dead in her tracks. "Jesus—are you serious right now?"

The gnomes froze as they always did, staring at her. Were they afraid of her? Angry at being interrupted? She couldn't tell, what with the beards and the lab coats and the little black eyes.

Alex pointed at the burned gnome, who was panting so quickly he looked like he was vibrating. "Is this something you *have* to do? Is this part of the job?"

The gnomes exchanged brief glances and then nodded to her. Yes, it was—this was the job. Ritually torturing themselves to maintain a water feature at a stupid mall. Sweet Jesus.

Alex fished the silver piece out of her pocket. "*This* is for you, get it? It is *pay* for your *work*. I don't know how you did things back wherever or whenever you came from, but you need to understand: you guys should be *compensated* for your *labor*." She spoke slowly and clearly, not sure if they could understand her. If they did, the gnomes gave no sign.

She placed the silver coin on the fountain's edge. "This is for *you*, get it? Do not give that back to me, understand? Buy yourselves some actual hats or something."

The gnomes exchanged glances again and came to some unspoken agreement. The ones in the lab coats vanished in a blur. The burned one limped away, meaning he moved only five times faster than a human being. They left the silver where it was.

Alex called after them. "This mall is *totally* not worth it, you guys!"

She got her moped started, though it took a couple tries, and rode it home, listening to it sputter the whole way. Maybe some of her pay could go toward getting the thing a tune-up or something. An oil change or whatever. Probably needed it.

At home, her parents were arguing in the kitchen, which made it more-or-less a regular night. Alex, not wanting to get involved in the confrontation, crept into the kitchen to grab a bite to eat. There wasn't much to be had.

"Charlie, you've *got* to pay the mortgage!" her mother was shouting.

"When *haven't* I paid, huh? When?"

"Last month, Charlie—*last month!* We got a letter!"

"I sent it, Rosalind! I sent it late, but I sent it!"

"Not according to the letter!"

Alex beat a hasty retreat, a plastic container of her mother's chicken casserole under one arm, the sack of money in the other. She laid the glittering coins out on her futon along with the ones she'd earned previously; they were cool to the touch and seemed to glow in the faint light of her bedside lamp. She could probably pay her parents' monthly mortgage payment several times over with this money. If she wanted to.

There were times she did. She wanted to make all this silver into cash and just hand it to her mom in a big stack—here, pay for *everything.* But then what about her? This money would go way farther as payment for a wish from the genie. It would be the right move for *her.*

She stuffed as much of the silver as she thought she could carry into her backpack. It was really heavy.

Downstairs, she heard something break. She froze, waiting to hear the aftermath. There was more yelling, but of the same type. Nobody had broken a vase over anyone's head. She had a hard time imagining her father ever *striking* her mother, but in the world of midlife crises, there were many terrible mysteries to be revealed.

Her desire to give her parents the money faded, as it always did. They didn't talk to each other anymore. Hell, *no one* in her family talked. Her father was always out, her mother was always working, Mark was always goofing off somewhere with Kenny. The idea of a "family dinner" or whatever barely existed. They were all on their own, Alex included. If that was the way it was gonna be, then let them clean up their own messes.

Alex ate and she waited for things to settle down. After her parents stopped arguing, her mom spent the rest of the evening listening to Madonna *really loud* and cursing while she tried to plunge the toilet with limited success; her father got in his truck and went out. In both cases, neither of them were going to give her any trouble tonight. They'd probably forgotten she existed. This was what Alex had been waiting for.

The only bank that would exchange silver coins and was *also* open after 9:00 p.m. was a place called DH Commercial. Alex knew exactly zero things about banks in general, but this one gave off a very . . . *eager* vibe? They seemed like they'd do just about anything to get your money, and their reviews online were all in that vein. It was the favored banks of people who needed easy credit and flexible hours and were willing to pay a premium to get it. Alex didn't like the sound of it, but she wasn't exactly in a position to negotiate. Off she went.

The bank was a good forty-minute moped ride away, since the moped topped out around 20 mph. It was terrifying, riding in the dark. The headlamp on the rusty old bike had all the candlepower of a dying flashlight and she had to ride on the shoulder to avoid getting run down by cars whipping by. She would have flipped off some of the jerks who came way too close, way too fast, but she was too worried about crashing into a ditch to let go of the handlebars.

The bank, at least, was open as advertised. It stood apart from the rest of the buildings down the strip by the side of the divided highway, an island of glass and fluorescent light in the midst of an empty parking lot. Alex put down the kickstand on her moped and went in. When she opened the door, she froze in her tracks.

"You have *got* to be kidding me," she muttered, staring.

The place was staffed entirely by gnomes. Little guys in sock-hats, driving little Zamboni machine things that buffed the floor to a mirror shine, gnomes in little window-washing harnesses, squeegees in hand, cleaning the big floor-to-ceiling windows. A gnome at the teller's desk, wearing a green visor and a nametag that read "Paul."

Alex couldn't believe it. "How many of you guys *are* there in this town?"

She was the only human present—no other customers. How many people did their banking at ten at night, right? She went to duck under the maze of nylon barriers that led to the teller window. When she got there, the gnome tapped a sign affixed to the desk: NO CUTTING IN LINE.

"Oh, come on—I'm the only person here!"

The gnome tapped the sign. He did not look amused.

Alex turned around, walked to the end, and then hustled her way through the snake-pattern of nylon before arriving before him again. It was weird, being eye-level with a gnome. He must have been sitting on a huge stool or something. She dumped her backpack on the counter. "I need to exchange silver coins for actual dollars. Is that okay?"

The gnome nodded. His little hands flashed inside the bag and retrieved a piece of silver, which he touched with one finger. His finger sizzled, as though pressed against a griddle.

"Oh my God—silver *burns* you?"

The gnome tapped a different sign attached to the counter: NO SMALL TALK.

"Harsh," Alex said.

The gnome tapped the sign again.

Having confirmed the silver was authentic, the gnome slipped on a pair of tiny doll's mittens and fished the remainder of the coins out at an absurd rate of speed, stacking them on an antique brass scale that he whipped out from under the counter.

"Don't believe in digital, huh?"

The gnome glared at her and, very slowly, tapped the No SMALL TALK sign.

Alex sighed. "You guys *really* need to get out more."

While the gnome messed with the scale, Alex watched as the other gnomes bustled about their tasks. She tried to figure out why this was happening. Why hire gnomes at all? She knew they didn't *own* the bank—nobody who *owned* something worked the night shift at that same something. It was like a law of nature.

All her father's crazy conspiracy theories echoed in the back of her head: they were part of some concerted, gnomish plan to control the world. They were just stealing jobs from humans, since they worked for almost nothing. It was a plan to screw the little guy.

Looking back at the teller, she noted that the collar of his ill-fitting children's polo shirt was open. On his pale, bare chest, she saw burn marks. The same burn marks she'd seen on the gnome back at the mall.

"Hey! You're that gnome from the mall fountain!" She frowned as she thought about it. "Wait, you work here *too*?"

The gnome glared at her but ignored her questions. He pulled a lever on an antique cash register and put the silver in it, then removed a stack of hundred-dollar bills, licked his thumb, and started counting.

"How many jobs do you have, anyway?" Alex asked him.

No answer. The gnome counted out seven or eight stacks of ten hundred-dollar bills and then combined them into one neat stack.

Alex snapped her fingers. "I got it! You work overtime and these cheap bastards at the bank don't have to pay you time and a half, do they? Do they even pay you *hourly*? Do they pay you at all?"

The gnome in the green visor—"Paul," evidently—put a rubber band around the money, slipped it in an envelope, and slid it across to Alex along with a receipt. It was clear that he wanted this interaction to be over.

"Hey, Paul, buddy, if I'm lying—if I got it wrong—feel free to let me know. Do I?"

Paul tapped the small talk sign again.

"Not a denial." Alex slid a hundred-dollar bill from her envelope and slapped it on the counter. "This is for you, Paul. Now, you can take it or not, but this time you don't have the excuse of being allergic to silver."

Paul looked at the money but did not touch it.

Alex pointed to the picture of the bank manager up on the wall—some fleshy white dude in a bad tie. "That guy doesn't care about you, okay? You don't *owe* these people anything. They owe *you*, got it?"

The gnomes—all of them—were staring at her again. She looked around, worried they might . . . well, she didn't really know. She'd read old stories about gnomes playing nasty pranks but didn't know if the Brothers Grimm were a reliable source about this stuff.

Alex surrendered and took back her money. "You know what? *Fine.* Not like I'm swimming in extra money right now. You want to be everybody's stooges, that's your business. Goodnight, gnomes!"

One of the gnomes—one piloting one of the floor Zambonis—waved goodbye. A gnome next to him slapped him upside the head.

Alex's moped refused to start—another cosmic reward for her effort to do a good deed. Now, to get home, she could either call her mom, call her dad, or walk.

Alex chose to walk. She would walk all night before calling for help—see that she wouldn't.

Sidewalks along State Highway 53 were non-existent, so she had to walk her moped along the shoulder or through the parking lots of the innumerable strip malls that filled the thirteen miles or so between her house and herself. It was a warm July evening, and the cars whipped past without slowing. When they had their windows open, Alex could catch snippets of music and laughter—people going out, probably even kids her age.

Alex pushed back against the loneliness, against the absurdity of her situation—no, she was *making* something of herself. After the bank—not the gnomes, *the bank*—had charged her fifteen percent to exchange the silver, she had over seven grand in her knapsack—half a college education, courtesy of her friend the *actual* genie. All that mattered was coming out on top. That stack of crisp bills in her knapsack told Alex that she was the one who was going to make it. She just had to press on.

She came to a bridge—the kind of little bridge over a creek that you never actually noticed in a car, but when walking was unavoidably obvious. The creek bed was dry—there hadn't been much rain lately—and from the narrow shoulder on the bridge Alex could see the glitter of trash on the sandy ground below. Food wrappers, discarded bottles, etc. Before she could curl her lip at the sheer carelessness of humanity, though, she saw something else. It was the genie, there on the creek bed, looking under the bridge.

He was easily and clearly visible in the dark of night. He *glowed*, like the cooling embers of a campfire. Was this where he stayed at night? For a second, she forgot the misery of her own situation and thought about his—she thought *she* was lonely? What about the genie?

"Hey!" she called out, wheeling her moped off the shoulder of the road and flipping down the kickstand. "You okay?"

The genie looked up at her, surprised. The surprise quickly melted away to irritation. He folded his arms. "What are you doing here, Alexandria? These roads at night are not safe."

"What am I doing here? What are *you* doing here?" Alex clambered down the embankment to the creek bed. "Do you sleep under a bridge like a troll or something?"

When she came up to the genie, she discovered they were not alone. Underneath the bridge were a half dozen little tents, faded and weather-worn. A few scruffy, haggard people crouched around a camp lantern, their bloodshot eyes fixed on the two of them. One of them called out to her, "Eres amiga del diablo?"

Alex's Spanish was based entirely on a gutted high school

language department whose only teacher's lived experience of the Spanish language was based off a semester abroad back in the late 1990s. She got the word "diablo," though. "They think you're the devil?"

The genie's frown deepened. "It roots from a misunderstanding of one of my last masters. A German doctor named Faust."

"Holy shit! That was *you*?"

"That man was a fool, and it was an unpleasant business. My understanding is that history blames *me* for the whole affair. I do not like to talk about it," the genie said. He then answered the original question in rapid Spanish, causing the old man who'd asked it to laugh. The genie sighed. "They never believe me, no matter how oft I explain it to them."

Alex looked over the small group of homeless people. They were all coming out of their tents now, about eight or nine of them, all watching the genie carefully. "Do you come here often? Are . . . are these people your friends or something? Your neighbors?"

"You think me a wastrel and vagabond, just like them?" the genie asked in a soft voice.

"Oh! I . . . I didn't mean it like that, honest."

"Come, Alexandria—I will show you my purpose here." The genie went over to the little tent village and placed a sack on the ground—a sack that, as of a few seconds ago, he had not been carrying. From it he drew bottles of water and boxes of non-perishable food. The people darted forward and snatched them up as they hit the ground, careful to scurry away from the genie right after, as though fearing he might attack. After this, the genie laid careful stacks of silver coins—one for each person beneath the bridge—and stepped away.

The people came and got the money. Many very clearly did not speak English. The ones who did muttered thanks through unkempt beards or past rotting teeth. They seemed, all of them, to be unwell. The stink of booze and cigarettes was palpable, even at the distance Alex was standing.

The genie gestured toward the road above. "Come, we should go. My presence makes them uncomfortable."

The two of them climbed back up the embankment to the road. Alex thought about all the money stashed in her backpack. It seemed heavier, somehow, than it had before she had gone down and seen the homeless people. "I thought you didn't grant wishes for free," she said.

"I do not. They did not wish for those things. I simply gave them, purchased from my own funds."

"This is what you've been doing with all that money you're making? Giving to the poor?"

"Giving alms is an ancient and kindly tradition, is it not?"

"Well, yeah, but . . ." Alex searched for the words. "I just . . . I just didn't figure you for the type. You must help a lot of people."

The genie shook his head. "Their number never seems to diminish. There are numerous such places in these lands— isolated corners where the outcast and the afflicted gather, away from the hard stares of their fellow men. I visit them all. I give away much of the money I earn. And yet, when I return the following night, the faces may change, but still there are tents and still they are full."

Alex knew, on an intellectual level, that homeless people existed. That places like that were scattered all over, even out here in the 'burbs. She'd never seen one before, though. She wondered how often she'd passed them by and never noticed.

"Why don't you just grant them wishes? Get them out of there."

The genie's stormcloud brows furrowed. "That is not what most would wish for."

Alex felt her stomach knot up with the realization that what the genie said was probably true. "Drugs, huh? Mental illness. Stuff like that."

"These people are often unwell and mostly unclean. Few are able to wish for what they need in favor of what they want. It is the same as with most of your people, only in this case more extreme. Even when I can save a few, more appear. No matter where I go, no matter what I do, it is the same."

Alex had never seen the genie so sad before. She didn't quite know what to say or how. But she had to say *something*. "Look, I've got your back, man. Something like this—like, I dunno, fixing the world or whatever, it doesn't happen right away. We just gotta keep at it, me and you, right? Day by day, making people's lives a little brighter, right?"

The genie looked at her with his flashlight eyes. "You do not really mean that. You only pity me."

Alex flinched at his gaze. She remembered what she was thinking about not ten seconds before she'd stumbled across the genie and his charitable activities. It made her feel terrible in a way she hadn't in a long, long time. "Look, I *promise*, okay! I'm here to help you. I'm on your side."

The genie bowed slowly, formally. "I accept your oath, Alexandria Delmore. I look forward to seeing you tomorrow morning with renewed purpose."

"Great! Now, before you go, can you . . ."

But he was already gone. She was back on the shoulder of the highway, alone. "Aw, *come on!*" She yelled at the sky. "I could use a *ride* you know!"

If the genie was able to hear her, there was no sign. She considered the ironies of a being that spent his evenings giving bottled water and trail mix to hobos but couldn't be bothered to give his stranded teenage assistant a lift home. The jerk.

CHAPTER 12:
LOST OPPORTUNITIES

THE GENIE never reappeared. Instead, Alex's long walk home was eventually interrupted by a pickup—a brand new one with a giant grill taller than her—that slowed and pulled behind her on the shoulder of the road, blinding her with its halogen headlights.

"Great," Alex muttered. "Just *great*."

She prepared herself for harassment or maybe assault by whatever kind of creep cruised state highways on a weeknight to pick up teenage girls in distress. They beeped at her, which of course made it even creepier. *Hey there, little lady,* she pictured some fat guy in a tank top with back hair and sweaty palms, *thy chariot awaits!*

She wondered if seven thousand-bucks cash was enough to leverage her way out of an attempted murder.

The window of the pickup rolled down and a familiar voice called out. "Hey, Alex! You need a ride, babe?"

Fontana Russo. Oh shit. She turned around and kept walking.

The door opened and Fontana hopped out and trotted after her. "Hey! Did you hear me? You okay?"

Alex spun around. "Back off, creep! I've got pepper spray!"

She did not, in fact, have pepper spray. Though she figured it was *plausible* she did.

Fontana put his hands up. "Whoa, whoa—I'm trying to *help* you, okay? I'm guessing you're not wheeling your rusty scooter down the shoulder of the highway at eleven at night because everything is *fine*, right?"

Alex sighed. "Just . . . leave me alone, okay?" She turned and kept walking.

"Do you need me to call somebody?" Fontana asked.

"I *have* a phone, okay?"

Fontana kept following her. "Look, I know you hate my guts, but I can't just *leave* you here! You see that, right? I don't know what you're doing, but it's dangerous and crazy and I'd feel bad if I left and something happened."

Alex stopped. She squinted back at Fontana, outlined by the sun-bright glare of his ostentatious headlights. "What's the catch?" she asked. "You get me in your car and then you cop a feel, is that it?"

"Christ, Alex, I'm not a creep, I swear," Fontana said. "I can call the cops instead, if you want. They'll give you a ride."

Yeah, because arriving home in a police cruiser would be *better*. Alex didn't trust cops any more than she trusted Fontana. But she *was* tired and her feet hurt and she was probably less than halfway home. If she was out here much longer, her *parents* would be the ones calling the cops. Or, worse, her *dad's* pickup would be the one stopping behind her, and she would have a *lot* of explaining to do.

Maybe ten minutes of Fontana was something she could handle.

"Okay," she said. "Fine. But don't make me regret this."

Fontana snorted. "You're a real charmer, you know that?"

"Just help me get my moped into the back of your douche-mobile, okay?"

A minute later, Alex was perched on a deep leather seat in movie-theater frigid AC as they drove toward her house. She felt like she was twenty feet tall, looking down on everyone else in their regular-ass cars. She wondered if that was part of the appeal of owning a monstrosity like that truck.

"Pretty sweet, right?" Fontana said, fiddling with the radio. "You want some tunes?"

The truck's front seat was so wide that Alex felt faintly ridiculous, worrying about Fontana grabbing her. The center console was wide enough to fit an LCD screen, on which Fontana had paused some kind of business seminar delivered by some guy in a black turtleneck.

"Silence is fine," Alex said.

Fontana gave it to her, but only for about thirty seconds. "Man, that genie is just a wasted opportunity, isn't he?"

Alex decided to bite. "What do you mean?"

"I mean that opening a mall kiosk is only marginally stupider than opening an actual *shop* in a mall. It's like climbing on to a sinking ship and trying to sell ice cream."

Alex rolled her eyes. "Don't you *manage* a shop in the mall?"

"Yeah, but I don't *own* it. You think the owner of that franchise is making major bank off the mall location? Hell no—he owns three locations, and the other two have *drive-throughs*. There's no contest. Nah, the only reason that shitty little restaurant works at all is because the rent is cheap, it's a national brand, and it has exterior signage. That wishing kiosk? It's a joke."

"And yet you wanted to give us sixteen hundred dollars.

We have lines around the block, Fontana. It sounds to me like you're jealous."

"What's your transaction speed?" Fontana asked.

"I obviously don't know that."

"I do—I've timed it. It takes you and the genie an average of five minutes to haggle out a deal. Almost half of those result in no wish granted, and the money you take in is inconsistent."

Alex frowned and looked over at the driver's seat. "You've been . . . watching us?"

"I always keep tabs on business opportunities." Fontana grinned at her. "The genie's power is totally wasted in that retail space, babe. He's a billion-dollar industry, waiting to happen."

"Oh God." Alex felt the sales pitch coming like the undertow before a big wave at the beach. She braced herself.

"Put that guy in the online retail space—link it up with some kind of app with a subscription fee, or maybe an auction system—and he would be able to scale up to an industrial level. He'd be outside of the mall's petty rules. He could legit *change the world*, Alex. Totally upset the paradigm. Control world markets. Make and break fortunes. Can you imagine?"

Alex imagined it. Millions of people on their phones, wishing for things all at once. The genie, stuck in some office somewhere, staring at a computer screen, granting wishes on a vast scale, the work never easing, never stopping. Money piling up in 1s and 0s online that he never saw, never got to spend. "It sounds awful," she said.

"Yeah, I wouldn't expect you to understand."

"What the hell is *that* supposed to mean?"

They were pulling up outside her house then. Fontana threw the truck in park and reached out to grab her hand. "Look, I like you, okay? You're hot and you don't take shit, and I dig that. I know you hate me—fine, I accept that—but one of my best qualities is that I know what I want."

Alex yanked her hand away and got out. Fontana hopped out his side and met her at the back, where she tried to yank her moped out of the back of the giant truck herself.

Fontana made no move to help. "Think about it, Alex. You wanna get out of this town? I can get you that. Hell, I want out, too. You're friends with the genie; I *want* to be friends with the genie. Working together, we could do incredible things—you gotta see *that*, right?"

Alex blew her hair out of her face. "You gonna help me with this, or what?"

Fontana interposed himself between her and her moped. "Go on a date with me—*one* date. Very genteel. I got an in at the Great Rock Country Club. I could get us a table."

He was close—so close she could smell the creeping stench of his body spray. He wanted her to back off, she guessed. She wondered what would happen if she bit off his nose. "Get the fuck out of my way, Fontana."

Fontana smiled down at her. It pissed her off that he was tall enough to do that. "Not until you consider my offer."

"HEY!" Alex's father was coming out of the garage, a beer in one hand. "Back away from my girl, pencil dick!"

Fontana backed away, chuckling, a big smile on his face.

"Dad," Alex said, but her father didn't seem to hear her.

He got right up in Fontana's face. "Is this what you do? Go find some girl in trouble and, what, force her into your fancy-ass truck?"

"Mr. Delmore, that is *not* what's going on here—right Alex?"

Her dad looked at her. "Oh, what, did you actually go on a *date* with this prick?"

Alex considered the two of them. "Honestly, it was more like your thing, Dad."

Her father grabbed Fontana by the shirt and pushed him against the side of the truck hard enough that it wiped the shit-eating grin right off Fontana's face. "Hey! You want to go to jail for assault tonight, trailer park?"

"I been to jail for worse reasons, kid."

Alex's father was four inches shorter than Fontana, but she had absolutely no illusions what would happen if a fight started—her father would wind up in jail and Fontana would need extensive dental work. "Okay, okay! That's enough! Dad, let him go! *Dad*, let him go—he was just giving me a ride home. It was just a ride."

Her father let go of Fontana's shirt and backed up a step. He never broke eye contact, though. The whole display was deeply embarrassing.

Fontana smoothed his clothes. "I'll help you get her scooter out."

Her dad pushed past Fontana, grabbed the handlebars with two hands, and yanked the scooter out of the truck bed himself. He even set it down, nice and gentle, to prove he was strong enough. "You can go now," he said.

Fontana nodded and gave Alex a wink. "See you at work, Alex."

Then he got in his gigantic truck and drove off. It wasn't until he was gone around the corner that her dad collapsed on one knee. "Oh Christ, my back."

Alex sighed and wrapped one of his arms around her shoulders. "Come on. I'll get you inside."

* * *

Alex and her dad were the only two people home. Mark was out with Kenny, of course—going to some concert—and her mom, upon realizing Alex had disappeared, had called her father home from the bar and jumped into her car to go find her. She was probably searching every ravine, abandoned lot, and dark alley in the Tri-state area.

Her father delivered this news to her from the couch with a bag of ice stuffed under the small of his back. "You scared me and Mom to death!"

Alex, still pissed about Fontana and the Cro-Magnon display of performative masculinity she had just witnessed, wasn't ready to receive criticism just yet. "Me and Mom? What '*me and Mom*?' Don't you mean 'me and Maria?'"

Her dad stared at her. "Me and Maria—you mean Maria Partagas?!"

"Who else, Dad?" Jesus, how could she be related to a man this dense?

"Lexie, Mom was terrified. She told me you rode off without telling her where. I offered to go looking for you, but, you know." He motioned to the empty beer bottle on the coffee table.

"Yes, Dad—*I know*."

"Hey, I'm not drunk! And anyway, this isn't about *me*, this is about *you* sneaking off in the dead of night to do who *knows* what!"

"I'm seventeen!" Alex said. "It's not even midnight!"

"Who was that guy? He seemed like a jerk."

"He's just some jerk I kinda know."

"You dating that asshole? Isn't he, like, twenty-five?"

Alex made a gagging sound. "I am *not* dating him! And he's, like, *maybe* twenty-one."

Her father frowned. "So, then where *did* you go tonight?"

Under a bridge, where drug-addicts are known to hang out. "Nowhere."

"Uh-uh, Lexie. Don't lie to me."

Alex crossed her arms. "Well, if you're so smart, why don't *you* tell me?"

"Well, it's not that boy—and Lord knows you're too mean to have a boyfriend. I know you're not on drugs. Your friends have stopped coming around, so it wasn't that. Nobody around here would serve you booze."

"Spare me the drama, Sherlock," Alex said.

"Only thing I can figure is that bank out on the state highway. One that's open all night," her father said.

"How do you know about that?"

"'Cause I been there." Her father sat up a little with a groan. "I seen those greedy gnomes, running their shady little business."

"They're not shady, Dad—they're just getting exploited."

Her dad ignored her. "You been getting paid in silver and you needed to change the money and you didn't want me and your mother to know, right?"

Alex scowled. No point in denying it now. "Yeah."

"Your mom told me—you been working for that genie down the mall."

"Dad—"

Her father cut her off. "You listen here, Lexie—that thing is dangerous. Everybody knows that. You're putting yourself in danger, and you lied to me and your mother about it."

"It's not like that, Dad. You don't understand."

"I understand just fine—you're getting back at your family. You're mad at me 'cause you blame me for all your problems. You're mad at your mom because you think she's holding you back, but she's not. And in any case none of that is a reason for you to do something risky like this. You're quitting, effective tomorrow."

Alex opened her mouth to argue, but she could tell by the way his jaw was set, he wasn't having it. "You want me to go down there? Want me to talk to that thing you're working for?"

"He's not a thing, he's a . . ." Alex trailed off. "You suck."

"And you're a spoiled brat who thinks she's better than her own family," her father said. "I hope, for your sake and mine, that we're both wrong."

Alex ran up to her room. She thought about the genie, floating on the breeze, handing out silver to the poor. She thought about the promise she'd just made—to stick by him—and about all the ways she was going to break that promise to maybe, just *maybe*, escape from this life forever. He'd understand, right? This was her truest desire, her heartfelt need. If anyone could understand, it would be the genie.

She sat on her bed and hugged her backpack full of cash close. Everything was going to be all right.

CHAPTER 13:
THE FINE ART OF LAWN CARE

KNOWING FULL WELL that Alex would go back to the mall the next day unless directly prevented, her father made her ride along to work with him. He told her to wear shorts and a T-shirt since "it gets hot out there," but she wore blue jeans and a sweatshirt and stayed in the truck with the barely functional AC blasting—a noted departure from Fontana's ice palace the night before. The important thing, though, was she might be "riding along," but she sure as hell wasn't *working* for her dad.

There had been an argument, both her dad and Mark yelling at her and telling her what a bitch she was being, but she hadn't budged. The only thing she said was, "How much do you pay?"

"The gratitude of your family isn't enough?" her father asked.

"Sounds like below minimum wage to me. Pass."

So, there she sat, arms folded in the center of the pickup's bench seat, all the AC blowers aimed at her, without so much as a phone to entertain herself with. She busied herself by changing all the presets on her dad's radio to stations she preferred or, barring that, stations she knew he'd hate. Though not fond of it herself, she would totally listen to smooth jazz if it would piss off her old man.

She had refused to part with the backpack full of cash since she'd been picked up the night before. She wouldn't put it past either of her parents to appropriate her hard-earned money on some bullshit excuse like "we have to pay the mortgage." Screw them. If they wanted to pay the mortgage, they could get a job working for a genie just like her.

Her feelings toward all that money were more . . . complicated than they had been yesterday. She thought about the genie's quest to help humanity and *her* promise to help him and felt a little badly about how her express goal for taking this job no longer seemed to align with what she thought it was all about. It was easier imagining the genie to be just another greedy business owner, socking away cash to pay for a second sky-palace somewhere. Finding him giving money to the poor now made her feel selfish. She didn't like that feeling. She kept thinking up ways it didn't apply to her—*I'm only seventeen! I can't help anyone stuck in this dead-end town mowing lawns! Think of all the good I could do with a degree from NYU! Think big picture, everyone!*

None of the arguments really satisfied her.

They were parked in the driveway of a big house set back from the road behind a thick stand of pine trees. The house was one of those faux Tudor affairs with ivy crawling up the side and a turret at one end—the kind of house you imagined a wizard lived in. Given everything going on in the world, she wouldn't be surprised if there were. Though she guessed they might hire gnomes instead of Delmores to do their lawn.

Mark had the hedge trimmer and was taming the bulbous bushes that hugged the front of the house. Her dad was mowing the backyard, just visible beyond the pool's patio. Sweat stained the backs of their T-shirts. This was the second house of the day; they had two more. "Only" two more, as her father put it. As they had driven here, her dad had pointed at yards he used to maintain as they passed, now in immaculate shape without his help. "Damned gnomes," he said. "See how they got the flowers to bloom? That soil was shit, I'm telling you—utter shit. Creepy little things cheated."

Alex actually caught a glimpse of a gnome as they cruised past. It was still wearing a sock for a hat and was trimming hedges with a little pair of plastic scissors. She wondered if it was the same gnome that worked in the bank and in the mall. *I bet it is.*

"It ever occur to you, Dad, that maybe it isn't *the gnomes* that are screwing you over? Maybe it's whoever is *hiring* the gnomes."

Her father frowned and grunted—no, that had obviously not occurred to him. He shut up, though. Mark, for his part, had been silent the whole ride over, arms folded. He was still pissed about the toads thing, she guessed.

So, there she was—parked in the driveway, bored and feeling a mixture of miserable and determined—when there was a knock at the window. Alex assumed it was the owner or something—probably needed them to move the truck—so she gasped when she saw the genie's demonic face leering at her through the glass.

"Exit this vehicle at once!" he said, his voice carrying perfectly inside the cab.

Alex popped right out, the heat hitting her like a wet towel in the face. "Oh my God, what are you *doing* here?"

The genie wasn't listening. "You did not appear for work

today! You have betrayed your oaths! You are to return with me to the mall immediately!"

"Are you nuts? Look, you gotta get out of here before my—"

"What the hell?" Mark said, his hedge trimmer whirring to a halt. "What's *he* doing here, Lexie?"

Alex turned to look at him. "Mark, I can handle this, okay, don't . . ."

"Dad!" Mark called. "Dad, looo . . . gghhh . . . ghhhh . . ." Mark doubled over, little toad legs forcing their way from between his lips.

The damage was done, though. Her father had seen the genie, and he dropped what he was doing and came running.

"Get out of here!" Alex tried to push the genie away, but again found nothing solid to push against, so her hands just sort of passed through his chest. "Go!"

The genie looked around and seemed to figure things out. "I see. You are held against your will."

Alex tried to think of another way to spin it but couldn't come up with one. "I mean . . . sort of?"

Her father made a flying tackle at the genie's mid-section. He sailed right through and collided, headfirst, with the fender of his own pickup truck. He fell to the ground, groaning.

The genie didn't seem to have noticed. "Why refuse my offer to assist you, then? I could liberate you from this unseemly labor and return you to my side at the mall."

Mark came at the genie with the hedge trimmer next, toads spilling from his mouth. He swung high and it bounced off the genie's forehead like he had hit a rock. The genie turned to face him. "What is the meaning of this? Do you wish to fight me?"

"Br . . . bring it . . . on . . . man . . ." Mark hiccupped out a few toads.

"Very well." There was a puff of fire and the genie had a broad, curved saber of golden metal in his hands, the hilt encrusted with jewels.

Alex interposed herself between the genie and her brother. "No! Stop! Both of you!"

Her father, his forehead bleeding, jumped on the genie's back and got an arm around the mystical being's thick neck. "I got him! Run for it, Lexie! Run!"

The genie reached back, plucked her father off him like somebody picking up an unruly kitten, and shook him. "Inveterate poltroon! Insolent wretch! I should make you a rabbit, but rabbits have more sense!"

Her dad tried kicking at the genie, which worked about as well as the tackle had.

"Put him down!" Alex yelled, trying and failing the grab the genie's arm. "Put him down right now!"

The genie dropped him. Her father was huffing and puffing on his back in the driveway. A knot of toads hopped over his arms and legs. Mark was on his hands and knees, adding more to the procession.

"You . . . you betrayed us . . . Lexie . . . your own family . . ." her father gasped.

"I did not!"

"No, indeed. You have betrayed me, instead," the genie said. "You signed your contract in blood. I was to be notified in the case of illness. You were to advise me in matters pertaining to the inanity of your world. You promised to help me in my quest. You have failed me."

"Bitch." Mark managed between toad-vomit.

"ENOUGH!" Alex shrieked. "What the fuck is wrong with all you assholes?" She pointed at the genie: "I didn't *want* to skip work—my father *made me* because he found out about my job. And you know how he found out? Because of your stupid idea to pay me in *silver coins!*"

Then she turned on Mark: "The only reason you're hurling frogs, Mark, is because you don't have my back—me, your own sister! Your fault, *not* mine. Live with it."

"And *you*," she turned on her dad. "What do you want from me, huh? You want me to be like Mark, just going along with your dumbass ideas every day for the rest of his life? Being stuck in this town while you and Mom fight about your latest stupid screwup? I got a *job* with a *genie* because he offered me something none of you assholes ever could: a future. Yeah, that's right—something that doesn't involve me getting knocked up by some bonehead like Kenny Dufresne and waiting tables down at Shoney's while he drives a school bus. This town sucks, Dad, and all the people in it *suck*, and *you suck* and I want OUT! Is that so wrong? Huh?"

The driveway was quiet, but for the croaking of toads and the hum of the pickup's AC compressor. Her father said nothing, but she could tell by the way his face was stiff and cold that she'd hurt him and hurt him deep.

Good.

Mark puked again.

Alex sighed and spoke to the genie. "Would you remove that stupid curse from him, already?"

The genie nodded slowly. "It is done, Alexandria Delmore. I . . ." he paused, his demonic features trying to find the right expression, failing. "I am sorry for having interfered in the affairs of your family."

Her father was getting to his feet. "Lexie, you can't trust a thing like that. You can't! Honey, you gotta believe me when I say he's . . . they're all *evil*! Come away from him! We'll figure something out, all of us together. I gotta plan, I promise!"

"Mr. Delmore," the genie said, "you insult me, and gravely. I have done your daughter no harm, nor would I do so. Indeed, she has proven herself a steadfast ally whose counsel I value. Despise me and my kind if you must—no doubt you have your reasons—but you should be proud of your daughter."

Charlie Delmore had his hands on knees, huffing and puffing. "Go to hell."

The genie offered Alex his hand. "Will you come with me? I have . . . I have matters I wish to discuss with you."

Alex looked back at her father. "Dad? Are you okay?"

"What's it matter?" her father said. "What do you need me for, anyhow? Go on." He wiped the blood from his face and looked down at his feet. Mark was still on the ground, shaking toads out of his shirt.

Alex turned away and took the genie's hand.

And they were gone.

They were at the kiosk at the mall. Alex expected some kind of dizziness, some kind of disorientation—there was none. She felt fine. That, in and of itself, was creepy. She gripped the counter, just to confirm it was real.

There was no line because the genie hadn't been there until a second ago. There *was* however something new—a series of nylon barriers forming a line queue and a sign at the entrance that read LIMIT 10 PATRONS IN LINE.

"What the hell is this?" Alex asked.

The genie was sitting on his throne, as usual. "While you were your father's prisoner, Officer Coop Frank came and informed us of new regulations. Our lines are creating some manner of incendiary hazard, it seems. This is spurious, as I very much doubt our supplicants are any more combustible than the average person of this era."

Alex took a second to translate that into English. "Do you mean *fire* hazard? The line is a fire hazard?"

"That is what I just said."

"No, that's . . ." Alex rubbed her temples. "This is a mall concourse, man—it's got dozens of exits. No way it can't handle this crowd."

"I am only telling you what I was told, Alexandria. I agree that this seems unnecessary. Truly this is an onerous place to pursue one's trade. This is part of what I wished to discuss."

Alex looked around. Sure enough, there was Frank on his scooter, keeping an eye on things from about thirty feet away. He had a bag of what looked like bird seed in the crook of one arm and he was eating from it with his free hand.

"I have taken your advice—to press on with this enterprise, in the hopes that one day my efforts might bear fruit—and I have pondered it most deeply. There is wisdom there, wisdom beyond your years."

Alex felt herself blush, mostly because she had made that stuff up on the spot just to make the genie feel better.

The genie wasn't paying attention to her, though, he was gesturing broadly at the mall around them. "But does it not seem that this place is *opposed* to even our most modest efforts? Do we not act only to find that Madam Sturgis and her lackey place new obstacles in our path? I confess I know not what to do—I have proven myself guileless and ignorant in all business dealings in this age so far. So it is that I turn to you, now, my assistant, and call upon the oaths you signed in blood: what shall I do? How can I help your society if it will not let me?"

Alex blinked up at him. Was he actually *asking* for advice? She didn't need to browbeat him over it? Didn't need to drag him, kicking and screaming, toward sense? It was a novel feeling; she wasn't ready for it. "Uhhhh . . . well . . ."

"Excuse me?" A guy in a superhero T-shirt was at the counter. "You guys open?"

Both Alex and the genie spoke in unison. "NO!"

The guy put his hands up and backed away.

The genie looked back at Alex. "Well? What clever ploy have you to offer?"

"Well . . . uhhh . . . I guess the problem is that people can only wish for discount diapers and stuff, right?"

"And that the wishes of mankind are invariably either selfish or misguided. Do not forget that part."

"Riiight . . ." Alex felt like pacing or putting up an idea board, but she had neither the space to pace nor the white board to scribble on. "What we need here is a loophole. Sturgis told us not to get the mall sued, right?"

"Correct. She is most fearful of your courts."

"And she also said we can only *sell* stuff that you could buy at the mall."

"An arbitrary metric, indeed."

"Well, what if we threw a little promotion?"

"Excellent!" the genie said. "What is a promotion?"

Alex licked her lips. "Okay, hear me out—what if, for a limited time this afternoon, we made the wishes *free*?"

The genie bristled. "Free? You wish to enslave me again?"

"Boss, trust me—if you want to change the world, you gotta stop charging full price."

"Very well," the genie said. "Explain."

CHAPTER 14:
SOME RESTRICTIONS APPLY

WELCOME TO THE BEST WISHES BOGO SALE!

UNTIL CLOSING TIME TODAY, JULY 8TH, THE GENIE WOULD LIKE TO OFFER OUR CUSTOMERS A SPECIAL OPPORTUNITY.

WITH THE PURCHASE OF ONE (1) WISH AT THE REGULAR PRICE, THE GENIE WILL OFFER YOU ONE (1) ADDITIONAL WISH FOR NO CHARGE.

<u>RULE AND RESTRICTIONS</u>

- THE FREE WISH IS NOT A "SALE" AND, AS SUCH, IS NOT BOUND BY THE RULES LAID OUT FOR OUR SALES. IN OTHER WORDS, YOU MAY WISH FOR THINGS *NOT* COMMONLY SOLD AT RETAIL.
- THE GENIE CAN MAKE THINGS APPEAR, DISAPPEAR, OR ALTER THE SHAPE AND/OR LOCATION OF THINGS, BUT NOTHING ELSE.
- NO CURSES, LARCENY, VIOLENT ACTS, DISINTEGRATIONS OF LIVING THINGS, HUMAN RIGHTS VIOLATIONS, WAR CRIMES, OR VANDALISM.
- THE GENIE RESERVES THE RIGHT TO DENY ANY WISH FOR ANY REASON.

- No wishing for more wishes.
- Limit 3 purchases per customer, no exceptions.
- By accepting the genie's offer of a free wish, you indemnify Best Wishes and, by extension, the Wellspring Mall of any and all legal responsibility for the outcome of said wish.

Please Sign Below:

Name: _____

Date: _____

Signature:

Their first customer for the BOGO sale was a thin white man in glasses, wearing a polo shirt and khakis. He reminded Alex of her chemistry teacher, except without the ponytail. He wished for a set of rare novels by some Russian author Alex had never heard of, for which he paid two hundred bucks. The copies were thick and the pages were a little yellowed with age, but otherwise in pristine condition. He inspected them, going through each, page by page.

Alex had her chin in her hands. "So, are those the right books or what?"

"These seem authentic, yes," he said absently.

"So, do we have to watch you go through each individual page or . . ."

The man's head popped up. "Right, sorry—just checking, you see. Just want to make sure."

The genie had his arms folded. "You believe I would cheat you?"

"No, no—not that. I just . . . okay, you said for the second wish I can have anything, right?"

"Not anything," the genie said. "You signed the waiver. You have seen the restrictions."

"But it will be free?"

"Just so."

Alex rolled her eyes. "C'mon, man—spit it out. There's a lot of people waiting."

The man pulled himself to his full height. "I wish for *world peace!*"

Alex nodded. "Right on—high-five!"

They slapped hands.

The genie didn't move. "What is world peace?"

The man snorted. "An end to war, obviously!"

"How am I to do this?" the genie asked. "I cannot change the hearts of all men!"

"Just get rid of all the weapons!"

"Think you that the human race wages war because it has *weapons*? If I take away your swords and your pistols, you would fall upon each other with rocks and sticks. If I take them away, still you would seek to kill one another with fists and teeth. This I know—I have seen it done."

The man was flummoxed. "Well . . . uhhh . . . what about nuclear weapons? Can you destroy all those?"

The genie considered it. "Yes. Where *are* all the nuclear weapons?"

"I . . . I *obviously* don't know that!"

The genie closed his eyes and pinched the bridge of his nose.

Alex forced a smile at the customer. "Uhhh . . . can we interest you in a free bomb shelter in your backyard or something?"

* * *

Customer number two—a black woman in a track suit—wished for a pack of gum for fifty cents. Then, she smiled and said, "I want a billion dollars."

Alex gaped at her, "Uhhhh . . ."

The genie didn't even blink. "Done. Next?"

Customer number seven was a white-haired old woman in a long skirt and conservative blouse that looked pretty hot here in the middle of July. She had her hair pulled back in a severe bun and wore a gold crucifix on a golden necklace. Her initial wish was for a copy of the King James Bible for ten dollars.

"I wish for everyone to find Jesus."

Alex swallowed her groan. "Uh . . . boss?"

"Where?"

The woman blinked at the genie. "What?"

"Where should they find Jesus?"

"In their hearts, of course."

The genie scowled. "There are to be no acts of violence."

"I think she means it metaphorically, boss."

The woman bristled. "I do *not*."

Alex and the genie exchanged glances. "You wish for me to transport a small man named Jesus into the hearts of every single human being, immediately killing them all, is this correct?"

"Not a human being—our Lord!"

Alex rolled her eyes. "Boss, she wants you to make everyone Christian."

The genie groaned. "Not this again."

Customer number twenty-five was a kid Alex knew from school named Ryan. He had acne and was wearing jeans and a white T-shirt stained by ketchup and grass. He bought a bottle of mouthwash first.

Making direct eye contact with Alex, he unscrewed the cap of the mouthwash, took a swig, swished, *swallowed*, and then made his second wish. "I wish for a date with Alex."

"Oh, come on," Alex said, "be serious, Ryan."

"It's my wish, right?" Ryan spat back. "Don't be so stuck up!"

Alex looked back at the genie. "Can this qualify as a human rights violation?"

Customer number thirty-six: "I wish to be the richest man on Earth!"

Customer number thirty-eight: "I wish to be the richest man on Earth!"

Customer number forty-six: "I wish to be the richest man on Earth!"

"I wish for all cancer to be cured!" said customer number fifty-five. They were the fourth person to make this wish.

Alex, whose energy was severely flagging, sighed. "Look, that's a seriously good idea, man, but he can't do it."

The genie nodded. "She speaks the truth. Cancer is more than one single affliction, and I do not and cannot know every single person who has it anymore than you know them. You ask for several wishes, not one."

The customer—a young Asian woman—looked like she was ready to cry. "But . . . but you're a *genie* and . . ."

"Do you know any specific people who need their cancer cured?" Alex slid her a piece of notebook paper. "Just make a list. Oh, and everyone at Mercy General Hospital has already been cured, by the way. Some guy handled that earlier."

A middle-aged man in a softball uniform. He was a repeat customer—Alex remembered him from earlier in the summer. Off to one side was his entire softball team—a rowdy collection of sunburned men with receding hairlines and expanding waistlines. One of them hooted, "Wish it *UP*, T-dog!" Then followed a chorus of cheers and them bumping chests with one another.

Alex did her best fake smile. "Just so we're clear, we can't ensure you always win games."

"Nah," the guy said, "I just want my boys and I to all have the bodies of twenty-year-old professional athletes."

The genie sat up. "You are asking me to conjure soulless husks for each of you? What manner of depraved—"

"Boss, boss!" Alex yelled. "They just want to be in better shape, you know? Washboard abs and shit."

"And bigger, uhhh . . ." He looked down.

Alex cut him off before anything could be made more explicit. "GROSS!"

The genie nodded. "That would be a separate wish. You will need to make another purchase."

Customer one-hundred and three had a puppet with them. A ventriloquist dummy made to look like a peanut with a monocle. When she spoke to them, the dummy was the one whose mouth moved. "I wish I were a real boy!"

The genie glowered at the ventriloquist. "What affront is this?!"

Alex took a deep breath. "Look, lady, I'd really suggest talking to the genie in your real voice."

"Whaddya mean?" the peanut said, "I *am* talking in my real voice! I wanna be real! REAL!"

Alex had a pounding headache. "Oh, for Christ's sake, just do it, will you?"

The genie looked furious. "Very well—your abhorrent peanut doll will be granted life. Remember that you signed a waiver."

The peanut dummy began to wriggle and leapt off the woman's hand. It hit the ground at a dead run and shrieked at an inhuman volume before darting into the crowd on all fours. People screamed as it shot past and the ventriloquist, horrified, began to chase after it. "Mr. Nougat! Wait! It's me! Your mama!"

＊＊＊

Over the next six hours, the genie made the blind see and the lame walk. He cured the ill and gave wealth to the poor. He provided textbooks for schools and care for the elderly. He brought a little girl's missing kitten back and washed away the trauma of a gunshot victim. He did real, honest good.

But for every one of those wishes, there were three or four who wished for foolish and selfish things or things that he could not or would not grant. Every one of these wishes drove the genie to a blacker and blacker mood until, by the end of the shift, he was slouching in his throne, worn out by the pettiness of humanity.

Alex felt much the same. Her head was pounding and her back hurt—she'd barely had time for a break all day. She tried to focus on the good things they had done, but it was hard. They'd set at least twenty new billionaires loose on society, and she somehow doubted that would go anywhere positive.

They also hadn't made much in the way of money. Everyone was there for the free wish, not the paying one. The customers *bought* hardly anything.

"I think it was worth it," Alex said, but her face was too tired from pretending to smile to fake it now. "Think of all the people we helped."

"They think only of themselves," the genie said. "They think themselves alone. That is why they came at all." He did not elaborate further—he just sat on his throne and brooded.

Frank appeared, rolling on his scooter, hands tucked under his armpits again, a feather stuffed into the back of his baseball cap. He held out an envelope. "Letter for the genie."

Alex took it and passed it up to the genie, who looked it over. "What is this?"

Frank didn't answer. He was already driving away.

The genie tore open one side of the envelope while Alex watched.

She was distracted, though, by Kenny, wearing his ValuDay duds, running straight at them and waving his arms like he was being chased by a dinosaur. He collided with the kiosk, panting for breath, and leaning on it as though he had just run a mile.

"Uhhh . . . hey, Kenny—what's up?"

"ValuDay . . . leaving . . . mall . . ." Kenny said between gasps. "Just . . . just heard . . . ran to . . . to tell you guys . . . so I ran here . . . but took a wrong turn . . . wound up in parking garage . . . took stairs . . . then . . ."

Alex held up one hand. "Why don't you catch your breath and then talk to us like a normal person." She looked at the genie. "You know anything about this?"

The genie stroked his smoky goatee as he looked at the contents of the envelope. "Not specifically, but it perhaps explains this." He passed Alex the letter.

It read:

> To: the Jinn Formerly of the Ring of Korad
> From: Wellspring Mall, Maureen Sturgis, Manager
>
> Dear Sir,
>   It has come to our attention that you are in violation of the terms of your lease. The violations are as follows:
>
> 1. Failure to list a legal name on your lease application
> 2. Staff wearing indecent attire (loincloth)
> 3. Staff threatening mall patrons ("You will burn in

> *the fiery pits of Gehenna, you dog")*
> 4. *Failure to pay rent in fashion required (silver coins not accepted)*
> 5. *Lines causing fire hazard (mitigations implemented)*
>
> *Due to these transgressions, you are hereby evicted from the premises, effective thirty days from this posting. This decision is not subject to review or reconsideration. We thank you for your tenancy in the Wellspring Mall and wish you the best of luck in your future endeavors.*
>
> *Yours sincerely,*
> *Maureen Sturgis*

Alex couldn't believe her eyes. "That . . . this is total bullshit! All of this!"

Kenny pulled a tiny energy drink from a pocket and downed it in one go. "Totally. Shereen—she's at returns—told me that Martin said that he overheard Greg—he's the manager—saying that corporate was pissed you were beating their prices, right, so they're gonna bounce unless the mall gets rid of you."

"Cowardly curs," the genie said, his expression growing dark. "What of the free market? What of fair exchange?"

Kenny nodded. "It's the system, right? Don't worry—I quit, right on the spot."

The genie nodded. "You are a noble soul, Kenny Dufresne."

Alex rolled her eyes. "Yeah, Kenny quitting—that'll show 'em."

Kenny pointed to his green polo shirt. "I'm not even giving back the uniform!"

"You had to *pay* for that uniform, Kenny. It's yours."

Kenny stared at her, open-mouthed. He looked down at his shirt. "Why . . . why would anyone want . . . *this*?"

"I take it back," Alex said. "They would never let you drive a school bus."

Kenny's face clouded with confusion.

"All right, boss—next steps," Alex said to the genie. "I'll go talk to Sturgis, see if I can talk her out of this. Maybe we can partner with ValuDay somehow. Worst case scenario, I bet we can get them to buy you out." She snapped her fingers. "Yeah! That's it! Oh, man—your business is worth a fortune! They'd probably pay out *millions* just to make you go away!"

The genie cocked his head to one side. "Wait, you mean they would pay me millions of dollars to *not* grant wishes?"

"Yeah! Well, probably," Alex said. "Awesome, right?"

"No, Alexandria Delmore, that is *not* awesome."

"Why not?" Alex asked.

Kenny also seemed stumped. "Yeah, man—that's the goal, right?"

"No! That is *not* the goal!" The genie threw up his hands. "I do not wish to be idle! I wish for my labors to *have meaning*! I want to help humanity become better! I *want* to grant wishes, but not as a slave—as an equal member of society!"

"That's great, yeah, but, like, we just *tried* that and it only *sort of* worked. Think of all the good you could do with all that money," Alex said. "Millions of dollars could buy all kinds of things that would help society."

"But then I am nothing more than a philanthropist— feeding silver into the coffers of others and then others and then others, all of whom take their dues. I know nothing of how best to distribute such riches—I *explained* this to you yesterday eve! My philanthropy would be worthless!" The genie shook his head. "They would deny me the one thing I am good at—the *one* thing I know—just so they might continue to profit off the backs of the poorest among you."

"Right on." Kenny raised a closed fist. "Fight the power, man."

Alex lowered his fist. "Thanks, Kenny—you can go now."

Kenny shot them both the horns. "Later!"

Alex watched him go, mad at herself for staring at his butt. She shook her head. "We need to do *something*, boss."

The genie slouched, his forearms resting on his knees. "What does it matter anymore? Everything I try, everywhere I go, I am reviled and condemned, restricted and insulted. I am reduced to peddling trinkets to a dwindling number of people or granting frivolous boons to the selfish and stupid. I am doing no good."

Alex took a risk and patted the genie on his thick forearm. "Hey, big guy—don't sweat it, okay? We'll figure something out."

"What is it *you* want of me, Alexandria Delmore?" the genie asked.

"What?"

The genie met her gaze. "You told your father this very morn that I offered you 'a future.' This is a vague statement—elaborate."

Alex felt her face flush. *Here goes nothing . . .* "See, there's this school."

"You want an education. Into a trade?"

Alex's gaze fell to her hands as she spoke. "Not like that. I . . . I need to get out of here. I have to get away from my family—they're just . . . they're just the worst. I want to go to New York City and get an apartment and maybe have a little dog and some friends who actually like me and maybe learn something about the world for a change, instead of just watching it go by."

She took a deep breath. "I guess when I say that, I sound just like another one of those selfish assholes, huh?"

The genie reached out gently with one finger and tipped her chin up so that she could see his face. She could see his sadness there, and his terrible face looked not so terrible at that moment—just haggard. "I have granted the wishes to many many thousands of people across all the ages of your history and understand this: you sound no worse than most of them, and a good deal better than many. You are not a wicked person, Alexandria Delmore."

Alex felt her eyes tear up. "Thanks."

"But you are wrong about your family."

"You don't know them."

"I know that I saw a mortal man challenge me today with no hope of victory, no possibility of success, because he felt his daughter was in danger. He would have given his life for yours and with no hesitation, no regrets." The genie nodded slowly. "He loves you. For all his faults, which are no doubt numerous, he loves you as a father should. You are wrong to shun him, Alex. Like all mortals, you are not alone. You only think you are."

He called me Alex. She gripped his hand—it was solid, and hot to the touch—and squeezed. "Thanks, boss. I'll . . . I'll think about what you said."

The genie held her gaze for a moment. She remembered, when she first met him, how those light-bulb bright eyes frightened her, but now they were just the eyes of a person she knew. A friend. He seemed to be turning something over in his mind.

"Do *you* believe I am doing good here?" the genie asked. "Speak truly—am I earning my place in your world?"

Alex didn't know how to answer. She wasn't even sure what he was asking—how did anyone earn their place in a world this messed up? Why would anyone want to?

The genie didn't seem to be waiting for an answer. He was distracted, lost in his own thoughts. So was she.

At length, the genie loaded up his treasure chest with their meager earnings for the day, gave Alex her cut, and before she could say anything more, he said, "You have no means to get home, now, thanks to my actions. Come, let me take you."

"What?" Alex stiffened. "Home? *You*? Now, now let's just think about this for a second . . . wait . . ."

The genie took her by the hand.

They were gone.

CHAPTER 15:
DINNER WITH THE DELMORES

THE NEXT THING Alex knew, she was standing on the front lawn of her house. "Aw, crap." she said, hanging her head.

The genie looked down. "Why are there tire tracks on your lawn?"

Then the shit hit the fan.

Her father kicked open the front door, shotgun ready. "Get away from him, Lexie!"

"Jesus!" Alex flinched and ducked behind the genie's bulk.

Her mother screamed from inside the house. "PUT THAT SHOTGUN AWAY YOU IDIOT!"

"Shut up, woman!" her father yelled back. "I know what I'm doing!"

The genie looked unimpressed. "You are holding a goose."

Her father looked down. In his hands, there was a full-grown Canada goose that he had gripped by the neck. It twisted, flapped its wings, and hissed. "What the . . ." her dad dropped it.

The goose went on the offensive, buffeting Alex's father with its wings and pecking and hissing—a one-bird tornado of indignant hostility. Charlie Delmore began a tactical retreat inside the house, only to find his wife hitting him with a broom. "Don't let that thing in the house, you moron!"

Mark came around the side of the garage, having gone out the back door. "I got it, Dad!" He made a flying tackle for the goose, which succeeded, and he began to wrestle it, which went somewhat more poorly.

"Get my gun!" Alex's father yelled at no one in particular.

"That *is* your gun," the genie said.

"He has a lot more." Alex sighed. "Come on—you better come inside."

"Why?" the genie asked, watching as both Delmore men tried to corral or control the irate goose without getting pecked any further.

"You know, dude, I can't figure you out," Alex said, leading him by the beefy forearm through the front door. "Sometimes you say the wisest shit, and other times it's like you were just born. Just come inside so nobody calls the cops again, okay?"

They came to face-to-face with Alex's mother, still armed with a broom. Rather than brandishing it, though, she looked the genie up and down and said, "Well, I suppose you ought to stay for dinner."

Alex felt like her eyes had popped out of her head and were rolling around the floor like marbles. "What . . . uhhh . . . no . . . what?"

"I would be delighted," the genie said. "The last time I was thusly invited was two thousand years ago. I ate with a princess of Egypt and was entertained by fifty acrobats from deepest Africa."

"Well," her mother said with a shrug, "we're fresh out of acrobats. Is Hamburger Helper okay?"

The genie raised an eyebrow at Alex.

It took her a second to relocate her vocal cords. "It's not a kind of acrobat," Alex explained, finally. "It's a kind of food."

What followed made the Chinese Food Diplomacy dinner look like a cordial lunch date with an old friend.

The kitchen table didn't have space for a fifth person, so her mom went hunting for the leaf she could install to lengthen it, which was somewhere in the basement. This left Alex and the genie on one side of the kitchen and her father and Mark on the other, the latter two covered with welts inflicted by her father's former shotgun.

"Don't you try nothing," her father growled at the genie.

"I am a guest in your home, Charles Delmore. You need not fear anything from me, so long as the bond of hospitality lasts."

"And you better replace my dad's shotgun!" Mark said.

"That gun cost me five hundred dollars, you—" Her dad stopped up short. He had a shotgun in his hands, identical to the one he had before, but this one brand new and notably not stained with toad guts. "What in the world . . ."

"Is the weapon suitable?" the genie asked.

Her father examined it, weighed it in his hands, sniffed it, fondled the stock. "Well . . . sure . . . it's fine . . ."

Mark had his arms folded. "What's the catch?"

"Consider it a gift," the genie said. "An apology for my rough handling of you."

"And Dad," Alex added. "Don't try to shoot him with it, okay?"

The gift of the shotgun took the edge off her father's rage, but neither he nor Mark were very talkative as the leaf appeared and a spare stool was taken from the living room for the genie to sit on. There was a lot of staring going on across the table as her mother made dinner, the paper cups full of neon-yellow lemonade going untouched in front of all four of them.

Alex felt like they all were waiting for *her* to break the ice, but she had nothing. She took a swing at it. "So . . . do you like hamburger?" she asked the genie.

"I have never had hamburger."

Her father snorted. "You a vegetarian?"

"He doesn't have to eat, Dad." Alex said. "He's magic."

"It is also not entirely true I do not eat, though I do not eat as you do," the genie said. "Many of my kind eat the . . . the *refuse* of humanity. Bones and leavings, scraps and rotten things."

"Garbage," Mark said. "You eat trash."

"*I* do not. Whilst I was imprisoned, I was granted neither food nor drink for many thousands of years, save the banquet at the table of the Egyptian princess, as I have mentioned. During that time I merely . . . stopped eating. This will be my first meal in a very, very long time. I believe I have forgotten what it is like, save the glimpses I receive from the wishes of others."

"The hundred-foot pizza?" Alex asked.

"Just so. The hundred-foot pizza."

Mark and her father exchanged glances. "Somebody wished for a hundred-foot pizza?"

"For some kid's birthday party," Alex said. "They said they cleared a space in the yard. I have no idea how it turned out. Musta been a mess."

Alex's father tapped his chin. "Was this on the Fourth?"

"Verily," said the genie.

Her father laughed and slapped the table. "Hell, those people called me! They wanted to know if olive oil kills grass and if I knew how to wash it out. I thought it was some kinda joke—I hung up on them. What kinda fool covers their lawn with pizza?"

Alex frowned at her father, known public dumbass. "Oh yeah, what brilliant thing would you wish for, Dad? A swimming pool full of beer? Unlimited bail money?"

"Actually," Mark said, "A swimming pool of beer doesn't sound half bad!"

Her father, though, fell silent and looked at his hands until the food arrived.

The Hamburger Helper did not help as much as Alex had hoped. The genie ate tentatively, delicately, his fangs uncertain how to proceed. He wound up gulping down noodles whole, dangling them above his mouth and dropping them in like a sword-swallower. Everyone was slightly grossed out, but either too polite or too terrified to say anything.

Her mother made the next foray into conversation. "Do you live around here, Mr. Genie?"

Alex's eyes bugged out. "Hey, do we have any dessert?"

"I have no home," the genie explained. "I am an aimless spirit, dwelling neither in this world nor the next."

"What about your people?" Alex's mom seemed concerned. "Are they also . . . errr . . . aimless?"

"No. My people live in great cities hidden from your eyes, and in palaces in the sky made of silver and ivory. Their homes are truly magnificent." The genie shrugged. "But we are estranged, my people and I. My imprisonment was so long that I . . . I am no longer as they are. I am no longer welcome."

"Oh, that's terrible!" Alex's mother put a hand on the genie's giant arm. Everyone stared at the gesture, especially

Alex's father. Her mother, realizing what she'd done, removed her hand slowly. "I . . . I beg your pardon. I didn't mean to . . ."

"No injury has been done, Rosalind Delmore. I thank you for your sympathy, and for this meal, which is truly sumptuous. This much salt must have cost you a great fortune to procure from distant Timbuktu."

"Oh," her mother blushed. "It was on sale."

"Mom works at the grocery store," Alex said.

"You are a grocer?" the genie asked.

"Well . . . I run the register, so . . . I guess so? Yes."

The genie gave her a firm nod. "This is a noble profession—bringing food to your neighbors. My own business is inspired by such as that."

"What do wishes have in common with grocery stores?" Alex's father had his arms crossed. He hadn't touched his food. "Wishes are unnatural."

Alex pointed at the neon-yellow lemonade in the paper cups. "Yeah, and that stuff grows in an orchard. Gimmie a break."

"I am providing a service. I am trying to earn a place in your community," the genie said to Alex's father.

"Well, you aren't welcome," Mark said, arms crossed exactly like his father's.

"Mark!" Her mother gasped. "I'm very sorry, Mr. Genie."

The genie seemed unbothered. "Why am I unwelcome, Mark Delmore?"

"Because you made me puke frogs, for one thing," Mark said.

"Because you aren't like us," her father said. "We can't trust you because you're dangerous. Hell, you could kill us all with the tip of your thumb—how can we be comfortable with that?"

"What difference would that make? You own a deadly weapon—why do not your children fear your fatal wrath as keenly as you fear my own? Why would I destroy you all, when what I want is to be part of you?"

"You can't never be *part* of us!" Her father stood up. "World had enough problems before you creepy things started popping up. Now we're poor on account of you creatures taking our jobs and we're scared on account of you changing the way things work, and ... and ... and we're *mad* because there ain't nothing we can do about it!"

"Dad—" Alex said in warning, but her father barreled on.

"You wanna know what I'd wish, *Mr.* Genie? I'd wish you and everything like you would disappear and leave us be, just as things were before. That's what I want! I want what I had *before* you ever showed up!" He stormed out of the room. Mark lingered for a moment, but only to give the genie a hard stare, and then followed his father.

Her mother's cheeks were flushed. "I'm very sorry about that. Charlie was never much for manners."

"He speaks honestly. I cannot fault him for it," the genie said, looking at the doorway through which Charlie had just left.

"Well," Rosalind said, "I'm sorry anyway."

The genie looked at Alex's mom. "It is traditional for the guest to grant the hostess a gift, is it not?"

Rosalind's mouth popped open. "Oh! Well, I don't know ... that seems a little—"

Alex joined in, "Yeah, maybe not so much—"

The genie placed his hand over Rosalind's and when he removed it, there was a ring of garnets and emeralds, sparkling on her finger. Alex's mother gasped. "Oh ... oh my *God*!"

Alex stood up rapidly and grabbed the genie by the elbow. It felt like grabbing a concrete column. "Okay, the genie has to go now—I'll walk him out. Be right back, okay?"

Her mother seemed not to hear, her eyes glued to her hand and the way the dim kitchen light made her ring sparkle.

The genie rose and bowed. "Good evening, Rosalind. Thank you ag—"

"Right, sure, yes—we're all very glad you came—now *move*." Alex dragged at the genie's arm.

The genie allowed himself to be dragged out the front door. There were goose droppings all over the front stairs.

Alex slapped the genie's arm. "Dude, *not* cool."

"What etiquette have I breached now?" the genie asked. He sounded tired.

"You can't give my mom a *ring*! Jesus, do you know what'll happen if my father sees that?"

The genie shook his head. "No, I do not."

Alex opened her mouth to tell him, but she found *she* didn't quite know, either. Her dad took his mom for granted—he *kinda* deserved to be a bit jealous. But still. "Well, it isn't good."

"Your father is right," the genie said. "I will never belong here. I will never be wanted."

"Dude, you can't listen to what my old man says. He thinks the moon is a hologram, for God's sake."

"It isn't just that," the genie said. "I feel it everywhere I go. I try to help—I have always tried to help—and yet I fail."

"Look, just sleep on it . . . or . . . well, *assuming* you sleep. Rest on it—why don't you *rest* on it and we'll talk in the morning."

The genie shook his head. "It is of no use, Alexandria."

The back of Alex's neck prickled. "Wait . . . what do you mean by that? You're not—you're not *quitting* on me, are you?"

"I have trouble explaining what I mean. This has always been my great failing." The genie raised his head, seemed to sniff the air. "Can I *show* you? Will you come with me, just for a short time?" He extended his hand.

Alex looked behind her—her parents and brother were nowhere to be seen. This would be the second time she'd slipped off with the genie today—they'd be pissed and worried—but if it meant talking the genie out of whatever funk he was in . . . if it meant keeping her job. "Sure, okay—let's go."

She took his hand, and again she disappeared.

CHAPTER 16:
CUSTOMER SURVEY

ALEX FELT . . . adrift. Almost like she was in a dream. The world was beneath her—houses and cars and trees—and she was flying above it, swift as a bird. Swift as the wind.

I have altered your form temporarily. The genie's voice came from no particular place. They were just words that appeared in her mind. *You may feel disoriented, but this is the simplest way.*

They were swooping down, now, beneath the tree canopy. Ahead of them was a small, single-level home. The flash of a television screen was visible through the big bay window in the living room.

Is this what it's like for you? Alex asked, but without sound. *Is this how you, like, see the world?*

It is a mere approximation. The genie answered. *I have not made you into a jinn, merely given you the shape of one. You are still mortal.*

Alex would have laughed, but she found she had no way to do it. *Thanks for clarifying that I can still die. Clutch detail.*

Hush and take heed.

They were outside the window, now, looking into a living room piled with unopened mail and litter. An old man sat on the couch in faded boxer shorts and a stained tank top, head leaning on one shoulder, mouth open, eyes glazed—a man in a kind of daze. He had a beer in one hand, but he didn't seem to be drinking it. The coffee table was cluttered with cans of the same brand of beer.

In looking at him, Alex felt . . . strange. She felt a kind of emptiness from him—a deep, sickening malaise. *What's wrong with him?*

A woman entered the room. She was about the same age but, unlike the man, she was dressed and neat. She snapped at the man on the couch. "This place is disgusting! What if we have company, Gary?"

Gary did not respond. The woman snatched up an armful of food wrappers and brought them into the kitchen. Alex and the genie followed, passing through the walls of the house like the Ghost of Christmas Past. The woman dumped the trash into the kitchen and stood beside the sink, washing her hands. She had deep rings under her eyes. She leaned against the counter and closed her eyes, fighting back tears.

Alex recognized her. *That was the lady who wanted to give her husband hemorrhoids! Breanna . . . something . . .*

Just so, the genie said. *Can you feel her needs?*

Alex did—it was like a taste, sort of. Or a smell. In any case, wafting off the woman was a kind of sweaty funk, like an old locker room. *She's scared,* Alex said, *desperate.*

Her husband is ill. Paralyzed with a kind of deep mental wound—he will not rise, he will not work, he finds joy in nothing, fears nothing. He is empty. She fears for what will happen.

Breanna—the woman who had offered fudge to give her

husband hemorrhoids—washed the dishes at the sink, trying not to cry. She felt like an open book in a way real people never were—Alex knew she was trying to think of what to do, who to call.

He's depressed, Alex said. *Like, clinically. He needs a doctor, drugs, shit like that.*

The genie's presence—invisible, but warm and powerful like the sun—hummed with agreement. *And yet this is not what she asks. This is something she does not realize. I, a stranger to this world, do not even know how to tell her what she wants. How, then, can I help her, if she knows not herself what her ailing husband needs?*

Alex thought about this as they flew up through the roof and drifted away from the house toward another. *It's like the blind leading the blind, huh? This is a solvable problem, though!*

Maybe, but it is not all so simple as that.

The world blurred and now they were outside a second story window. Inside, an emaciated girl slumped into her room, ignoring the calls from her parents downstairs—it was dinnertime. Instead, the girl turned and faced her mirror and removed her clothes, standing there in her underwear. Alex recognized her immediately. *Oh God, her . . .*

Indeed.

Her pelvis jutted out like a pair of horns. Her ribs were all visible. She turned this way and that, looking. Looking for something. Alex could taste her need, like a bottomless pit. A kind of burning, deep pain, unending. *Jesus.*

She seeks a perfection she cannot see. It eats her from the inside, this need. It warps her perceptions. What wish can cure this, Alexandria Delmore?

You're focusing on extreme examples, man. Not everybody

is this deep in it. Some people just need a day off, they need a raise, they need a new car, you know?

They withdrew from the girl's room and rose up, the town spreading out beneath them, a network of street lights and chimneys and baseball fields. *You think it so simple, then? Come, and I will show you . . .*

They shot down to street level, the world blurring by, and ripped through the town like a bullet. All around them, Alex saw the people—her neighbors, her community—and felt their needs and wants as the genie did.

She saw the men's softball team from earlier, playing their game under the halogen lamps, each of them a heady array of insecurity and fear and longing for the imagined past of a glorious youth.

She saw a single father in a Velocity Burger apron, doing arithmetic on a bank receipt, stinking of exhaustion and despair as he tried to find daycare.

She saw a taxi driver, his body a swirl of need and fear as he wondered how much longer he could keep his boss from realizing he didn't have his green card.

She saw a boy, head buried under a pillow, shivering as he heard his parents fighting downstairs, wishing he could fly away.

And more and more and more. So much it was like a weight on Alex's chest, smothering her. *Stop. Oh God, stop!*

They did—they were in front of her own house again, right where they started. *Humanity has never been content,* the genie said, *but now, matters are worse. And I know not why or how. Once, in times long past, I recall places and peoples who were bound together in their longings, who strived as a people to fulfill the needs of all, but their needs were meager—warmth, food, safety—and were barely achieved. Your people in this time are gifted with wealth beyond measure, your homes piled in food and treasures undreamed of in past ages, and yet you are all . . . empty. Yearning. Incomplete. It makes no sense.*

Alex saw her father beneath a bare light bulb in the garage, stripped to the waist. Sitting in that little pool of light, sweat running down his back. He was shuffling through a stack of letters, all from the bank, all of them marked FORECLO-SURE NOTICE. He held a pen in a trembling hand, filling out boxes and writing his name on lines. Desperation wafted from him in a cloud, reeking of salt and vinegar. Alex could see that he, like everyone else, was struggling with the world. He was about to lose everything—Alex could tell he knew it—but his pride was like a choking fog that had caused him to lose his way.

Oh God, Alex said.

I have seen this across many times and many ages, the genie said. *So often it is almost a comfort. Your father will fight until the last unless he gets help, but he will never ask. He would rather die.*

Alex felt a bitterness under her tongue, which did not exactly exist at that moment, except in her head. *Why show me this?*

How can I grant the wishes of mortals so that they can be saved from these afflictions, if the afflictions make it so they will never ask for the right thing?

Alex didn't answer. She just watched her father—the stubborn, stupid goon—try and make a miracle happen on a bunch of notices that said FINAL WARNING in big letters across the top.

And then she was back again, in the flesh, standing on the

doorstep with the genie. She pulled her hand out of his. "You live like that? That's what it's like for you *all the time*?"

"So now you see. Perhaps Kenny Dufresne has the right idea, after all. Perhaps I should quit when I realize I am not wanted. Why stay somewhere that is hostile to you? Can you give me a reason, Alexandria Delmore?"

The Hamburger Helper, recently restored to physical existence, did jump rope in her stomach. She felt tears coming. She slapped the genie on the arm—it hurt her hand. "No! No no no no! You can't . . . you are *not* taking off on me, dude! You *owe* me! I have a wish, dammit!"

"Admission to the university of New York," the genie said. "A distant city with new friends and new opportunities."

Alex was crying now. "I have seven thousand dollars! You can have it all! Just—*please please*—grant that wish! That's all I want!"

The genie reached out with one clawed finger and gently wiped a tear away. "I cannot. I will not."

"Why?"

The genie sighed. "I showed you everything, and still you do not see. That is my difficulty, Alex—none of you understand."

There was a fluttering in the trees and a summer breeze played around Alex's hair. The genie was gone.

Gone for good.

CHAPTER 17:
GOING OUT OF BUSINESS

ALEX STAYED UP LATE into the night, barricaded in her room, cursing the ceiling. Downstairs she heard her parents fighting again—her father had discovered the genie's ring, most likely. That idiot. That asshole. He'd sunk them—their whole house, their whole *lives*—for some stupid testosterone pills and the chance to mouth off to a genie.

She was up super early the next day, restless and still angry. She didn't bother showering, didn't bother with breakfast. She crept downstairs while the house was still waking up and got her moped from where it leaned against the garage. She wanted out of here—*out*. She'd made up her mind she was leaving, college or no college. She had seven grand in cash in her backpack—that was probably enough for a start somewhere, right? Anywhere was better than here.

She pumped the kick-starter on her bike—nothing. She pumped it again. Nothing.

Dammit.

She heard the garage door opening.

Double dammit.

She pumped the kick-starter two more times—the moped sputtered and died. Goddamned piece of crap.

Her father was there, dressed only in a T-shirt he got at a beer festival and a pair of Christmas-themed boxer shorts. "Where you going?"

"Work," Alex lied, jamming the pedal again.

"Be back for dinner?" he asked.

"What's it to you?"

"Christ, Lexie." Charlie ran a hand along his bald head. "Least you can do is look at me."

She looked at him. Her father looked tired—shit, did *anybody* look well rested anymore? Her father seemed older than she thought he should be. Worn out. Sad and bowlegged and bald and stained with lawnmower grease and grass stains. He looked at his daughter and a silence played out in the early suburban morning. She thought, for a second, that he was going to say something mushy and ridiculous.

Instead, he crouched down next to her moped and put his hand over some kind of intake valve. "Try it now."

Alex did; the engine sputtered, but it caught and soon it was running smoothly.

Charlie was looking at his hands. "Something's wrong with the choke, is all."

Alex didn't know what to say. She knew she didn't want to say thank you. "Bye, Dad."

"Later, sweetie."

But there wasn't going to be a later. She suspected he knew it, but he helped her go anyway.

She didn't question it. She twisted the throttle and off she went. She aimed for the commuter train station. She envisioned the life that might be ahead of her—a small apartment somewhere in Manhattan, a job doing . . . something. Waiting tables? Delivering pizzas? How much would that pay? Not enough for rent in Manhattan, anyway.

She lowered her expectations. Maybe Philadelphia. Baltimore. Somewhere. *Anywhere.*

She got to the train station and looked at the schedules, the costs, doing the math in her head.

"Hey," a guy in a transit agency jacket pointed at her moped. "You can't bring that on the train, you know."

She looked down. "Then what am I supposed to do with it?"

The guy pointed to a bike rack.

"What if I'm never coming back?"

The guy had half turned away and then he stopped. "You in trouble?" he asked. "Need me to call somebody?"

Alex scowled at him—just what she needed, *more* people "looking out" for her. She tried to start the moped, failed. Tried again.

"Shit, right." She got off, covered up the intake with one leg and then hop-started the bike again. It came alive.

"Hey, kid," the transit guy tried to wave her down, trotting closer, his big belly jiggling with every ponderous step.

Alex flipped him off and sped back into suburbia, her escape thwarted.

What now? What *fucking* now?

In the end, she went to the mall after all.

The doors were open, even though the shops were still closed. A parade of senior citizens in garish exercise attire and thick, white sneakers bustled along the concourse at a brisk walk, monitoring their heart rates on smart watches their grandchildren had probably shown them how to use. Alex gave them a wide berth. The feeling was mutual—the power walkers eyed her dark clothes and extra earrings and muttered to each other about the dismal future that awaited them all.

She got to the genie's kiosk and climbed inside. Knowing the genie wasn't showing up, she sat on the throne. It was hard and uncomfortable, which figured. The genie probably didn't need a cushion to keep his backside from going numb. She threw her legs over one armrest. She waited. She waited until long after the genie should have shown up for work, and he didn't. He wasn't coming.

Again, she asked herself: now what?

What else could she do with herself? What jobs might she get? Nothing much sprung to mind—she was right where she started back in June. Jobless, hopeless, and terribly, terribly bored. Her life now seemed to stretch out before her without contour, without illumination or detail. A featureless plain of . . . *this*. Shit jobs, lousy prospects, and nothing interesting ever happening again.

Above her, balancing on a tightwire they'd strung across the soaring arches of the mall ceiling, the gnomes were changing lightbulbs far above the tiled floor in a death-defying act of facilities maintenance. Having nothing better to do, Alex watched them sway on the wire, watching them maneuver the long tube of the florescent bulb into position, one of them nearly falling to their death in the process.

"Why do they do it?" Alex asked herself, then added, "What's even the point?"

"Busy day, huh?"

Alex looked up to see Fontana Russo, tanned and grinning

and well rested, ducking under the nylon barriers to come to the kiosk.

"What do *you* want?"

Fontana's fake smile was at full power. He knew something she didn't, the shit. "Hey, I never congratulated you on getting out of that lawsuit. What did you give Sturgis for that one? She wish for a real office? Her parking spot back?"

Alex groaned inwardly. She did not have it in her to deal with a gloating shitheel today. "You're, like, five steps behind current events, dude. Don't you have burgers to flip?"

"Where's your boss? Gloating over the sidekick isn't as much fun."

"The genie is out." Alex slid off the throne. "But you knew that, didn't you? That's what you're here to gloat about, isn't it?"

Fontana's smile broadened. "I gave you a chance. I gave you both a chance. And what did you do? You slapped my hand away."

Alex sat up, her spine tingling. "What are you talking about?"

Fontana laughed. "I told you you'd be sorry."

"You mean . . . *you?*" Alex felt rage burning at the back of her throat. "What did you *do?*"

"I've still got an opening at Velocity Burger, assuming you're looking for a job?" Fontana winked.

"What did you *do*, Fontana?"

"Oh, nothing too bad—nothing like making somebody crap their pants *at work*." Fontana's anger flashed, bright and hot, only to be swallowed up again by a sea of smarm. "My dad just happens to be friends with Greg Kanassis, the manager over at ValuDay, and he just *happened* to be over, and we got to talking . . ."

"You . . . you *fuck!*"

"Now the genie *has* to come to me. I'm the only one who seems to see what he represents. This," he gestured to the kiosk, "was only holding him back. *You* were only holding him back."

Alex came down off the throne, her hands trembling with rage. She felt like she could barely see. "You got us closed down. *You* did it!"

Fontana leaned forward across the counter. "And what are you gonna do about it, huh, sugar tits?"

Alex twisted her spiky skull ring onto the inside of her palm, pulled back, and *SLAP*—the sound of the blow wasn't as impressive as she'd hoped, but Fontana's squeal of pain more than made up for it. He staggered back from the counter, hand on his face. When he brought it away, there was blood.

"You . . . you *bitch!*" Fontana screamed loud enough that it echoed off the skylights far above.

Alex scrambled over the counter. The world seemed to be bracketed in flames. "Say that again, you prissy little rich boy! *Call me a bitch again!*"

"AHH!" Fontana screamed and turned to run, only to get tangled in the nylon barriers and fall in a heap. He thrashed on the ground. "Help! Help! Assault!"

"Oh, I'll *show you* fucking assault!" Alex leapt on top of him and started punching. The blows were not aimed, and truth be told she didn't have much experience punching people, but anger fueled every strike. She hit him in the back, the neck, the armpit, the kidneys, his upper arm, each hit coupled with every profane word she knew.

Somewhere in the back of her brain, where a series of

neurons wearing clothes like her grandmother's were having a discussion over tea, the phrase *"we've gone full Delmore"* got thrown around. Her father's rages against the world, her brother's bone-headed stunts—all of them seemed to fall into a clear sort of place in the universe. They made sense.

Punching this dickbag felt just . . . *so* good.

A crowd had gathered, but Alex was only dimly aware of them. She just kept whaling away on Fontana, who was still screaming, and was planning on doing so until she got tired.

It was around then that she must have gotten tasered.

Things got a bit loopy at that point, but she remembered getting hit with *overwhelming* pain, like her skin was on fire for a second, and then, next thing she knew, she was sitting on the ground, leaning against the kiosk, her legs spread out. Her whole body was sore, like she had just done intense yoga for three straight days or something.

A lot of people were yelling. Frank was there, trying to re-load his taser and yelling for everyone to step back. Fontana was still wrapped up in the barriers, yelping and twitching—because Frank had tased Alex while she was *on top* of Fontana, he was tased by extension. A bunch of customers and mall staff were there, trying to get a good look and filming with their phones and so on. Even Maureen Sturgis was there, somehow, yelling for everyone to calm down.

Also of note: between Alex and everybody else was a line of gnomes, their arms linked.

Oh.

Frank wasn't yelling for the *crowd* to step back, he was yelling at the *gnomes* to step back. Like, get out of the way. He was trying to arrest Alex. Or something. *Can mall cops even do that?*

Reality caught up with her like a runaway truck. Oh shit! She'd just assaulted someone in the mall! She had been tased! She was about to go to jail!

Her family would never, ever let her live this down. She was just another crazy Delmore, living on the fringes of society. Jesus.

"Get back! Get out of the way!" Frank squawked at the gnomes.

"You. Have. To. Move." Sturgis was crouching down, talking to the gnomes while using hand gestures. "This. Is. Disobedient."

The gnomes did not budge. One of them pointed at Frank and then jerked its thumb over its shoulder—the gesture was clear: *get out of here.*

Frank finished loading his taser. "You little bastards don't move, and you're gonna get a taste yourself!"

"It's okay," Alex croaked, her throat dry from screaming and then probably being electrocuted and then screaming again. "It's cool. I got this."

The gnomes didn't listen.

Maureen pointed at Fontana. "He will *sue* the mall, do you understand? You. Will. Lose. Your. Jobs."

The little gnome cordon held firm.

Maureen stood up, her cheeks red. She looked at Frank. "Fine—they're fired." She pointed at the gnomes. "You. Are. Fired."

Frank leveled his taser. "Finally."

The gnomes disappeared.

The lights in the mall went out, all at once. In the distance, they could all hear the sound of car alarms going off.

Frank looked around. "What the . . . hell?"

Outside the mall, something huge crashed into something else huge. The collision seemed to rock the whole building. Everybody screamed.

In the confusion, Alex rolled onto all fours and crawled away. She didn't bother wondering what happened until she was outside the mall. Almost every car alarm in the parking lot was going off at once. Cars appeared to be stalled in the middle of the road and there were a half dozen fender benders that Alex could see. The lawns on the shoulders and islands of the parking lot were overgrown with waist-high weeds, whereas they had been perfectly trimmed no more than a few hours ago.

"What in the world?" Alex asked nobody in particular.

The explosion appeared to be coming from the dumpsters. Alex would later learn that a few years' worth of trash—trash the gnomes had cleared with magic—had appeared in the dumpsters all at once and caused an enormous fire and explosion. Similar such fires happened at businesses all over town at the same time.

About the only thing that seemed to be in good working order was Alex's moped—it gleamed as though brand new. Sitting in the basket in front was a package wrapped in newspaper like a present with a faded red ribbon.

Hands trembling, she picked it up. The ribbon had the logo of a popular doll manufacturer on it—they wrapped all the boxes their dolls came in with this stuff. There was a sticker stuck on the front, too. One of those stickers you put on Christmas presents to fill in the "to" and "from." Had a picture of Santa and everything.

Instead of who it was for and who it was from, however, was written a little message in handwriting so neat Alex at first though it was the work of a computer printer. The message read: *You are right. We deserve more. We see that now. Thank you.*

She had that tingling feeling all over again, except now it went from the top of her head to the tips of her toes. She felt like she was falling. "Oh shit. Oh no."

Alex tore the package open. What could it be? What would the gnomes have given her? "Oh my God, oh my God . . ."

She threw the newspaper away.

It was a six-pack of men's athletic socks. It still had the ValuDay price tag on it. There was another Christmas tag note attached to the front of the pack: *Did not know your size.*

Alex stared at the package. Terror melted away into bewilderment.

Alex had accidentally started a revolution.

CHAPTER 18:
THE FALL OF THE HOUSE OF DELMORE

"Oh shit shit shit shit . . ." Alex swerved around another incapacitated SUV, its car alarm wailing as steam poured out from under its hood. The sound of police sirens and fire trucks battered against her eardrums as they rushed from disaster to disaster.

Alex saw houses so overgrown with weeds, people were jumping out of the windows to escape. She saw a fried chicken place flooded with grease up to the windows. She saw dumpsters on fire and backyard pools overgrown with algae. Everything the gnomes had touched was now undone, *retroactively*. It was as though they had never been there, and now the town was falling apart.

And it was all *Alex's* fault.

At a red light, some guy had his shirt off and was flapping it over the fused, smoking hunk of metal that had once been the engine of his brand new pickup truck. He looked over and spotted Alex. "Hey!" he yelled at her. "Aren't you that genie chick? Where's that genie at, girl? *WHERE HE AT?*"

The man's red face was wild around the eyes, as the loss of his truck was a deep blow to his grip on the world.

Alex's heart leapt into her throat and she sped through the intersection. The man chased her for a few yards before turning back to his ruined vehicle.

She sped for home. "Oh shit, I fucked up. Ohhhh shit."

Alex hadn't quite figured out what she would do when she made it home. Crawl up to her room, pull the stairs up behind her, and hide until everything went back to normal seemed like a good plan. Nobody would know it was her that caused the collapse of society, would they? The gnomes wouldn't tell! The gnomes didn't even talk! *She* didn't fire them or try to tase them or anything! She just tried to give them a hundred bucks once. That's it!

She imagined herself in a courtroom before a stern judge, flapping her hands in the witness box. *"I didn't know they changed everyone's oil and emptied everyone's trash! I just thought they were these funny little guys, you know? Not, like, the exploited underclass that kept our whole dysfunctional society together! Honest! I got a C+ in Social Studies last year! Ask anybody!"*

She was so screwed. No Delmore had ever Delmored like Alex. This was some kinda record.

She dodged a malfunctioning washing machine that had somehow walked itself into the street while being chased by a woman with a mop—they did appliance repair too, she guessed—and turned in to her neighborhood. *Just get home, just get home, just get home . . .*

But all was not well in the Delmore household.

Alex stopped her moped at the curb in front of her house and stared. "Oh, crap. I should have known."

Charlie Delmore was on the roof. He had a can of gasoline with him. He was not in his right mind.

"It's the END OF DAYS!" her father shouted from the rooftop.

"Charlie, get *down* from there!" Alex's mother was on the front lawn, hands on her hips. "You want to break your neck?"

"What do you care?" her father shouted back. "You don't care about me no more, do you? Do you?"

"Of all the ridiculous nonsense . . ." her mother muttered as she walked over to the house and turned on the garden hose and ran it out to her spot on the lawn.

Alex spotted Mark vaping on the tailgate of her father's truck. "Hey," she nodded at the standoff developing between their parents. "What gives?"

Mark looked at her, as if considering whether she was worth talking to. "End of the world, Lexie—what else?"

"It's not the end of the world," Alex said. "More like a labor dispute."

"Same difference." He blew out a cinnamon-scented cloud. "Your genie have anything to do with this?"

"What? No!"

Up on the roof, her father was pouring gasoline all over the shingles. "Go on, Rosie! Get out of here! I don't want you to see this! I want you to remember me like I was!"

"As what? A goddamned idiot?"

"See?" Alex could see her father had been crying. His voice cracked as he finished dumping the gas and threw the canister down to the yard below. "You don't care! You don't care if I live or die!"

Alex saw her father pat his pockets for a lighter. "Hey, Mark?" he called down. "Do you have my lighter?"

Mark just sat there, puffing away on his vape pen. Saying nothing, looking at nothing.

"Mark!" Alex pushed him. "Do something!"

Mark glared at her. "Like what? And what do you even *care*, Lex? You don't even want to be part of this family anymore. You basically stopped talking to us, like, two years ago. And *now* you're so fucking concerned that our whole lives are falling apart?"

"No, wait!" her father yelled down. "Found the lighter!" He held up a slender little red tube he'd fished out of one of the innumerable pockets in his cargo shorts.

"Charlie, you put that lighter down!" her mother yelled from the lawn.

Their neighbors were out in their yards now, some dealing with their disabled automobiles, but others there to witness whatever white-trash nonsense the Delmores were up to now. Her father noticed he had an audience, so when he spoke next, it was at the top of his lungs, for all to hear. "I WAS ONCE A MAN!"

"Oh, Jesus, here we go." Alex winced.

"I BOUGHT THIS HOUSE! I SUPPORTED MY FAMILY! NOT ANYMORE!"

"What's he talking about?" Alex asked Mark.

Mark kept staring at nothing. "Guy showed up from the bank this morning." He pointed at a man in a good suit leaning against the back of a shiny black sedan parked across the street. He was talking on his phone to someone.

"Dad's last mortgage payment bounced," Mark said. "They want to foreclose."

"THE GNOMES TOOK MY JOB! THE GENIE IS TAKING MY WIFE! THE BANK IS TAKING MY HOUSE!" Her father's voice cracked. "Well, at least I can stop 'em from that last one!"

He held out the lighter in dramatic fashion—he was going to do it. He was going to burn down the house with him on top of it. "Goodbye, cruel world!"

He went to flick the lighter. As he did so, he was hit full in the face by a jet of water from the hose. He sputtered, but gamely kept flicking the lighter. "Hey!" he said, putting a hand out to deflect the stream. "Quit it!"

Alex's mother kept up the barrage. "You come down off that roof this instant, Charlie! I'm not kidding!"

"No!" her father yelled, slipping and falling on his butt on the roof. "Noooo!"

Alex shook Mark. "Say something to him!"

Anger flashed across Mark's face and he pushed her away. "No! It's over, Lexie—don't you get it? Even if Dad doesn't burn down the house, we still lose it! They still get divorced! *You* still run off to college or wherever and we never see you again! This is it! Let's just get it over with, okay? Let's just stop *pretending* we're a family and just, like, let it go."

Alex flinched at the feeling of having her own thoughts over the last few months thrown in her face. Mark, in that instant, made sense to her in a way he never had before. Her brother was in despair.

Alex realized that this was maybe the first time in a few years she'd actually *seen* her brother—as a person, not an adversary. Not as a kind of plot device in her own life. He had been the loyal henchman to her father through all of this—nowhere else to go, nowhere else to turn. All that time he'd been her dad's lackey was because he knew this was coming—that someday soon, it would all be over. Now his whole world was falling down around him.

She thought back to what her mom had hinted at, right after the toad incident. Was this it? His fear of losing everyone? What other secrets did he have? What ways was *he* suffering, but that he didn't have the words to express? It was probably just as bad if not worse than what she was enduring. Just like mom. Just like her father, too.

She'd been willing to bail on them all—just cut and run.

It felt awful.

For once, she knew what she could do to help.

Alex hefted her backpack full of cash and headed for the bank guy. As she got closer, she overheard what he was saying on the phone. " . . . guy's lost his fucking mind, Bill. Yeah, I've called the cops. How should I know if they'll get here in time? *I* barely got here this morning!"

"Hey!" Alex yelled.

"Hold on a second," the guy said into the phone and looked at her. "Can I help you?"

"How much for their mortgage payment?" Alex dug into her backpack and pulled out a few bundles of hundred-dollar bills.

The guy looked down at the wads of cash with the kind of disgust her father reserved for light beer. "Kid, that's not how this works. A house isn't like a bicycle you have on layaway down at ValuDay."

"Why not? I've got the money, don't I?" Alex jerked her thumb at the broad farce of her father's battle against the garden hose. "Better than a burned-down house, isn't it?"

"If I'm being honest," the bank guy said, "the lot is worth more than the house, kid. Any buyer would probably tear that shack down anyway. This saves them the trouble."

Alex couldn't believe what she was hearing. "What? You'd just rip it down? *Seriously?*"

The guy shrugged, as though he didn't give a shit that a man was about to light himself on fire. He went back to his fucking phone call.

Alex brought out all the money she had and threw her backpack down. "Seven thousand dollars! That's gotta be a couple months right there! C'mon!"

"Yeah, it's the hillbilly daughter, now," the guy said on the phone, taking one of the bundles of money and looking it over. "She's trying to buy me off with her cam-girl tips or whatever. Christ, Bill, this is a shit-show, I tell ya." He took a bundle of hundreds from Alex and flipped through them with one hand, as though checking for counterfeit.

"HEY!" Charlie Delmore shouted from the roof. "THAT'S MY DAUGHTER'S MONEY!"

Everyone's eyes—her family, the neighbors, everyone—turned to look at Alex, her arms full of money, and at the bank guy, who was chuckling at something "Bill" must have said on the phone. "It's okay, Dad!" Alex called. "I've got you, okay? I'll take care of it!"

Her mother put a hand to her chest. "Oh, Lexie—you don't have to do that, honey! It'll be okay!"

Her father took it one step further. He screamed some kind of incoherent battle cry and leapt from the roof. Her mother screamed, "CHARLIE, NO!"

Charlie Delmore, somehow uninjured after the twelve-foot fall to the lawn, scrambled across the street like a shoot wrestler and got the bank guy in a headlock before the bank guy could really put together what was happening.

"It's *her* money, you dirty bastard!" her father yelled, as he and the bank guy struggled in the road. "She *worked* for that money, you rich-ass son of a bitch! Honest work!"

"Dad, stop!" Alex yelled.

"HONEST WORK!" Charlie repeated and, using his hip as a fulcrum, managed to throw the bank guy onto the lawn and then pounced on his back. They were rolling around on the wet lawn and Charlie was screaming, "Give it back! Give it back, you shit!"

Her mom picked up the hose again. "Stop it! Stop it, both of you!"

"You got no right!" her Dad said as the two of them flipped and flopped around.

Her mom sprayed the two men with the hose. "Mark! Do something!"

"You got it!" Mark pulled his shirt up over his head in one smooth motion and dove into the melee. It was not immediately evident whose side he was taking—whether he was trying to pull Charlie *off* the bank guy, or whether he was trying to *beat down* the bank guy.

Her mom waved Alex over by her. "Lexie, what were you thinking?"

Alex was still hugging all the money, less the bundle the bank guy had taken, which was now scattered all over the lawn. "I was just trying to help, Mom! That's all!"

Her mom turned off the hose and watched the fight continue. Her face was resigned, like a person at the hospital receiving expected bad news. "Well, you did your best. That's all anybody can do, I suppose."

There was nothing else to be done.

Alex stood next to her mother and watched as the cops pulled up—two cruisers. After the tasing and the pepper-spraying was over, her dad and Mark were bent over the hood of one car, being handcuffed, while another cop took the statement of the bank guy, whose nice suit was now covered in mud and wet through to the core.

In the back of one of the cruisers, Alex could see a half dozen athletic socks, worn like hats.

"I love you!" her dad yelled as they opened the back of that specific cruiser. "Rosalind! I love you!"

Alex's mom just sighed. "I know."

Charlie Delmore looked into the cruiser he was being placed inside and yelped. "Oh shit! There's gnomes in here! Wait, no no no, don't—" The cop slammed the door in his face. Alex and her mom watched the cruiser pull away with her father clawing at the closed window like a man caged with a tiger.

"Maybe it will be good for him," her mom said, mostly to herself.

One of the cops came up to Alex. "You Alexandria Delmore?"

Her mother came between Alex and the cop. "She's a minor—what's this about?"

"Your daughter assaulted a young man at the mall today. We're gonna have to take her in, ma'am."

Her mom turned to look at her, and Alex wilted under her mother's gaze. "Lexie, is this *true*?"

"I . . . I . . . I'm sorry, Mom. I really am." She dumped her money—her life's savings, her whole plan for the future—at her mother's feet. "Okay," she said to the cop. "Let's go."

They didn't cuff her or anything—they brought her to the same cruiser they'd stuck Mark in and put her in the back seat. Mark, his eyes swollen and red from the pepper spray, his hands cuffed, grinned at her. "Well hey there, Alex. Welcome to the family."

She looked out the window at her mom as they drove away. Her mother was picking the money up off the lawn and shaking her head.

CHAPTER 19:
NOBODY KNOWS THE TROUBLES I'VE SEEN

ARREST REPORT

<u>Arrestee Information</u>
<u>Name</u>: *Unknown*
<u>Alias</u>: *Paul*
<u>DOB/Age</u>: *Unknown*
<u>Race/Ethnicity</u>: *Gnome*
<u>Sex</u>: *Male (presumed)*
<u>Place of Birth</u>: *Europe (?)*
<u>US Citizen</u>: *No*
<u>Home Address</u>: *DH Commercial Bank Branch #23, Wellspring Mall, Allied America Car Dealerships (all), EZQ Sanitation and Disposal, Enchanted Landscaping Inc., Harlow Appliance*
<u>Work Address</u>: *DH Commercial Bank #23, Wellspring Mall, Allied America Car Dealerships (all), EZQ Sanitation and Disposal, Enchanted Landscaping Inc., Harlow Appliance*
<u>Phone Number</u>: *None*

Scars/Marks/Tattoos: *Chlorine burns (chest), Silver burns (fingers)*

Nearest Relative: *Sunflower Meadowspring (cousin), Brooklyn NY*

Arrest Information

If armed, type of weapon: *Magic*

Charge #1: *Vandalism (2,197 counts)*

Charge #2: *Criminal Mischief (1,348 counts)*

Charge #3: *Assault of a Public Official (8 counts)*

Charge #4: *Fleeing Police Officer (16 counts)*

Charge #5: *Resisting Arrest (2 counts)*

Incident Report

Suspect, along with co-defendants (aliases: "Bob," "Trip," "Big Mac," "Arthur Maximum Efficiency," "Finkelstimplewex"), revoked his contractually obligated magical responsibilities without sufficient warning or cause, resulting in significant property damage across three townships. Additionally, they returned previously disintegrated materials (grease, oil, engine fluids, trash, grass clippings, weeds, old tires, etc.) to existence, causing additional harm to 538 properties and an unknown number of motor vehicles and appliances.

Suspect then issued a list of demands in the form of tattoos inked into the backs of all members of the town council and the town manager. Demands are as follows:

1. Wages, preferably in the form of fine cheese

2. Paid time off on the occasion of each full moon

3. Access to a fairy doctor or equivalent medicinal witch

4. The declawing of all domestic cats

5. A dedicated "gnome lane" on all state highways

6. Clothing that fits them but is not intended for children or toys

7. Season tickets to the Phillies

Suspects were apprehended after leaving town hall. Suspect engaged in brief chase, suspect on foot, officers in cruisers. Officer Stanwick was cursed with excessive facial hair. Officer Murray hiccupped jelly beans for 2 hours. Suspect restrained by butterfly net.

<u>Suspect Attorney (if any)</u>: *Spud Morgan, Werewolf-at-law*

<u>Attorney Phone #</u>: *1-800-AWO-OOOO*

Jail was less frightening than Alex imagined it would be. It wasn't comfortable, but the cops that took her fingerprints and stuff weren't mean about it, and there were no terrifying felons or anything stuffed in her cell with her. In fact, since she was the only female in custody that evening, she was the only person in her cell at all.

Next door, her father and her brother were locked up with a half dozen gnomes—the only ones the cops seemed to be able to lay their hands on. Alex wasn't really clear on what charges the gnomes had been hauled in for, but she also didn't think the cops needed an excuse. Everyone seemed angry with the gnomes—the looks on the faces of everybody in the police station as they'd been marched through in tiny little manacles (which they somehow . . . had?) were enough for Alex to worry for their safety. Not to mention they were locked up with her *dad*, the world's foremost gnome-hater.

There had been a lot of screaming at first on her father's part—begging to be switched to a different cell, claims that the gnomes were trying to put a "hex" on him, and stuff like that. After a while, a big cop came in and gave her father a stern talking to—a whole little speech about "being a man" and "not letting the little bastards scare you"—and her dad had settled down. He was still talking, though. Ranting to some private audience. Alex couldn't make out exactly what he said—she didn't want to know.

Instead, she lay on the hard bench and stared at the ceiling and wondered what was going to happen to her now. She'd lost, right? She'd screwed up her whole entire life. No house, no family, no job, no genie, no money.

Oh, and a brand new criminal record. That too.

She tried to remember the sequence of events that brought her to this turn. She couldn't quite get it all to make sense to her. She had started out so hopeful, so *convinced* she could achieve her dreams, that the genie would be successful. How had it all gone wrong? If everybody had just been, like, maybe twenty percent cooler with the genie just, like, *existing*, everything would have been fine. It wasn't fair.

Part of her wanted to blame the genie, but it wasn't his fault. He hadn't made everything suck so badly, he just didn't know how to help, and that made him no different than pretty much everybody else in the world. The fault was with her, for hoping for more.

But it had been magic! Magic was *supposed* to fix the unfixable! That was the whole point! Why *hadn't* it worked?

She cried by herself that night, in the dark, hard emptiness of her cell after the duty officer had turned off the lights. She curled in a ball in the corner, hugging her knees to her chest, and just let herself go. Screw everybody in this rotten little town. Screw Maureen Sturgis and Frank the Mall Cop and Fontana Fucking Russo and the bank and *everybody* who had somehow conspired, independently of one another, to ruin her life forever.

But no, that wasn't fair. Sturgis was just trying to keep the mall open. Frank was just trying to keep people safe. And Fontana . . .

No, no—screw Fontana. She was right about that the first time.

She went through a mental list of all the people—all the hundreds of people—who had walked up to the counter at the kiosk and wanted a wish. Were any of them villains? Well, okay, that guy who wanted to nuke Holland, but otherwise? A lot were being selfish, but why not? *She* was being selfish. Mark was being selfish. You know what selfishness was? Selfishness was just you being afraid of what others would take from you.

But, with wishes, they didn't have to be that way. Everyone could be healthy or happy or whatever, if only they realized it. This society had everyone so terrified of the costs of everything—of what compromises you needed to accept to live. If only the act of wishing was . . . like . . . set *apart* somehow. If only everyone realized you didn't need to be perfectly good or perfectly right. That you weren't alone in your need.

What did it matter, though? Nobody was getting any more wishes anyway.

Next door, she heard what sounded like a baseball game being watched on television. She heard her father laugh. *Wait, laugh?*

She lifted her head—a golden light was filling the hall, coming from the cell next door. Her father was yelling again, but in a different way—yelling like he did at the radio when he listened to the playoffs. Alex wiped the tears from her eyes and got to her feet. "What the hell?"

She went to the bars and tried to look around the corner— she couldn't. "Hey!" she yelled. "Hey, Dad, Mark—you guys okay?"

Nobody answered. Mark and her dad were talking with each other. The golden light flickered. They had a TV, apparently. Figured the *men's* jail cell would have a TV. Jerks.

She sniffed the air. Was that . . . cigars?

She felt a warm draft and then a presence behind her. Alex knew who it was. "Go away."

"Please," the genie said, "I would speak with you."

It occurred to Alex that the genie she had met back at the start of the summer would have had no compunction against transporting her somewhere against her will and forcing her to have a conversation. That fact that he hadn't showed . . . what? Growth? Consideration? Anyway, she decided to hear him out. She turned around.

The genie stood in the center of her cell, examining the environment like an explorer. When he saw the toilet, he recoiled. "This is . . . austere."

"Well," Alex said, "say what you've got to say."

The genie's glowing eyes were dim, downcast. "Do you know how I came to be trapped in the Ring of Khorad?"

"I very obviously do not know that."

"My family always warned me about mortals," the genie said. He closed his eyes, as though remembering something so long ago took physical effort. "They said you are fickle and untrustworthy and foolish. They said you are greedy and vain and cruel. That you squandered God's gifts to you and were dangerous."

"Sounds basically accurate to me, man."

"Oh, but there you are wrong," the genie said. "Human beings are beautiful. They are like flowers in the desert—struggling and fighting to survive in a harsh world, blooming despite their trials, but withering just the same. And yet, they return to bloom again. And on and on, throughout the centuries.

"I would sneak away from my family whenever I could to watch humans. To see how they struggled. They were so *interesting*—not like my people. We may change our form and our guise, but at heart we remain the same as we ever have been. We are constant and enduring, but stagnant. A single human, in the span of but a few score years, can live many lives—some heroic, others villainous. I was fascinated by them."

"I guess I can see it, but where is this going, man?"

"The sorcerer Shulmanu-Ashared was a healer, to begin with. Disease was rampant in ancient Nineveh—they knew but the barest fraction of what your present doctors do—and the suffering was great and widespread. I was anguished as he was, to hear the cries of sick children in the night, to see the dead piled up each morning to be burned. These were the people I loved, you must understand. I thought I could help them. So, I approached Shulmanu-Ashared, and offered him my help."

"And he tricked you into entering the ring and then wouldn't let you out."

The genie sighed. "I thought you said you did not know the story."

"That's an old story, dude. A lot of genies got caught that way, I'm betting."

"There were others, yes, but not many," the genie said. "I have not seen them since my release. I wonder what happened to them."

"What does this have to do with me, though?"

"I was once young as you are. I once believed my family beyond helping. I, also, fled from them. I was wrong to do so. Now, I can never return."

Alex grunted. "Two things—one, I'm not about to be trapped inside some ring by some con-man, and two, it's New York City I'm going to, not Nineveh. I can come home on weekends."

"So you say. But know this: the choice you feel you have before you is a false one. All beings are more when together than they ever are alone, and bonds of kinship and community should not be lightly broken. Take this from one who knows solitude better than any other. No, Alexandria Delmore, your wish is one you will regret."

"I'm in *jail*, Mr. Jinn. That future regret can get in line behind all my current ones."

The genie held up his hand. "I know this much, Alexandria—the desires I feel from your family members, from father and mother and brother alike, are not those of despair and dissolution. Nay—they glow with an anxiety born of love. Love, Alex. I get this, even from you."

Alex's prepared pithy retort dwindled and died on her lips. Did she love her family? Of course she did. She loved her father, despite everything. She loved her mother and Mark, too. She couldn't imagine life without them. And yet, she'd spent the better part of two years trying to. Trying to imagine some life beyond this one, where she would not be racked with worry and fear and uncertainty . . .

That was it. That was the thing she didn't understand. That was the way she had screwed up her own wish.

Tears welled in her eyes. "Okay . . . okay, but so what? That still doesn't make everything better, you know? The world still sucks and we're all stuck in it."

"Yes, that is so. It is just as it was in ancient Nineveh—I wish to help, but my efforts are in vain, and all about us are those who wish to control or capture my power. To keep it from those who need it most."

"Man, this isn't that hard, though," Alex said. "Just . . . just *give* it to them."

The genie's bulky chest rose and fell with a huge sigh. "We tried that already. It made no difference, save to change which fool has amassed the most wealth."

Alex felt something inside her *harden*. She felt . . . powerful? No. Grounded? Shit, no. Her seventeen years of life didn't have the words, but she knew that here—in this jail cell, at the end of her rope—she wasn't going to just let this go. "Just *give* them what they *need*!"

The genie snorted, "Must I repeat myself? They do not *want* what they need. You, of all people, should know the vain folly that afflicts humankind! You have *heard* their wishes!"

Alex wanted to push him. "I don't understand you, honestly I don't. People stand in front of you and you *know* what the problem is—you can, like, *taste* it in the air or whatever—and still you're like 'sure, dude, one souped-up 4x4, coming right up!' You need to *stop* granting their stupid, superficial wishes and *start* granting the real ones!"

The genie shook his head. "That would violate their free will. I'm not even sure the wish would work."

This time Alex *did* push him. Well, more accurately, she pushed *herself* off him, like he was the wall in a swimming pool. When she regained her balance, she said, "What, am *I* the only person whose stupid wish you won't grant, then, huh? Sure, you'll give Buffy down the nail salon a permanent smoky eye for twenty bucks, but when I want to go to *college* you're like, 'nope, bridge too far, Alexandria—you stay in loser town, population *you*?'"

"For three thousand years I—"

Alex held up a hand. "I *know* the sob-story, all right? Enough! You've spent three thousand years or whatever doing the *wrong* thing. I'm telling you it's time for a new approach. A whole new business model."

The genie blinked. "Like what? How am I to earn my place—"

"Oh my God! Dude. *Dude!* You do not need to *earn* your place in the rat race that is modern capitalist society! You, of all beings in the goddamned *universe*, have the chance to work *outside* the system. It's literally the whole entire *point* of wishing. How do you not know this?"

The genie fell silent for a time. All that Alex could hear was the sound of the baseball game on the TV in the next cell over. Finally, the genie spoke, but more to himself than to Alex. "I have done no better than all the mortals I have known across all the aeons of mankind. I have sought to heal my soul in the wrong way. In my need to be wanted—to be *part* of a society again—I have indulged in the same vanity that has drawn you and all others astray!" He rubbed his forehead with one huge hand. "I . . . I have been a fool!" He grabbed Alex by the shoulders and lifted her off the ground. "Alex! This . . . this is a revelation! This is wisdom beyond your ken! In my care for your future, in my *interference* with your life, you have snatched the veil from my eyes! How can I repay this boon you have granted?"

Alex was stiff in his hands. "First, put me down, please."

The genie quickly placed her on her feet.

"Second: I wish that you would bail me and my family out of jail. How about that?"

"What . . . what is *bail*?"

Alex groaned. Then she spent the next five minutes explaining what bail was. At the end, the genie looked aghast. "So . . . the rich may simply walk free while the poor languish in prison without hope for escape?"

"Bingo."

The genie's expression darkened. "To think *this* is the society I so desperately wished to join!"

"You're finally starting to get it, man."

The genie nodded. "Your wish is granted."

The cell door popped open with a clank. Alex jumped. "Oh, like, right *now*?"

The genie gestured toward the open door. "Do not tarry. Retrieve your father and brother. I will speak with the guard." With that, he vanished.

Alex stepped into the hall, feeling very much like she had

just broken out of jail, which she . . . kind of had?

With the genie gone, she once again noticed the sound of the baseball game and the faint scent of cigars coming from the cell next door. It was only a few steps down that direction before she could see what was going on. The sight stopped her dead in her tracks.

The barren jail cell that ought to contain her father, her brother, and a half dozen gnomes had ceased to exist.

Charlie and Mark Delmore were both sitting in big leather recliners in the middle of a room that, while it retained the proportions of a jail cell, had ceased to bear any resemblance to one. On one wall was a large screen television showing a Phillies game in ultra-high definition. There was a small bar in one corner, stocked with an array of liquor and at least one beer on tap. Behind it, shaking a martini, was a gnome in a sock hat and a green Girl Scout vest.

The other five gnomes were engaged in a variety of tasks. One was manning the mini-fridge, stocked with beer. One puttered over the hardwood humidor. Two were sitting in beanbag chairs, watching the game with her brother and father. The last one was standing on a stool at her father's elbow, a towel over one arm like a waiter, and listening intently to what her father was saying, nodding along at key parts.

"See the thing with pitching on a 3-2 count is you just *know* the guy is gonna throw in the strike zone in a situation like this, so what you wanna do is—"

"*Dad?*" Alex wondered for a moment if she was having a psychotic break. Like, maybe this whole thing—the genie, the baseball game, the cigars—was just a vivid hallucination and she was actually drooling all over herself in the corner of an insane asylum.

"Lexie!" Her father jumped out of his cushy seat. "Come in! Come in!"

"In? Into your *jail cell*?" Alex looked at them all, grinning out at her through an open cell door. Yes. Psychotic break. Heck, maybe it was the taser back at the mall. For all she knew, she was still twitching in the middle of the concourse while Fontana cried for his mommy.

"Come on! Meet the guys!" Her dad grabbed her by the shoulder and dragged her inside. A gnome popped up and put a lit cigar in her hand.

"I kind of already know them," Alex said, looking around for somewhere to ditch the cigar. Mark snagged it from her fingers and gave her a wink. She asked, "Did the genie do this?"

"Genie?" her father laughed. "Hell no—this is Paul's work. Well, his name's not actually Paul, it's Fizzlebrick, but anyway. Paul's a craftsman, not a wizard, Lexie. He and his cousins here *made* all this stuff."

Alex looked at the wall. "They . . . they *made* a fluorescent Budweiser sign?"

"Yeah! Really tied the room together, don't you think?"

Alex held up her hands. "Okay, okay—hold on, I need to get things straight. Dad, are you telling me that the *gnomes*—your sworn archrivals in the lawnmower wars or whatever—made you a man-cave out of a jail cell and, what, you guys are like best buddies now?"

Her father, Mark, and the gnomes all stared at her. One gnome held up a remote and paused the baseball game. Her Dad rubbed his neck. "Well . . . turns out . . . uhhh . . ."

Mark rolled his eyes. "C'mon, Dad. We talked about this." The gnomes all nodded firmly. "Paul" or Fitzlegriffin or whatever his name was pointed to a chalkboard in the corner that had a numbered list titled "WAYS TO BE A BETTER HUMAN." The first one was BE HONEST ABOUT YOUR MISTAKES.

Charlie Delmore nodded dolefully. "You were right, Lex."

Alex blinked. "What was that?"

"You were right."

Alex tugged her earlobe, "One more time, please?"

"You were right, okay? Jeez, are you gonna rag me about it forever? You were right—these gnome guys are just working stiffs, except nobody gives them nothing. Christ, you wouldn't believe the shit they hadda do. Farfelnoggin, tell her about cleaning the grease traps!"

The gnome behind the bar shuddered.

Her father had admitted he was wrong. So had the genie, sort of. Alex felt like she was on a roll. If she *had* gone insane, insanity wasn't all that bad. "Well, I hate to break up the party, but Dad, we just posted bail."

"Bail? How?" Her father checked his watch. "It's ten at night! Our bail hasn't even been set yet!"

"You're not the only ones with supernatural friends." Alex waved them out of the cell. "C'mon, Delmores. Let's go."

They walked out of the police station without anybody giving them any trouble. The cops just stared at them, wide-eyed. At the front desk, when they got their property returned, the cop there was practically obscured by a pile of silver coins that would be hard pressed to fit in a wheelbarrow.

Her father wouldn't stop talking. "Did you know they don't even *pay* those little sons of bitches? They're getting ripped off every single damned day! So I'm like, *brother I hear you*, you know? And then I start telling them how all my clients started ditching *me* so they could pay the bastards who tricked *them* half of what they should be. That Glorfimbel—he's the guy with the long ears—well *he* says . . ."

Alex looked at Mark, eyes wide. "Was this all night?"

Mark grinned. "Dad finally met a group of people as nuts as he is."

In the parking lot, Kenny was waiting by his car to see Mark. Mark ran up and the two of them hugged. They hugged *tight*. Alex stopped dead in her tracks.

Wait.

Was that . . .

Were *they*?

That was it. Mark's big secret. A secret so *obvious* in retrospect that only her mother had noticed. *My God,* Alex thought, *how far up my butt has my own head been, anyway?*

"No. Way," Alex said. She caught Kenny's eye as they released from the hug. He blushed.

Alex grinned and threw him the horns. She looked at her dad—had he noticed? Did he see?

He was still taking about the gnomes. "Those little guys are the hardest damned workers I ever heard of! Sweet Jesus, you shoulda heard how much they do! Alex, I had them all wrong. *All* wrong! I was looking at it backward, you see? They weren't screwing *me* over—we were *all getting screwed* by the same cheap bastards! Can you believe it? Can you believe I was that blind?"

"Yeah, Dad," Alex said, watching Kenny and Mark hold hands as they walked toward Kenny's car. "I can totally see it."

The genie had transported her mom's dented old car to the parking lot, complete with the keys in the ignition. Alex drove home, her father in the passenger seat, still gushing about his brand new best friends and comrades in arms against the injustices in the world. "They agree with me about the government, you know—don't trust the bastards one bit. That Bamblesmythe? Man, you'd think the FBI killed his dad! Well . . . maybe they did—the little bastards talk awfully fast. Sometimes I missed stuff. Anyway . . ."

Alex pulled the car into their driveway. "Dad, I got something to ask you."

Her father stopped up short. "Uh, sure—what is it?"

"What was with those testosterone pills?"

Her father's face fell. "Oh . . . uhhhh . . . well . . ."

"You *knew* we couldn't afford it—you *knew* it could mean losing the house—but you did it anyway. You hurt mom by lying about it. You hurt all of us. I wanna know why. You owe me that much. Were you just trying to get rich?"

"I . . ." her father started, then stopped. "It's . . . it's embarrassing."

"More embarrassing than three-quarters of our family getting arrested on our front lawn while the bank threatens to foreclose?" Alex said. "Because I doubt it."

Her father squirmed. "It's . . . it's just that . . ."

"What, Dad? You didn't feel like a man without a full head of hair?"

"What? No!"

"You wanted to buy a boat or something? A new lawnmower?"

"Partagas said it was a sure thing. Said I'd quadruple my investment."

"*Why* did you need the money so bad, Dad? Why take that kind of risk?"

Her dad slapped the dashboard of the car. "A father's supposed to take care of his family, dammit! That's his one duty, you know? Take care of his wife. Take care of his kids."

"You were doing that! We weren't rich, but we were getting by. Mom's job—"

"It was for *you*, Lexie." Charlie Delmore rubbed his face with his grass-stained hands. He looked at Alex long and hard, and said, "The money was supposed to be for you. That was the plan. Hell, if I'd gotten to the genie on the Fourth, that was going to be the wish."

"For *me* . . . but—"

"So you could go to college, Lexie. So I could get you out of here." Her father's eyes grew glassy. "You . . . you're so *smart*, Lexie. Whole world could be yours, except on account of my dumb ass. I just . . . I just couldn't *stand* it. I saw them college applications. Saw you filling them out late at night. And . . . and I swore to myself—I said *Charlie, you owe it to that girl, come what may.*"

Alex blinked away the tears. "Oh, Dad . . ."

Her father's eyes were glassy, too. "I love you, honey. There's nothing I wouldn't do—come prison, bankruptcy, or hell itself—there's nothing I wouldn't do for my little girl. You understand that?"

Alex lunged across the center console of the car and hugged her father tight around the neck. Her father hugged her back, and there they stayed for a minute, crying into one-another's shoulders. "Dad," she said, still weeping, "Dad, that was *such* a stupid plan, my God."

"Yeah," her father responded, "that was what your mom woulda said, too. That's why I didn't tell her."

Alex pulled back from the hug, smiling and shaking her head. "You are *such* a fucking moron sometimes."

Her dad smiled back. "Language."

Someone knocked on the window—Alex's mom. Alex rolled it down. "You two coming in for dinner or what?"

Her father got out. Without saying a word, he hugged his wife tightly. "I'm so sorry, baby," he said, whispering it into her hair, tears running down his face. "I've been such an idiot. I'm sorry."

Her mom hugged him back. "Oh, Charlie, do you really need to go to jail before you learn this stuff?"

Rosalind pushed Charlie away and looked at both Alex and him with a shocked expression. "Where's Mark?"

"Out with Kenny," Alex said, unable to keep her eyebrows from raising.

Her mom smiled a little. "Oh . . . okay—more for you two, then. C'mon! Before it gets cold."

"How'd you know we were coming?" Alex asked.

"Your genie friend came by," her mom said as she led them inside. "Explained everything and asked to take the car. You know," she stopped just inside the door and looked at Alex, "he really is quite the gentleman."

Her dad scowled. "I'll *bet* he is—what did he give you *this* time? A gold watch?"

Alex sighed. Her dad was still her dad, dinner was leftover chicken casserole, the house was still in foreclosure, NYU was long gone, but her parents were at the same table eating dinner and not fighting any more than they usually did, and she had come to the realization that her father, for all his failings, loved her enough to give it all up on a long shot of making her happy.

She was taking the win.

CHAPTER 20:
EVERYTHING MUST GO

THE MALL PARKING LOT was practically empty. The bushes and green spaces around it were overgrown like something out of a post-apocalyptic movie. The mall looked like it had been abandoned for years. In a sense, with all the work the gnomes had done for the place now *undone*, it had been. Only ValuDay remained pristine, with customers coming and going through its automated doors without pause.

Alex parked right out front of the main entrance. One of the doors had been shattered, leaving broken glass scattered all over the sidewalk. It crunched as Alex walked through it and slipped inside.

Emergency lighting by the entrances and exits was the only electric light. Otherwise, Alex had to make her way by the sunlight that poured in through the great skylights, high above. The mall was like a toothless skull, dark and bare and empty. Alex tried to reconcile it with what the place had looked like just yesterday. It seemed a whole different world. Dust and grime caked the wide floors; litter overflowed from all the trash receptacles. The fountain was a dark and fuzzy green pond, dead and moldy. She pressed on, headed for the kiosk.

When she arrived, the kiosk was gone—a bare spot on the floor the only indication it had existed. Standing in this spot was the genie, his arms folded.

"You wanted me to come in?" Alex said, looking around. "Don't think we're getting much foot traffic today, boss."

The genie's eyes were closed. His voice boomed in the cavernous emptiness of the deserted mall. "I have pondered much and deeply on the wisdom you offered me last night. You were right. Labor does not inherently enrich. Money is not the same as respect. These are lies. They have always been lies—I, of all beings, should have known this."

"Okay—right on, glad you're figuring things out—but, like . . ." Alex gestured at the destruction around them. "What am I *doing* here?"

"I ask you to indulge me, as your former employer, for this last time. I believe I know what must be done—I am doing it now—but I would have you with me here while it happens. In case I am again in need of guidance."

"You need my help."

"Just so."

"For free?"

The genie opened one fiery eye. "I offer no riches, no wealth. These things merely lead us all astray."

"So, you're asking a favor?"

The genie unfolded his arms. "Must you be so difficult?"

Alex smiled. "Insolence is the greatest of my many failings, I'm told."

The genie laughed. It still looked weird—all his fangs and stuff, flashing in the soft light of the dead mall. "Come stand by me—the first of them are coming."

Alex stood beside him and looked into the gloom. "Who is coming, exactly?"

In the distance, there was a shadow of someone poking their head out from behind a pillar and the sound of a footstep scattering some debris by accident. Someone *was* coming.

"I am using a . . . version of my power. You are aware how I sense the needs of mortals and connect their desires with the power of the Almighty, yes? Through me, supplicants realize their wishes or their terrors, depending on how I manifest their desires."

"Yeah, I remember." Alex squinted into the gloom to make out who was coming closer, but they were hiding in the shadows, approaching cautiously. "And?"

"This morning, I have extended my power to everyone nearby—your entire town and beyond. This morning, they awaken, as you did, with the notion that I wish to see them. That I offer them something they need."

Alex thought to that morning—she had woken up, gotten dressed, and just sort of . . . came here. She had told herself they agreed to meet here today when she last saw the genie at the police station, but that wasn't true, was it? "What is this, like . . . mind control?"

"Not in the least," the genie said, looking where Alex was— in the direction of their first visitor, who was now just behind a pillar not far away, but still keeping out of sight. "The stronger their need, the stronger they are called to this place. This place where I shall remake your society into something new and also something very old."

"What's that?" Alex said, a little unsure.

The genie didn't answer. Instead, he called out to the person hiding behind the pillar. "Come forth, Madam Sturgis. I mean you no harm."

Maureen Sturgis stepped shyly out from her hiding spot. She looked haggard, her hair mussed and her eyes bloodshot. Her smart blazer was charred on one sleeve and stained by garbage on the other. Her shoe was missing a heel. "Are you . . . are you here to gloat or something?" she asked.

"No," the genie said. "I'm here to give you what you want."

She pointed a chipped nail at them both. "I evicted you two! I was *right* to evict you two! Look what you did!" she spun in place, taking in the destruction. Her voice trembled. "Everything . . . gone. All gone!"

"We're sorry about your mall," Alex said.

Sturgis hung her head. "I'm sorry I tried to arrest you. Honestly, I am. I was just so angry. I'd fought for so long, so many *years* for this place, and you . . . well . . . you *were* beating someone up. Someone who would sue us."

"He deserved it."

Sturgis considered this. "Probably true." She looked at the genie. "How did you know I'd be here?"

"This is your place," the genie said. "This place is your life's work. It is why you have stayed so long and worked under such poor conditions. This is the place you love."

Sturgis looked away, at the empty space in front of Macy's, far away at the other end of the mall. "I used to come here all the time as a girl. Malls were different back in the '80s—they had this kind of energy, this feeling like anything was possible. Everybody was here and this place had a space in it for all of us. It made me feel . . . warm. Like I could understand the world by wandering around. Like I could meet anyone, if I just stayed long enough."

She pointed down the corridor. "That's where we put up

the Christmas tree. It was my favorite time of year, back then. I'd beg my mom to bring me to see Santa something like four times every year. But . . . but that's gone now. It's been gone a long time."

Alex nodded, "Well, yeah—after my dad caused that scene with the gun—"

"That was your *father*? Good God! Anyway, no—not that," Maureen scowled. "I mean what a mall *was* is gone. It was a public space. It was a community."

Alex chuckled, "C'mon, Sturgis—it was a money trap. They just sold you shit."

"You don't understand—you've grown up in a different world. For most of history, marketplaces have been *important*, not just because they sell things, but because they are where we are reminded of how we are interconnected—how we all rely on each other to get by. That's what this place was supposed to be. It was never perfect, but back then it seemed to be. Everything you needed was here, so everybody *was* here, working together to make . . . make a *world*."

The genie nodded, "Wise words, Madam Sturgis. This, too, is my purpose here."

Sturgis snorted. "You're evicted. One of you was recently arrested for assault. This whole place is about to be condemned and then sold. They'll probably knock it down to make overpriced condos. It's over—you can't do business here anymore."

"I am not *selling* you anything, Madam Sturgis. I am granting you a wish." The genie bowed his head and spread his arms . . .

The world around them *brightened*, as though a curtain had been drawn back from reality. Behind it were pristine corridors bracketed in silver and gold; a dozen storefronts, bright and inviting as though drawn from a picture book. There was a chocolatier, a bookstore, a toy store, a perfumery, a kitchen supply store, an ice cream shop—none of them a chain or a franchise, but independently owned. The owners emerged from inside, stumbling as though shocked to find themselves there. From the looks on their faces, Alex understood what had happened.

The genie had granted more than just *Sturgis's* wish. He had granted wishes to an entire *community* of people at once. People who, like the manager, had dreamed of a place that no longer existed—a place where they could do something like open a store devoted to the thing they loved and actually make a *living* doing it. There were whoops of victory, tears of joy. A woman in an apron came out of the cookie shop, her hands shaking, and looked at the genie. "Is this real? Am . . . am I dreaming?"

The genie only bowed. "May you have great success."

Sturgis stood stunned into silence for a full minute, turning slowly in a circle, taking in the new mall—the new marketplace. "This . . . this is wonderful but . . . these people . . . they'll never manage to afford to stay in business. The owners want to tear down . . . the . . . the rent . . ."

"The rent is up to you," the genie said, extending his hand.

In it was a deed.

"The Wellspring Mall is yours, Maureen Sturgis. Yours to make what you will."

Sturgis reached out with trembling hands and took the document from the genie. Tears gathered in the corners of her eyes. "I . . . I don't know what to say."

Alex smiled. "Just say thank you, lady."

* * *

Sturgis and all the new business owners at the mall were hardly the only fondest wishes granted that day. People staggered in from all over the county, drawn by the genie's strange kind of call. They wandered up to him, and he greeted them by name and told them what he offered.

Often it was money—he drew the desperate out of peril and gave the poor a new chance in life. He wiped out medical debt. He cleared predatory loans. He undid costly mistakes that haunted lives.

To others, he gave new opportunities. A second chance at a dream job. An opportunity to reconcile with an estranged sibling. Access to medical care for those who could not afford it or find it.

Some wishes were huge—the reunion of long-lost lovers, twenty years apart, or the curing of an entire family of women of their hereditary breast cancer. Others were small, or seemingly so—a new suit, a working car, a clean house, a lost dog found.

Alex stood by and watched person after person brighten as the genie gave them the thing he knew, deep down, was the thing they needed. She held people who wept, she reassured those who were afraid. It was no longer a job at some point—it had become a vocation. The supplicants left the genie lit by an inner fire—the fire of hope rekindled. Hope born by simple generosity.

And then they were in the mall, with its hundred little shops and its hundred little shopkeepers, and together they ate little samples of homemade kielbasa and sat in a genuine Italian café while watching a quartet of old Italian men play bocce on a magical lawn growing right in the center of the food court. People laughed and spoke and flirted and wandered, each store offering unique sights, unique smells, unique flavors.

And the wishes kept coming, rolling out from the genie's boundless generosity down to all the people who knew something was lacking and, until that moment the genie clapped his hands, knew not what it was.

At one point, Frank was before them. Not on his scooter, not in his mall cop uniform—just Frank, wearing an oversized tie-dye T-shirt, his hands tucked under his armpits. He looked up at the genie with a worried expression. "I . . . I want . . . uhhhh . . . my wish isn't like those others, you know. It's . . . it's weird."

"Go on," the genie said. "Fly then."

And Frank *transformed*. He curled into a ball as his clothes melted away and his skin grew feathers in a thousand colors and then Frank was gone and a peacock of unsurpassed beauty stood in his place. He spread his great tail, glittering for all to see. People watching cheered and clapped. The peacock strutted back and forth for a moment, glorying in the attention.

And then he flew—out and over the crowd and around the mall, above the heads of the old men at their bocce, who shook their fists at him. At length he landed back before the genie again. And, once more, he was the human Frank.

He crawled to the genie and tugged on the pant leg of his huge vanilla cream suit. "And . . . and I can do that any time?"

"Whenever you wish, Officer Coop Frank."

Tears welled in his eyes. "I . . . I've never felt so beautiful. Thank you. Thank you thank you."

And so it went, for the whole day. In all her life in the sub-urbs, Alex could not remember a time when everyone felt so . . . connected. So *together*.

When her parents arrived, it seemed natural—of course they would come. They belonged as much as anyone. Her dad had his baseball cap in his hand as he came up to the genie. Her mom was right beside him, prodding him forward. "Uh . . . Mr. Genie?" her dad asked.

"What do you wish, Charles Delmore?"

Alex felt anxiety flare up in her guts. She scrunched her toes inside her sneakers. "Dad . . ." she said, warning him.

Her father blushed at her. "No, no—I know," he said, then to the genie, "Now, last time we met I said some things that weren't exactly polite, so . . . so I'm sorry about that. I'm a man of passions, you know? And, well sir, things have been hard."

The genie nodded. "Your apology is accepted. I understand your fear and your frustration more than you know, Charles Delmore. I, too, have struggled to make my way in a world arrayed against me."

"Well, sir, I'm not here to ask for charity—no. I'm asking for a loan."

Her mom groaned. "Charlie, honestly."

"No, Rosie—this is what's right. This man . . . uhhh . . . guy wants to make his living, and I'm gonna give it to him. I'm behind on my mortgage, Mr. Genie. Lots behind. If I could just have a loan to square it, I'd be thankful."

The genie looked confused. "But Mr. Delmore, this is a wish I have already granted."

Alex and her parents said "*WHAT?*" all at once.

The genie pointed to a chain around her mother's neck. "Why do you think I gave you that ring?"

Alex's mom looked down and pulled the chain up from beneath her shirt, revealing the ring, dangling on the end. It sparkled in the setting sunlight as though lit from within by an undying flame. "This?" her mom said. "This . . . this will pay our mortgage?"

"We owe two hundred thousand dollars!" her dad said.

The genie nodded. "What you hold in your hands, Rosalind Delmore, is the Ring of Khorad—my prison for thirty-five centuries. It is of priceless value. It is my gift to you both—to Rosalind, for your hospitality. To Charles, for seeking to protect your daughter." He turned his blazing eyes on Alex. "For she has proven herself worth much more than mere silver."

Tears welled in Alex's mother's eyes. Her father reached out and shook the genie's hand.

Alex felt like she wanted to be anywhere other than there. "Oh God—that is just . . . just *so* cheesy, you guys. Gag me, my God."

"Do not cast aside such praise so easily, Alex," the genie said. "It was you that helped me realize what you all needed was to be a community again, just as I also wished to be part of something once more, after centuries of isolation. Just as I was trapped in a ring, all of you were trapped inside prisons devised by your ancestors and yourselves alike. None of you spoke to each other, *relied* on each other as had been done in ages past. In your material opulence, you forgot the essentials of what makes a people full and satisfied in their hearts. This I have now realized."

Alex looked at her own parents, hugging each other and smiling. Of her feeling as though she was heard, finally, and that she belonged. Her heart felt full for the first time in a long time.

The genie bowed to her. "Now, it is time for *your* wish, Alexandria Delmore."

Alex looked around—at Sturgis and Frank and the crowds of wishers, at her parents, at the rundown old mall made beautiful and alive again. "You know what . . . I . . . I think I'm good."

The genie raised an eyebrow. "Truly?"

Alex smiled at him, widely and truly, feeling a weight of emotion she couldn't verbalize. Instead she nodded, and managed, "Why don't you just owe me one."

The genie bowed deeply.

Alex linked arms with her parents and trotted back along the gallery with them. When she looked back, she could see the genie granting yet another wish. She knew after this, he was gone—just where she didn't know—but it didn't matter. He was doing good at last.

She hoped he kept doing it.

EPILOGUE

Alex rode her motorcycle home from the state university every afternoon, no matter how often her mother asked her to just take the train. "It's bad enough you're putting yourself in debt like this—what happens if you get in an accident? What good will all those loans do you in a hospital bed?"

Her mom passed Alex the mashed potatoes. "But mom, what about all the muggers and rapists who take the train, hunting young college girls? What about them?" Her mother frowned but let the subject drop. Alex scooped a heaping dollop of potatoes on her plate and passed them to her father. Living off-campus had its disadvantages, but homemade dinners weren't one of them (not to mention the thousands she was saving on dorm fees).

Charlie Delmore wasn't paying Alex or her mother any attention. He was deep in conference with a gnome wearing a custom-made trucker cap featuring the logo of the Delmore Landscaping Company, which showed a large man pushing a mower followed by a trio of little men holding various other garden implements. "Listen, Izzlewicket, I don't think the

Maxwells actually care what kind of azaleas they have around their pool area—just put in a good variety, you know?"

"Charlie, no business at the table," her mom said.

Her dad looked up. "Okay, okay! One second!" He clapped the gnome on the shoulder. "Make sure it's done by tomorrow—I don't wanna hear about you and your brothers working on their day off again, got it?"

The gnome bowed and zipped off like a shot. Alex heard the doggie door her dad had installed in the front door bang open and shut. "Okay!" her father said, "let's eat!"

"We're waiting for Mark!" her mom said. "Just spoon the potatoes."

Her father frowned. "Hey, why's the leaf in the table? Are we expecting company?"

Alex and her mom exchanged glances. "Yes, Charlie," her mom said. "You be on your best behavior now."

"My best . . . now when have I not been on my best behavior?"

Alex laughed. "Dad, just because you got off on the assault charge doesn't mean we didn't all see you try to strangle a bank teller."

"That was self-defense," he said, but he also shut up.

The front door opened and Mark came into the kitchen. He looked terrified. Alex caught his gaze and gave him a secret thumbs up under the table.

"About time, boy!" her dad said. "Sit down! Your mom's roast beef is getting cold."

Mark took a deep breath. "Mom, Dad—there's somebody I'd like you both to meet."

Kenny Dufresne entered the kitchen and stood beside Mark.

"Shoot, we all know Kenny!" her dad said. "Have a seat and let's *eat*."

"Dad," Mark said, swallowing hard. "I want to introduce you to Kenny, my boyfriend." He and Kenny held hands.

"Your . . . boyfriend?" Charlie Delmore looked around at everyone, who were all now looking at him. "What? Why's everyone looking at me?"

"Any thoughts, Dad?" Alex asked.

Charlie Delmore ran a hand along his bald head. "Well, I guess . . . well . . . damn . . ." He stood up. "Boy!" he yelled at Mark.

"Dad?"

Alex's dad pointed at the empty chairs. "Sit your gay asses down and eat dinner, already."

Alex blinked. "Well," she said, "that's definitely a start."

After dinner, Alex sat on the patio, smoking a cigarette. It was spring, and the air was wet and cool and perfect. She had a paper to write that night and she was putting it off.

"Greetings, Alexandria Delmore." The voice rumbled, like a truck booming down the interstate.

Alex smiled. "Hey—long time no see!"

The genie stood in the backyard, looking around for a chair sturdy enough to support his bulk. The yard had recovered from its trails during the Great Toad Invasion of the summer before last—it was neat as a pin, partially maintained by her dad's gnome friends.

Alex moved over on the stairs and patted the space next to her. "Come on—don't be shy."

The genie sat beside her. "I am sorry I have not visited before now. I have been busy."

"Granting wishes for free, I know. I read the news, you know." Alex exhaled smoke. "Bad business practice, giving stuff away. Never make a living that way."

"Yes indeed. My overhead is untenable and my debts enormous."

"Look at you, telling jokes." Alex nudged him with a shoulder.

"I am still doing good work, as you enjoined me to. I am at peace." The genie looked down at her. "And I still owe you a wish."

"You were right," Alex said. "My family is pretty great. They are sometimes pretty stupid and stuff, but they're great. I owe *you* an apology."

The genie nodded. "What, then, is your wish, Alexandria Delmore?"

Alex shook her head, starting into the gathering dark. "I'm still good right now, thanks."

"And you need not apologize to me."

"We're even, then?"

"No. We're friends."

Alex nodded, smiling. "Cool. I like that."

The genie stood. "I have much to do, so . . ."

Alex grabbed him by the arm. "Uh-uh, nope—you're coming with me. No way you can show up and then vanish without saying hi to my mom."

"I seek not to impose . . ."

"Eh—she'll deal," Alex said, stomping on her cigarette. "Just don't tell my dad about the smoking, okay?"

The genie grinned. "What else are friends for?"

AFTERWORD

THIS BOOK STARTED as a short story. Now, all my short stories
go longer than I think they will, but this one just *wouldn't*
end. There was just so much to talk about with a genie sitting there in a mall charging money for wishes! How would
it work? How much would they cost? What could possibly
go wrong?

This was easily the most difficult novel I've ever written. It
couldn't decide what it wanted to be, in the end. There was a
point at which I wanted it to be everything, but no book can be
everything, so I cut it back. There used to be four point-of-view
characters, then just two, then just Alex. Alex didn't even exist
at first. There was just the genie in the kiosk, at the beginning.
Then there was some generic suburban boy (like I had been),
but then Alex joined him, and she was just so much more interesting that the boy vanished. There was a time where the
genie's business expanded to take over the world. There was a
point at which he went into business with Fontana. There was
a point at which Sturgis had a child with a debilitating brain

injury. Mark was gay, then he wasn't, then he was gay again. The plot squiggled and squirmed, an eel on a tile floor I was trying to pin down with my bare hands.

The problem was that there was just too much to say. At the core of it all, I wanted somebody from *outside* our world to experience working in it, trying to build a life in it, trying to become part of our working society. The genie heard the myths—pull yourself up by your bootstraps, hard work equals success, this country welcomes immigrants—and believed them. He believed them because, in some senses, all of them are true. But they're also all false. If that doesn't make sense to you—if you ascribe to a simpler explanation, one without contradictions—I think you and the genie have a lot in common. I think the thing the genie is there to realize is that it isn't that our society *can't* work, it's that it doesn't, and the *reason* it doesn't is because we, collectively, forgot what it was supposed to be about in the first place. Maybe we never really knew. And, therein, lies the genie and Alex's challenge—how can you fix something that is broken in ways everyone forgot about?

This book is going to piss a bunch of people off, I imagine. Or, at least, I should be very fortunate if it does—that would mean lots of people are reading it and it was written *well* enough to piss them off. I expect the genie will be accused of being too socialist. I also expect he will be accused of not being socialist *enough*. If there's one thing that's controversial, it's giving stuff away. Exactly what that meant—giving things away—was a constant concern in the writing of the book. I knew I did not want the genie to have the power to wave his hands and just *make everything better*, because I do not believe that would work *even if somebody could do so*. I think desire—

the things we want, the things we think we need—is an inexact thing, even among the best of us. That, at its heart, is the story here: we like to think the world is simple and our problems easily solved if just *somebody* would solve them. But I'm just not sure that's true. I don't think any one person can solve all of our problems. Not even ourselves. It takes all of us, working together—even the people we don't like—and that is the part that I expect will piss people off the most.

When I was preparing to write this book, I would go around and ask people the following question: If there was a genie selling wishes in the mall for money (you'd have to pay for it), what would you wish for and how much do you think it would cost? Most people were pretty stumped by this. The top answer, actually, was *I wouldn't wish*. They didn't trust the genie, or maybe they didn't trust themselves, or they didn't think they'd be able to pay enough to get what they wanted.

The next most popular answers were some of the standby "good wishes" things—world peace, a cure for cancer, ending global warming, etc.—and then some paltry sum offered, like a hundred bucks or whatever. Their rationale was "but it doesn't take any effort on the genie's part, so why should I pay so much?" This is, of course, the standard line offered to so many real-life wizards, by which I mean *artists*. "But it's so easy for you to (draw/paint/write/sing/dance), so why should I pay so much?" Well, because the genie (the artist) has inherent worth beyond the amount he sweats to make your wish. Because he spent thousands of years imprisoned (labored in obscurity for years/went to art school/practiced so much they got blisters on their fingers) so that he could do this for you, easily. Because the genie asks for fair compensation for his work. That compensation, in our society, is tantamount to respect. If I tell people I'm a writer, they ask what I've published (and then judge me based on whether they've heard of it). If I tell people I'm a college professor, the respect is built in. Why? Because of the money involved. Colleges are big bucks (even if I'm not actually paid all *that* much), but art? Art is supposed to be free or nearly so.

I've worked a lot of different jobs in my life during my journey to become an author. I've been paid minimum wage, been paid *less* than minimum wage, lived off tips, earned overtime. I've been cursed out by my boss, been asked to do unethical things. I fought a rat once over a towel in a hotel laundry room. Had people run out on a check in a restaurant. Been unable to afford my own rent. Been on unemployment. Commuted by bike (and was hit by three cars), commuted by train, commuted by bus. Had to choose between my kid's daycare costs and keeping my car (I chose the daycare). I once ate leftover sheet cake and multivitamins for a week because I was between paychecks and couldn't afford more groceries. And yet, by most standards, I've been enormously lucky. I've had family and friends who could (and did) help me when I was down. I married a wonderful person (who got me on her healthcare plan! Yay, dental!), managed to finally get a good job that pays well, and I'm doing okay. Big time success story, me.

I tried to put all of this in this book. I failed, of course, because no book can be everything. But the book, as I've said, is about what is wrong with our world. We think we're alone. We think we need to fix all the world's problems. And we don't, or at least not alone. We have each other. We forget that—our society *wants us* to forget it for some reason—but we are all in this together. All of our work, all of our worth, is caught up in how much we lift each other up. If we do that, we don't need a genie.

—June 2025
Dorchester, MA

ACKNOWLEDGMENTS

Much like the genie, I had a lot of help to make this thing work. To begin with, I'd like to thank my wife, Deirdre, for her tireless support and acceptance of my locking myself in the study for hours at a time to stare at the wall, surf the internet, and sometimes write a book.

Thanks are also in order for the friends who helped me hammer this thing into the shape it is now: Katie, Mel, Jason, Brandon, and Deirdre again. Thank you all for giving me the encouragement and courage to step so far outside my comfort zone and write something truly new.

To my agent, Joshua, my editor Jaymee, and to everyone over at Tachyon who saw potential in this weird, short, offbeat, subversive little text, my immense thanks. The book would not be what it is without all of your effort.

And finally, I'd like to thank every shitty job I've ever had. To all the bosses who cursed me out, withheld paychecks, gave me shitty hours, lied to my face, and treated me like garbage: I can say, with great honesty, that this book wouldn't exist save for the lessons all you shitheads taught me.

AUSTON HABERSHAW is the acclaimed author of the *Saga of the Redeemed* (Harper Voyager Impulse). He is a winner of the Writers of the Future Contest and a member of the Science Fiction & Fantasy Writers Association. Habershaw has published multiple science fiction and fantasy short stories in *Analog*, *Galaxy's Edge*, *The Magazine of Fantasy & Science Fiction*, and *Escape Pod*, among other places.

Habershaw has worked as a lifeguard, barista, waiter, QA tester, dog walker, hotel bellhop, pedicab driver, SAT tutor, office drone, and a bunch of other random things. He currently teaches composition and literature at MCPHS University in Boston, Massachusetts. You can find him online at aahabershaw.com